LOVE UNDERCOVER

Jessica stared at Cary's hands. She loved men's hands and his were beautiful with long, slender fingers, strong palms, and solid knuckles. "I'm glad I met you, Cary. You're a nice guy." She trembled as his hand lightly stroked her cheek.

"You're a nice woman, Jessica, which is why I won't do what I've been aching to since I first saw you in the lounge."

Jessica met his tortured eyes. Their warm depths were black and she felt the tension and heat radiate from his body. The atmosphere in the room suddenly shifted from their teasing playful tone to something darker and richer. Something Jessica was beginning to understand. "What do you want to do, Cary?" she whispered.

Jessica's eyes grew wide as Cary leaned closer to her. Then their lips met and somehow her eyes closed. At first, he merely nipped her lips and teased the corners of her mouth with his tongue. Then he carefully drew her closer and placed his full mouth over hers. She felt the heat of the kiss on her toes, the tips of her fingers, throughout her entire body. Then she knew he was the ocean wave and she was drowning in his arms.

LOVE UNDERCOVER

Tamara Sneed

ARABESQUE
BET
BOOKS

BET Publications, LLC
www.bet.com
www.arabesque.com

ARABESQUE BOOKS are published by

BET Publications, LLC
c/o BET BOOKS
One BET Plaza
1900 W Place NE
Washington, D.C. 20018-1211

First Printing: September, 2000

10 9 8 7 6 5 4 3 2 1
Printed in the United States of America

Prologue

As the silence in the room uncomfortably hovered in the air, Cary Riley stared past the woman's perfectly coiffed black hair and out the window. Even though the woman kept a professional smile on her face, he could tell his behavior frustrated her. That was his reason for silence in the first place. Cary liked to read people. His life depended on his ability to predict a person's thoughts by watching their body movements, listening to their unspoken words, and observing their little, uncontrollable facial expressions. Dr. Lydia Myers was frustrated because after spending ten hours over the last two weeks with Special Agent Cary Riley, she still could not understand him. Cary didn't want her or anyone else to ever understand him.

"I think you need to take a vacation," Lydia finally said, since they both knew Cary would not break the silence.

"I don't want a vacation," was his only response. He met her eyes, daring her to contradict him.

He should have known that the Group would pick psychiatrists who weren't easily intimidated. "This is for your own good, Cary. Your last assignment was very difficult, both emotionally and physically. You need time to rest, to think, to be a normal person for a little while. You need to clear your head."

Cary shook his head but knew she'd already won. Dr.

Myers would tell the director of the Group, Maurice Iverson, and Iverson would order Cary to take a leave of absence. "I don't even know where to go," he protested lamely.

"You could go home," she suggested softly.

Cary quickly shook his head, feeling one of his headaches start. The heavy throb usually began behind his left ear, then traveled behind his eyes and finally rested in the center of his forehead. "That's not an option."

Dr. Myers glanced uncertainly toward the closed door, then opened her desk drawer. He looked at, but didn't touch, the colorful brochure she placed on top of her desk. "I know this is against procedure but . . . my husband and I were planning to vacation here for our three-year anniversary. It's a small inn in northern California, very quiet. I think you'd enjoy it."

Cary picked up the brochure and stared at the white, sprawling house pictured on the front page. Hadley's Inn was written across the top of the page in elegant cursive. "Hadley's Inn," he murmured more to himself than to her. He finally looked at Dr. Myers and nodded. "I guess I'll tell you all about it when I get back." Dr. Myers smiled, looking relieved and slightly smug.

A nondescript Black man, dangerous in his commonness, stood in a phone booth a few blocks from an unlabeled FBI adjunct building in Northern Virginia and placed a collect call to Jubumga, West Africa. He waited for the correct code word then said, "Hadley's Inn." He quickly replaced the receiver and walked down the street to meet his colleagues for lunch.

One

Cary glanced across the quiet lounge of Hadley's Inn. Five days ago, he'd packed his Jeep with clothes and food, and started from his home in Virginia toward the other coast. He reached Northern California at the same time as a September rainstorm and drove straight to Dr. Myers's suggested retreat, Hadley's Inn. Hadley Hansot and her husband, Jake, were extremely friendly people who made him feel at home the second he stepped onto the porch. But, aside from being friendly, they were incredibly nosy.

Cary told the Hansots he was a marketing director for a sports apparel company in Chicago, with several business cards to confirm the story. The truth was entirely different. The truth was much less honest and tidy than the lie, Cary thought. In his line of work, Cary learned people liked to believe lies. Even if every piece of evidence pointed toward the contrary, a person believed only what he or she wanted to believe.

Cary smiled bitterly at the direction of his thoughts. His thinking was the precise reason that Dr. Myers had suggested he take a few weeks off, and Iverson had ordered Cary to follow the directions. Cary was losing all ability to separate himself from the job. Being an undercover field agent during the last five years for the National Intelligence Group, an ultra-clandestine department within the FBI, made it difficult to separate. The employees told their parents, spouses, and friends they worked for the FBI, which was technically true, but there was much more involved that they could not tell them.

Cary's last assignment involved infiltrating a West African terrorist group on American soil. He was captured and shot in the left arm after his cover was blown. He spent a pain-filled night in the terrorists' jail, not fearing or caring for his life. When the Group didn't hear from him at the appointed check-in time, a team stormed the underground headquarters. Cary watched as all ten men in the terrorist group were unmercifully gunned down. He didn't feel remorse for their deaths and that was what scared him. He hadn't dated in over a year, he hadn't seen his brother or sister since he'd joined the Group, he didn't even have friends he could call for a basketball game, and none of that mattered to him. He was lying constantly to people— about his job, his name, his birthplace—and Cary knew he was about to crack under the pressure.

Cary stood to stoke the crackling logs in the fireplace. The inn boasted a maximum occupancy of fifteen guests, and the owner, Hadley Hansot, told him he was the fourth and final guest to check in that night. There had been cancellations due to the storm. The large inn felt quiet and lonely at night, surrounded by only trees and mountains for several miles. Cary was glad. He had to think, like the psychiatrist had ordered him to.

He walked over to the window and watched the pouring rain pound against the trees and the front porch. He smiled slightly, as he realized that as horrible as he felt, whoever was stuck outside in the rain was in a much worse position.

Jessica Larson kicked the tire on her motionless, mechanically dead black Honda Accord and cursed as the rain unforgivingly continued to pour down. She kicked the tire once more in anger, as she thought of the report she was supposed to be revising that waited on the kitchen counter in her dry San Francisco apartment. Jessica pulled thick brown hair from her cinnamon brown face and glanced down the ink-black two-lane highway. She couldn't see ten feet in front of her, much less where the road disappeared. Jessica grabbed her purse and began to blindly stumble down the highway. The night was too cold and dark for her to sit in her car and pray for help to come. And since Jessica never was one to rely on someone else to rescue her, she decided to walk to the nearest gas station or house.

Jessica was hopelessly lost on a deserted highway in the middle of a raging rainstorm, but she realized she wasn't as upset as she probably should feel. Since graduating from Stanford University five years ago and becoming a financial consultant at a prestigious firm in San Francisco, her life had been relatively problem-free. She had her own apartment, her own car, and enough extra money to have already paid off her credit-card bills and student loans. However, even with financial security, Jessica was slowly starting to realize something. She was lonely.

She had her friends, although most were either married or practically married and spent any free time with their men. There was her older brother, David. He spent time at work, or with his own "flavor of the week," or scheming with their mother to get Jessica married and pregnant. She knew she could find an acceptable man on her own, without their help. She was fairly tall at five-feet-eight with cinnamon brown skin, brown eyes, and long brown hair that was too thick to wear down, so she mostly pinned it away from her face. Since she ran every morning before work, she was thin and in peak physical shape. Almost too thin, her brother complained.

Jessica didn't think she was drop-dead gorgeous or insulting to the eye. She'd had her fair share of sleazy come-ons and catcalls. And before her realization, she hadn't been overly worried about her single status. She thought she was too busy with work to think about a man or a relationship. But lately, at night, in the dark of her room, while laying on her large queen-size bed, she thought about her future.

Jessica realized this wasn't the time to examine her life, as she nearly fell into a ditch in the road, covered by the darkness. She cursed herself for being so ridiculously stubborn. Her mother had told her not to drive back home that night in a storm, but Jessica wanted to return to her small apartment in the city and her report. Now, she could only think of the headlines for tomorrow's newspaper about a drowned Black woman who had been stupid enough to drive 400 miles in a storm.

Jessica turned excitedly as two car lights burst through the wet blackness. For a second, she thought of *Unsolved Mysteries* and *America's Most Wanted* stories about hitchhikers and seriously considered hiding in the bushes on the side of the road. But, she felt the sting of the rain and noticed the stretch of lonely road in front and behind her and decided to take her chances with the potential murderer. She waved wildly, jumping up and down on the road, until the van slowly rolled to a stop next to her.

The words "Hadley's Inn" were scrawled on the side doors and the driver rolled down his window, looking suspiciously like her grandfather. The ramrod-straight posture, meticulously groomed facial hair, and open smile on his dark brown face made her instantly nostalgic for home, even though she'd only left a few hours ago.

"You look about ready to drown out there." He motioned her inside the van with a warm smile. "Hop in."

Jessica immediately climbed into the passenger seat and slammed the door. "I appreciate this so much. Is there a mechanic nearby? My car stalled about half a mile back." Jessica briefly closed her eyes as the warmth from the interior of the car seeped through her wet sweater and jeans. The man pushed a few buttons on the console and she heard and felt warm heat push harder through the vents. She sighed in appreciation.

"You won't be able to do much of anything about your car until this storm lets up. No one's supposed to be driving in this weather, especially along this area, where there are always mud slides. I was the last car to get through the roadblock."

Jessica rolled her eyes in exasperation. "Now what am I supposed to do?"

"You could think about this in the morning after a good night's sleep," he offered.

"At Hadley's Inn, right? Are you Hadley?"

The man laughed, shaking his head. "Hadley's my wife. I'm Jake, Jake Hansot."

"Jessica Larson. Onward to Hadley's, I guess."

Jake carefully started the van down the dark, unlit road, their progress slow from the rain and thick darkness. "What's a young lady doing by herself in the middle of a backwater road during a storm?"

Jessica tried to pull the clinging, wet sweater from her body, to no avail. "I wish I knew. I visited my mother in LA this weekend. I was heading back home to San Francisco when I thought I could save time by taking a shortcut. My shortcut somehow landed me here. Where is here, exactly?"

"You're in Blue Moon Bay, about an hour and a half southwest of San Francisco."

Jessica shook her head. "So close, yet so far away. I bet my mother is worried sick. She told me not to drive in this weather."

"No boyfriend or husband to call in San Francisco?"

Jessica stared out the window and slowly shook her

head. Usually, she would have bristled at that question from a complete stranger, but tonight she merely remained silent. Since her father had left her family when she was five years old and her brother had gone through puberty, men had been a complete mystery to her. "No," she finally whispered.

"That's hard to believe. A beautiful young lady like yourself."

Jessica smiled at his compliment. "I guess I just haven't found the right guy. Besides, I'm very busy with my career. I was recently selected as one of the recipients for a prestigious award of recognition given by the Bay Area Professionals."

"Congratulations."

"It's a very coveted award," Jessica continued, mostly because she couldn't stop herself, although she thought Jake could care less. "Every professional in the city under thirty years old wants the recognition. Just being nominated is a huge honor and guaranteed to open doors in the business community for the next ten years. As you can probably tell, I wouldn't have time for a relationship even if I wanted one."

"Of course," Jake replied. Jessica heard a slight hint of amusement in his voice.

"You don't believe me?"

"I believe you. I guess I'm from the old school where a person always finds time for that right person."

"Things change," Jessica replied, staring out the window. "I wake up early, go to bed late, and all the hours in between are spent at work."

"You do sound busy," Jake said, with the same hint of amusement.

Jessica noticed a gold medal dangling from the rear view mirror and grasped at the change in conversation. "I've seen this before. I think my grandfather has one."

Jake grinned. "It's a World War II veteran medal."

Jessica listened for the next twenty minutes as Jake regaled her with war stories, until he turned off the highway, onto a gravel road. A three-story, sprawling white building with the dark glow of warm candles reflecting through the windows appeared through the curtain of rain. Jessica smiled, surprised at the inn. She liked the quiet, relaxed feeling emanating from the place. An older Black woman in a flowered dress that whipped around her ankles in the wind stood in the doorway beckoning to them. Jake helped Jessica from the van and they rushed into the warmth of the house.

"Hadley, look what I found," Jake announced to the smiling woman, shaking water from his coat. He led Jessica to a small counter that stood across from the open doorway of a large room, with a fire raging in the stone fireplace. Jessica stared longingly at the fire.

"You poor dear. Do you have any dry clothes?" Hadley asked, briskly rubbing Jessica's arms.

"I brought a change of clothes in my purse, the rest are in my car. Is there any room?"

"Of course, of course," Hadley said, nodding, her eyes assessing Jessica's bedraggled state.

Jessica nervously smoothed dripping hair from her face and glanced at the puddle of water forming at her feet on the gleaming hardwood floor. "How much for a room?"

"For you, free," Jake answered before Hadley could speak.

"No," Jessica protested. "I know how much a room in a wonderful inn like this can cost. Please—"

"Here's a key to a room down the hall, with a great view of the forest, which would be nice if you could actually see fifteen feet in front of you outside," Jake said, ignoring her protests.

"I couldn't," Jessica refused.

Jake shook his head and closed her hand around the

key. "I forced you to come here. The least I can do is show you a little hospitality."

"Take it, sweetie," Hadley encouraged, then not-so-gently pushed her toward the hallway. "Now that's settled. Get out of those wet clothes and come to the lounge where I'll put some hot chocolate out. Dinner will be ready in about forty-five minutes."

Jessica felt tears in her eyes and was surprised. She didn't normally encounter truly nice people in the world of consulting. "Thank you both so much." She met their matching grins, then turned to follow Jake's directions to the room.

The relatively small room featured a large four-poster bed, an antique dresser, bay windows that showcased the darkness, and a door that led to a private bathroom. Jessica took a quick hot shower and changed into her dry clothes, taking the time to rejoice in the feel of dry cotton against her skin. She combed through her wet, tangled hair, leaving it to fall around her shoulders to dry naturally, then practically ran to the lounge to stand in front of the fireplace.

Jessica sighed in relief, closing her eyes as the heat from the fire slowly seeped through her skin and warmed her blood. She finally admitted to herself that she was relaxed. She could feel each muscle and joint in her body slowly melt into place. Even the muscles in her face slowly uncoiled as the flames from the fire purged the worries from work out of her mind. The report she had been rushing home to complete was completely forgotten, along with other projects at work that usually hovered in the back of her thoughts.

"You seem to be enjoying that fire," a deep voice vibrated through the room, interrupting her thoughts.

Jessica's heart began to race as she noticed she wasn't alone in the room. A tall, lean figure stood near the window in the shadow-filled corner of the room. He slowly stepped into the light cast from the fire, and Jessica with-held a gasp as her stomach dropped to her feet. He was beautiful. His smooth caramel-brown skin glistened in the firelight as he walked toward her. He had a defined nose, full lips, and beautiful brown eyes that slightly frightened her because of the intensity that burned inside them. There was a current surrounding his body that she knew would electrocute her if she allowed him to stand too close.

She found her voice before he decided she was a gap-ing idiot. "I . . . I was lost on the highway and Jake found me."

"You must be cold," he replied in a neutral voice.

Jessica relaxed as she assessed the situation. She was a plain Black woman, and this gorgeous Black man obvi-ously thought she would throw herself at him, like all other women probably did. Jessica wanted to assure him he definitely wasn't her type. Because if she ever decided to seriously date a man, her list would not include intimi-dating men with piercing eyes.

His eyes openly traveled over the length of her body, from her feet to the top of her wet hair, and she rolled her eyes in annoyance at his typical display of male atti-tude. Then she realized he wasn't looking at her like a man checked out a woman, but almost like a rancher would analyze a piece of beef for his farm. He was sur-veying her for flaws or defects and, for some reason, that made her angry.

"I am cold," she muttered, then turned back to the fire to signal the end of the conversation, but instead he walked closer. Instinctively she knew he would never harm her, but her skin tingled and she wondered if he could hear the loud thumps of her heart against her chest.

"I saw you come in. Why were you walking outside in the middle of a rainstorm?" he demanded.

Jessica glared at him. She was normally a nice person,

but his sharp words and invading eyes made her blood boil. She had been enjoying the fire, relaxing, until he intruded and made her stomach rumble with an unexplainable emotion. "I like to walk in storms," she bitterly spat out. "I like to get soaking wet and possibly catch pneumonia. It's a hobby of mine. In fact, I'm the world's leading expert on walking in storms. I travel across the world teaching others how to walk in the stinging cold rain of your garden-variety winter storm, instead of staying inside with a fire."

Judging from his narrowed eyes, he didn't miss the sarcasm in her voice. He took one step closer and Jessica straightened her back, meeting his eyes. She had too much pride to recant her immature words, although she immediately wanted to; but she also had not been successful in business by yielding every time she was afraid or said something she regretted. Then a ripple flashed across his face, and Jessica thought for a split second that the mystery man would laugh.

"Well, that's an interesting hobby," he finally replied with an impassive expression. Jessica had the strange notion that he wanted to salute her, but he abruptly turned and walked from the lounge. Stormed was the more appropriate word, she thought. She turned back to the fire and closed her eyes, still feeling the air from his presence sizzle around her. She tried to recall the relaxed feeling in her body before her strange encounter, but the man stayed before her eyes. She briefly wondered what he looked like when he smiled. Jessica squeezed her eyes shut. She doubted a man like him ever smiled, unless he was making some woman miserable.

TWO

There were three other people in the small dining room when Cary arrived for dinner. The two newlyweds, whom Cary had encountered earlier and would have cheerfully strangled, occupied one table in a dark corner of the room, giving a free demonstration on how to ram a tongue down another person's throat. Then there was an older man from Louisiana in the other corner of the room. He nodded companionably to Cary and Cary waved, but chose a table in the opposite corner near the kitchen. Cary definitely didn't want to listen to John Maison's tirade on women again. Cary sat in the chair, with his back to the wall.

The dining room glowed from the light of soft candles placed in the middle of each table. Cary would have preferred electricity, but the Hansots were apparently trying to create a romantic atmosphere, or there was no power. Cary tried to hate the soft lights and intricate flower arrangements on the tables, but the soft haze that hung in the room made him want to relax. He watched the newlywed couple taste the soup, then each other, and realized he was more jealous than annoyed. A woman had never looked at him with such love and trust. A woman had never willingly turned her face into his hands, smiling only for him.

Common procedure for any agent in a room full of

people was to sit with his back to the wall and face everyone in order to spoil any nasty surprises. That was one
of the first lessons the instructors drilled into young re-
cruits at the training academy. Cary liked to think he
followed instinct and training, but the real reason he
watched the entrance to the dining room walked into the
room. The woman from the lounge. After leaving her
that afternoon, Cary had thought of little else.

As soon as he met her eyes, Cary felt an emotion he
rarely allowed himself to feel—fear. The woman was gorgeous. Her long brown hair reflected the candlelight, and
her brown eyes seemed larger than that afternoon by the
fireplace, when he'd made an idiot of himself. Her brown
skin shimmered in the bright light of the candles, as if
they glowed brighter because she walked into the room.
With her curly hair, she looked like a live mermaid come
from the depths of the ocean to imprison his heart and
drag him back with her.

Cary wiped the suddenly damp palms of his hands on
his jeans as she walked across the dining room toward
his table. He was prepared to stand and leave the table
for her. He could barely breathe when she was across the
room; how could he act normal if she sat across from
him at the table? He could not imagine eating food across
from her, when his only thought would be nibbling on
her lips. An unrecognizable emotion curled through his
stomach and settled in his groin as she finally stood before his table.

"Hi." She smiled nervously and Cary remained in his
seat. It was the first time she'd smiled at him and he was
mesmerized by the dimple that appeared in her left cheek
and by the shine in her eyes. "Would you mind if I join
you?"

Cary shook his head and motioned to the empty seat
across from him. He felt the sweat on his forehead and
was momentarily puzzled. He had stared down guns, ter-

rorists, and assassins without blinking, and he was now completely flustered over this woman. This one incredibly sexy, gorgeous woman, he reminded himself.

The sudden object of his erotic fantasy nervously laughed as she sat in the chair. "I'm really sorry about earlier. I'm not usually so rude."

Cary withheld his laughter at her concept of rude. He had asked a stupid question about walking in the rain and received a stupid answer. He felt he deserved that and more. "It's not a problem. I'm sorry for asking such a dumb question."

She grinned, and Cary clenched the napkin in his lap as an almost painful jab of desire punched him in the stomach and lower regions. He couldn't decide if he wanted to stare at her eyes or her lips. Her eyes seemed to glow more gold in the candlelight than brown, and the light emphasized the fullness of her lips that he would have given his left arm to taste at that moment.

"My name's Jessica. Jessica Larson." She stared expectantly at him and Cary met her gaze. He decided he wanted to stare at her lips, especially when she dragged her tongue across them. He knew he was not going to make it through dinner. "Um . . . what's your name?" she asked.

Cary shook his head, cursing himself for acting like an adolescent moron. "Cary."

"A boy Cary?" She teased, wrinkling her nose. "My older brother, David, had everyone calling me Jesse James until I graduated from high school. You definitely must have been teased."

"Unmercifully." Cary had become so accustomed to not volunteering any more information than necessary that he didn't know how to handle a conversation. But, as Jessica smiled at him, he decided to try to pretend he was a normal man who could easily handle normal social interaction. "I was the quarterback of the football team in high school and at every school we played, the crowd would laugh when my name was announced."

"Scarred you for life, huh?" she asked.

Cary nodded, laughing at the surprisingly happy memories. His laugh sounded forced and hoarse to his own ears, but it certainly felt good. "My mom was an old movie fanatic, a Cary Grant fan. That's where the name comes from. She would always say that I should be thankful Humphrey Bogart wasn't her favorite actor."

Jessica stared open mouthed at this Greek god that had descended from the heavens to tease her. She'd already admitted to herself he was gorgeous, but when he smiled, a hazy glow formed in front of her eyes. Before dinner, she convinced herself to be mature and apologize for her rude behavior in the lounge. Jessica did not want to believe that a man could affect her so completely and make her behave rudely or strangely, but she found herself in that position.

His smile gave his face another quality that his vicious gaze did not. When he smiled, he seemed like the type of man who would play dollhouse with his daughter and play catch with his son on the weekend. Jessica couldn't understand how one man could seem like two completely different people.

Hadley walked over and set a bowl of soup in front of Jessica and Cary. Jessica didn't miss her smile at each one of them. Jessica wanted to reassure Hadley they were just two adults, passing the time by talking, but she knew there was more to it than that. At least, from the feelings consuming her. She realized he was asking her a question and forced herself to listen instead of drooling over how beautiful his brown eyes were. "So, what were you doing walking in the rain during a storm?"

"I'm originally from LA, but I work in San Francisco. I went home for the weekend and I planned to stay until Sunday, but I discovered I left important work papers at my place. I needed them for a project and I drove back. I wanted to shave twenty minutes off my driving record so I decided to try a shortcut. I took a wrong turn somewhere in all the rain, and my car stalled. Jake found me, wandering down the highway, probably toward a cave of hibernating bears."

Cary was amused by her story and laughed. Jessica wanted to comment on his laughing at her misfortune, but she was again shaken breathless by his smile. She wasn't usually the type of woman to gawk or stare at any man, but with Cary she didn't seem to have a choice. "Were the papers really that important?" Cary asked with a cocked eyebrow.

Jessica laughed. "Of course not. It's just . . . Families . . . Can't live with them and . . . can't live with them."

Cary's expression suddenly sobered and Jessica wondered if she'd said something wrong. She reached across the table for his hand, but took her water glass instead. He didn't seem like the type of man to want to hold hands or be comforted. He spoke slowly. "My sister's name is Margaret. When I was little, we called her Maggie the Cat, another invention of my mother's old movie obsession. She also loved Elizabeth Taylor."

If he wanted to pretend everything was fine then Jessica would too. "That's one of my favorite Paul Newman movies, *Cat on a Hot Tin Roof*. For a long time, I wanted to be like Maggie the Cat."

Cary grimaced. "If I remember correctly, Maggie wasn't the most loved person in the Tennessee Williams play. Her husband hated her, her in-laws hated her, the whole town hated her."

"I wanted to be like her because she was like ice—cool, confident, and beautiful. That's how I wanted people to see me, which is hard when you're fourteen years old and wear braces. Every day at work when I'm confronted with a difficult situation, I ask myself, what would Maggie the Cat do? How would she respond to this irate client? And that usually helps me decide how to act."

Cary stared at her until she blushed and finished her soup. Jessica usually only confided her insecurities to her brother and mother. She didn't know why, but she trusted him. He cleared his throat. "What work do you do exactly?"

"I'm a financial consultant at Jannings & Associates."

Cary whistled at the name and Jessica felt her face flush even more. She knew he would be impressed by her employer and she wanted him to. The thought shocked her. After years of rejection from other men's insecurities because of her intelligence or her job, Jessica had developed a thick skin and an apathetic attitude. For some reason even she couldn't comprehend, she wasn't apathetic around Cary. "That's a very prestigious firm."

Jessica wanted the surly, glaring Cary back, because she couldn't deal with this grinning and teasing Cary. She could barely bring the soup spoon to her mouth as he looked at her. "Thank you."

"Do you like your job?"

"Surprisingly, I really love what I'm doing. I don't save lives or the environment, I just make a lot of people who are rich, richer. There's a thrill I get from examining numbers and predicting market fluctuations that I can't explain." Jessica looked at him for approval and mentally kicked herself for doing so. She had never apologized for her job choice to anyone before and she wasn't going to start with this man.

"As long as you're happy," he said simply, smiling at Hadley as she replaced their soup bowls with the main course. "Compliments to the chef, Hadley. Everything is delicious."

As Hadley fussed over their plates, Jessica glanced around the room to escape Cary's intense gaze. She wasn't going to survive the meal if he kept staring at her lips. Her attention became riveted on a couple in a dark corner of the room, who mostly groped each other, ignoring the food in front of them. Jessica watched the man smile into the woman's eyes, then devour her mouth. Jessica wanted to turn away, but she couldn't because she realized she wanted that tonight. She wanted to feel Cary's hands on her back, on her arms, and on her breasts. She turned back to Cary and was surprised to find him watching her.

Jessica forced a smile and motioned to the couple. "Sickening, aren't they?"

Cary shrugged, briefly glancing at the newlyweds, not wanting to take his eyes off Jessica for any longer than was necessary. "Pretty much, except I think they'd disagree." He noticed she immediately became interested in the teriyaki chicken and her hair dropped over her shoulder, hiding her face from him. Cary watched her jerky movements in confusion until he realized she was a virgin. He held back his smile. He would be the first one to touch her center, to bring her to fulfillment, to praise her breasts. Cary knew he would be the first, because he'd decided about two minutes into their conversation that before the night was over, they would be with each other. He just needed to taste her once and he knew this practical obsession he was developing over her would end.

Jessica broke the silence when she looked at him again. "So, what are you doing at Hadley's Inn? Did you get caught in the storm?"

Cary debated which version of his invented life to tell her and surprisingly told her one as close to the truth as possible. "Lately, my work . . . My job, has been difficult. I just completed a rough assignment and I needed time off. I was actually ordered to take time off. I packed my Jeep, left Virginia, and ended up here."

"What do you do?"

Cary heard the concern in her voice and cursed himself for having to lie to her. "I'm a marketing director for a sports apparel firm." The lie sounded hollow to his own ears. He could see a million questions in her eyes, but she must have heard the same flatness in his voice because she nodded.

"Sometimes we all need a break," was all she said. Cary felt his daily headache begin as she averted her eyes to her plate. She was visibly nervous around him and he knew it was because he was staring at her. But he couldn't stop himself because before his very eyes, Jessica was making him fall in love with her. Cary gulped the remaining beer in his bottle and blamed his thoughts on the setting. A quiet inn in the middle of nowhere, a beautiful woman, a little alcohol, and, certainly, his thoughts would turn amorous. He would still have her, but that was all that would happen. He would make love to her then disappear into the night, like he was trained to do.

As the two explored the inn after dinner, Jessica felt she would melt into a puddle at Cary's feet if he kept pinning her with his heated gaze. She didn't know if he looked at everyone as if he wanted to eat them or just her, but the experience was unsettling and addictive. She figured he was falling victim to the environment, the candlelight and fire, and she doubted he would act on any urges. Not that she would stop him if he did. Jessica shocked herself. She had never been with a man for a variety of reasons, of which fear was a big one. The thought of sleeping with a virtual stranger was not how she had envisioned her first time. She'd imagined satin sheets, expensive lingerie, champagne, and a man she had known for more than three hours.

They finally walked into a large, empty room, with a

wall of windows and wooden floors. There was no furniture and Jessica figured it was probably off limits to the guests, but Cary walked in and Jessica followed him. She leaned against the chilled window and watched the rain, glad to see anything besides his eyes promising her something unnamed. Cary was like an ocean wave and she was an unsuspecting swimmer about to be pulled under by his sheer force.

"You like the rain?" Cary said, smiling.

"I love the rain when I don't have to fight traffic to get to work or I'm not wearing slippery heels," Jessica said softly, because the room seemed to require hushed voices. "I bet this storm is causing massive damage. We Californians don't deal well with natural havoc."

Cary laughed. "I've noticed. At work, there's one native Californian and he always becomes non-functional in the middle of winter."

Jessica turned to find Cary intently studying her. She brushed loose strands from her face and nervously smiled. "What?" she said, shaking her head in confusion.

"I just was wondering how you . . . I guess, why some guy hasn't hounded you until you gave him a chance. You're intelligent, beautiful, you even like beer. I just don't understand."

Jessica laughed at his confused expression and felt a slight flutter in her stomach because he thought she was beautiful. "It's mostly by choice. I'm concentrating on my career right now, that's my first priority, and the men I've met want to be the first priority. Anyway, I don't think men really like me."

"I find that hard to believe."

Jessica studied his face and realized he was sincere. She normally saw through come-ons and lines, but she actually thought Cary was serious. "No, it's true. I work insane hours, I'm not affected by their silly games, and I actually dare to voice my opinions. The men I meet either let me walk all over them or try to cut me down to their size."

"Maybe you just haven't found the right guy," Cary tried.

"I know. I have this theory about love." Jessica laughed at herself for blurting out her true emotions to a complete stranger. She hadn't participated in a real conversation in months. At work, she was always careful to talk only about job-related topics and she had not found time to really talk to her best friend in weeks. "Do you want to hear it?"

"Hell, yeah."

Jessica laughed and they both sat on the cramped window seat. Her knee brushed his solid thigh, but he didn't seem to notice. Jessica became excited as she began her theory. "In a college Greek Mythology course they taught us this old tale and I believe it. Long ago, when the gods still roamed the earth, a man and woman were one person, two halves of the same person. After the gods came down and saw all the sin and greed, they punished us, separating the two halves and spreading them across the earth. They vowed they'd make it as hard as possible for the two halves to ever find each other again. Somewhere, my other half is roaming around the earth looking for me, just like I'm looking for him."

"I like that. So, you're not just looking for Mr. Perfect, you're looking for your other half that some god has strewn on the opposite side of the world. So, your other half could be in China or Iraq—"

Jessica lightly punched him as he laughed. "I'm serious, Cary. But, there's more."

"Somehow, I knew there would be."

"I think the Fates, who probably felt sympathy for the sinful humans, throw the two together for a split second in time, to give them a chance to find each other. And it's up to you to make the move. Wink, grab his hand do whatever it takes to become whole again. And if you miss that split second, you miss your chance to be reunited."

"A split second, huh?" Cary became somber. "That's kind of sad."

Jessica stopped smiling. "I know."

There was a long silence as Cary stared out the window. He grinned and looked back at her. "That's the most creative thing I think I've ever heard."

Jessica couldn't resist teasing him in return. "What about you? No special woman in your life?"

Jessica watched in amazement as his cheeks flushed. He was blushing. "No, not for a long time."

"Why?"

"Long story, but I guess that's not a good answer," he said, as Jessica crossed her arms. He laughed, then held up his hands in mock surrender. "Okay. I guess I just haven't found the right woman. Truthfully, I haven't been looking lately. I'm kind of out of the relationship business for a while."

"Did someone hurt you?" Jessica didn't want to be intrusive, but the way his eyes looked everywhere but at her made her curious.

"No. I've hurt a lot of women . . . I guess I just haven't found my other half yet."

"It's a good escapist answer, huh?"

Cary laughed, then looked at his watch. "I didn't realize how late it was."

Jessica stared at his hands. She loved men's hands and his were beautiful with long, slender fingers, strong palms, and solid knuckles. "I'm glad I met you, Cary. You're a nice guy." She trembled as his hand lightly stroked her cheek.

"You're a nice woman, Jessica, which is why I won't do what I've been aching to, since I first saw you in the lounge."

Jessica licked her lips and met his tortured eyes. Their warm depths were black, and she felt the tension and heat radiate from his body. The atmosphere in the room suddenly shifted from their teasing, playful tone to something darker and richer. Something Jessica was beginning to understand. "What do you want to do, Cary?" she whispered.

Jessica's eyes grew wide as Cary leaned closer to her. Then their lips met and somehow her eyes closed. At first, he merely nipped her lips and teased the corners of her mouth with his tongue. Then he carefully drew her closer and placed his full mouth over hers. She felt the heat of the kiss on her toes, the tips of her fingers, throughout her entire body. Then she knew he was the ocean wave and she was drowning in his arms.

He nudged her mouth open and Jessica felt the power of his tongue. Burning need pooled throughout her body, gathering in her stomach. Cary's strong, confident hands roamed over her back, around her stomach, and almost to her breasts. His fingers barely brushed the full sides of her breasts and Jessica shuddered at the sparks left from the mere touch.

When the two finally separated, Cary drew in air with great effort and Jessica stumbled to the wall. She could barely see. Then she gasped, as without warning, Cary grabbed her arm and brought her back to him and his lips in one fluid motion. Their lips met with a force that nearly blinded Jessica. She didn't have much experience with men, but her body seemed naturally to know what to do as she surged against his hips and met his tongue in their contest to please each other.

With incredible human strength, Cary finally pulled away from her. He stared at her with blurred vision and knew she was as shocked as he was. Cary had never felt these emotions with other women. She tasted like a hot drink, after being in the cold. She tasted like home.

Cary's hands itched to rip her blouse apart and wipe away the questions that were already apparent in her eyes.

"I'm sorry, Jessica," Cary whispered, ashamed. He could tell she was about to bolt from the room at any second. "I don't know what came over me. I'm not in the habit of grabbing women and forcing them to kiss me."

"Don't apologize. I wasn't forced."

"No, this was inexcusable. I'm sorry. We've had a nice night and I've ruined it. I'm leaving early in the morning and I hope . . . Good night." Cary started for the door, cursing himself for acting like a Neanderthal with no self-control. He had never forced a woman to do anything in his life and he knew if he stayed in the room for one more second, Jessica would be on the floor. The thought sickened him, but all he had to do was look into her large brown eyes, and he became harder than he thought humanly possible. He wanted to bury himself so deep in her that he wouldn't be able to tell where he ended and she began.

"Cary, wait." Cary stopped but didn't turn to face her. She didn't know how close she was to being dragged to the nearest flat surface. As the silence lingered, he forced himself to turn and face her. One more, he was struck breathless by how beautiful she was, by how vulnerable she made him. While the thought of her power over him should have made him run from the room, Cary could only watch her.

She took a small step toward him. Cary waited. He forced himself to wait. He had a feeling if he made one move, or even breathed, Jessica would be gone. She would disappear like a dream. And for a man who didn't believe in dreams, Cary wanted to believe in her.

"Cary—" Her soft whisper trailed off as John Maison walked into the room. Cary silently cursed, as whatever Jessica wanted to say was gone. Cary watched with growing anger as John's eyes traveled from Jessica's flushed face, down the length of her body, to her shoes. Cary felt his hands automatically ball into fists as John's perusal continued, past the point of being polite, until even Jessica began to fidget. Cary had disliked the man after meeting him in the lounge, now he decided he hated the man. He also decided that if John continued to stare at Jessica, he would have to break his arm.

"Are you lost, John?" Cary's voice boomed across the once silent room.

"I hope I didn't interrupt anything," John responded, with a wink in Cary's direction. Jessica nervously cleared her throat and took a noticeable step away from Cary.

Cary didn't acknowledge John's sly grin, as he said, "We're finished in here. The room is all yours." Cary took Jessica's elbow and steered her toward the double doors.

"I can't blame you, Cary. I would keep her to myself, too," John said, laughing.

Cary glared at John, but Jessica pulled him out of the room and toward the stairs that led to the guest rooms. All murderous thoughts of John fled his mind as he realized the night was over. Jessica would leave and he would never see her again. The fact that his heart skipped a beat at the thought didn't even phase him.

"He's harmless, Cary," she said, squeezing his hands.

"Who?" he asked blankly.

"That man." She nodded in the direction of John Maison.

"He's harmless," Cary repeated, then glanced to the top of the stairs. He couldn't believe that in one night the idea of not spending one second with her could affect him. "I guess . . . I guess you want to go to your room. You have that long drive in the morning and . . ." His voice trailed off as he realized that she was smiling at him. Then he realized that she still held his hands.

"I'm not tired. Are you?"

"No."

"Good." She grinned and led him towards the lounge. Cary ignored the small voice that told him he would follow her anywhere.

Three

Jessica walked across the lounge as Cary lingered by the fireplace. She snuggled into the cushion in the window seat and just watched him. She could watch him all day. He was the most gorgeous man she had ever seen. If she had seen him on the street, Jessica knew she would have dismissed him as arrogant and not her type. But Cary was the opposite of everything she had ever believed a gorgeous man like him would be. In one night, he had changed all of her thoughts and preconceptions about men, and she knew for that reason she would always remember him. That reason and the amazing kiss that still had her knees weak with desire.

Then Cary turned to her and grinned. Jessica knew that for this one night, he was hers. She could tell from the soft expression in his eyes that he found her attractive, interesting. She knew it was the weather and the isolation that made him even remotely interested. He was a perfect specimen of a human being, and she was skinny, with practically no hips or behind to fill out a pair of jeans. She should have run from the room, but his intense, arousing gaze made her feel incredibly desirable and sexy. She subconsciously touched her fingers to her lips, still tingling from their kisses. His kiss had made her feel like the only woman on earth, as if she were his and he would be hers forever. She would think about reality—

that he would probably forget her name with the morning light—tomorrow.

"What are you thinking about?" Cary asked, as he settled on the cushion next to her.

"This has been a perfect night," she responded truthfully. He stared at his hands and Jessica cursed her inexperience as she realized that she had destroyed the evening. She had voiced her feelings, a cardinal sin in the world of male/female relations. "I only meant considering how the night started. I was walking down a dark road in the middle of the worst storm in years and then—"

"It has been perfect," he interrupted in a soft voice. She swallowed the lump in her throat as he met her eyes. She almost could see the loneliness on his face, but she dismissed that thought because she knew a man like Cary could not be lonely. He would have only to nod at a woman, and he would have company for the rest of his life. He abruptly changed the subject and said, "Hadley and Jake seem very happy together, don't they?"

"They almost make me believe a happy marriage isn't just something you see on television."

"You know you have a very skeptical view of marriage," he said, laughing.

"My parents divorced before I was born." She stared at her hands, not certain why she wanted to share this private part of her life with him. She hadn't told the majority of her friends the truth about her father. "I haven't seen my father since I was eight years old. There's an occasional phone call, but . . . I just know too many unhappily married people. I don't have much faith in the institution of marriage."

Jessica could feel Cary's intense eyes still on her and she finally looked up and met his eyes. "You know that was his loss, don't you?" he said softly.

Jessica smiled brightly. He could not have said anything more perfect if she had told him to. She wanted to brighten the mood before she cried and never stopped. "What about your parents?"

"They were married for thirty years and acted like newlyweds every day. Once, while we all were still in high school, my brother came home early and Mom and Dad were going at it in the living room. None of us were able to watch TV in there for a while afterward." Cary wrinkled his face in disgust as Jessica laughed hysterically.

"I hope I have the sort of marriage where, thirty years from now, I'll still be glad I married him."

"And then in the thirty-first year, you'll slap him with the divorce papers," he teased, nudging her shoulder.

Jessica laughed and playfully pushed him from her. She couldn't understand how Cary could make her feel so many emotions in one night. She went from lust to desire to humor, all because of the shift in his eyes or his smile. It almost frightened her how much control he had over her emotions; over her. She reminded herself once more of her vow to enjoy the night and not question her growing feelings.

"You have to admit that there are a lot of unhappy couples in the world," she said once her laughter had subsided.

"There are," he said, with a shrug. "Then I think of my parents or I see people like the newlyweds at dinner, and I think that maybe I haven't experienced all that love has to offer. And maybe if I had one moment like that, I wouldn't ever doubt love's power again."

"Have you ever been in love?" she whispered.

Cary didn't meet her eyes as he answered quietly, "Never."

"Have there been women?" she asked, curiously. The strange look he sent her made her bite her lower lip to restrain her laughter. He looked offended, as if she had insulted his sexual prowess.

"Of course there have been women," he responded in a self-righteous huff.

"But never one who made you want to act like your parents?" she prodded curiously.

He silently shook his head then asked, "What about you?"

"No one."

"Have there been men?" He repeated her question with a hint of irritation in his voice.

Jessica hesitated as she stared at her hands. She finally said, "No." She heard Cary's sharp intake of breath, before she forced herself to look at him. His wide eyes and open mouth made her realize that she hadn't imagined his surprise.

"When you say no . . ." He obviously struggled for the right words as he continued to gape at her. "What do you mean by no, Jess? Do you mean you've never been close to love or do you mean—"

"I mean, that I'm twenty-six years old and I'm a virgin," she blurted out. His shocked silence didn't offend her. In fact, she laughed. She almost felt liberated, like a fifty-pound weight had been lifted from her shoulders. She no longer had to pretend to be anything that she wasn't with him. Since Cary looked like he was on the verge of collapsing from shock or disbelief, she tried to explain. "I dated a few men in college who definitely tried to get me to see the need for sex, but . . . I never felt like it was right. I never trusted the men I was with enough to try . . . Now, I'm too busy at work to even find a man I would want to try with, and I don't exactly have a long list of potential men standing in line at my front door."

"Are the men in California insane?" he practically shouted in outrage. "You're still a virgin?"

"I think I still have some choice in the matter, Cary," she snapped dryly, glaring at him. Cary abruptly laughed and Jessica crossed her arms over her chest and tried not to pout. Her amusement with the situation rapidly disappeared. "You can stop laughing now."

"Are you waiting for marriage?" he asked, obviously unaffected by her anger as his lips twitched from the desire to laugh.

"I'm waiting until I'm sure."

"Sure of what?"

"Of him . . . of my feelings for him," she said uncertainly. She eyed him suspiciously as he studied her as if she were a creature from another planet. "Are you through laughing?"

"I'm sorry, Jess . . . Not that you're a virgin, but that I'm acting like an idiot." He leaned across the few inches of the cushion that separated them, and her anger instantly disappeared as she saw the raw desire in his eyes. She could feel his warm breath on her lips as he whispered, "I wasn't laughing at you. I was laughing at the expression on some man's face when he realizes that, out of all the men in the world you could have, you waited for him." She could feel the heat spread across her face and she quickly stared at her hands.

"I know how strange it sounds, all my friends tell me enough, but I—" He placed his fingers against her lips, effectively silencing her. She met his eyes and the butterflies once more started crawling over her body. All of her nerves concentrated on the touch of his fingers on her mouth.

"You don't have to explain anything to me or anyone else," he said, all traces of his laughter gone. His hand slid from her lips and Jessica withheld the whimper from the loss. His touch made her forget all of her promises to herself, all of her vows. "I hope you find him soon, Jess, the man who will make you whole."

"Me, too," she whispered, as she wondered if she already had. She found herself leaning toward him, her body moving of it's own will. Just as her eyelids fluttered closed and she prepared herself to experience the over-whelming emotions that followed kissing him, Cary cleared his throat and jumped to his feet.

"A checkers board," he said in a strange voice she didn't recognize as he stared across the room at a book-shelf packed with board games. "Do you want to play?"

Jessica momentarily sagged against the cool window, al-lowing the disappointment to surge through her body. When he sent her a questioning glance, she forced a smile and said, "Sure. Why not?"

Four

The early dawn light filled the lounge as Cary watched Jessica sleep. He gently stroked her soft hair, fanned out on the cushions of the couch, and marveled at the feel and vitality that seemed to flow through even the lightest strand. Around three o'clock, after checkers, card games, and hours of talking and laughing, Jessica's eyes had drifted closed and she was sprawled next to him on the couch. Cary had pretended to fall asleep on the couch next to her, but he couldn't sleep. He didn't want to spend one moment not experiencing the strange feelings that rushed through his body at her touch, her smile, or her laugh.

When he was with her, Cary felt something he hadn't felt in years. He felt like he could actually trust another human being. He knew he could place all of his trust in her and she would never disappoint him or be disappointed by him. Cary almost had half-convinced himself that he should try to make things work with her. To kiss her when she offered, to be the first and only one to introduce her to making love. He had spent half the night on the couch next to her in a state of painful anticipation of making all of his dreams a reality.

But, as Cary watched her, he also knew Jessica deserved a knight, a hero, someone to know exactly what she wanted and needed. She had dreams and ambitions that he couldn't possibly fulfill. She needed a husband who wasn't constantly looking over his shoulder and could give her all the love she needed. And those were all things that he knew he could never offer her.

"Good morning," Jessica mumbled as her eyes fluttered open. She stretched, causing the shirt to pull across her chest, and weakening his already shaky resolve. Never before had a woman made him feel tenderness and desire that made his hands shake simply by opening her eyes. She didn't notice his silence as she asked, "How long have you been awake?"

After a full night of dreaming about what could have been, Cary didn't have the strength to resist her anymore. Before he could stop himself, he kissed her. Not the hungry, searching kiss from last night, but with tenderness and caring and promise. Her tongue met his in a slow, lazy dance that made his heart expand in his chest.

Even when her hands grabbed the front of his shirt and he could feel her desire, he took his time, memorizing her mouth, the smell of her, the feel of her hair in his hands. She tried to move faster, to demand more, but Cary continued to show himself what he would miss, what he would always miss. He concentrated on the slick taste of her mouth, the softness of her neck as his hands moved to trace the length. He ignored the yearning that cried from the depths of his soul. Jessica would be in danger only if she were in his life. He told himself that she would be unhappy within a few days, regretting any decision to be with him.

Cary finally forced himself to pull away and the loss made him groan. He met her dazed eyes to force his gaze away from her swollen, moist lips. She continued to clutch his shirt, but Cary forced his hands off of her and he gripped the edge of the couch.

"Cary—"

"The rain's stopped." He interrupted her whisper,

even as he saw the unspoken consent to continue their kisses in her eyes. No matter how much he tried, he couldn't prevent the heavy note that entered his voice as he said, "I have to go, Jess. I need to get back to Virginia. It's a long trip."

"You have to leave now?" she asked, softly. His heart broke a little more at the entreaty in her brown eyes. He wondered if he were leaving to protect her or himself.

"Yes," he finally answered.

"Then drive carefully," she said, as her hands slowly disentangled from his shirt and uselessly dropped to her lap.

Cary couldn't prevent the disappointment that floated into his heart as he stood. Some part of him wanted her to grab his arm and yell at him for thinking of leaving her, but she probably realized he wasn't her other half anyway. He wanted to ask her a question. What if people were confused? What if one half recognized the other, and the other didn't realize it?

"Thanks." He couldn't resist one last touch, and he leaned down and wrapped his arms around her. He inhaled her sweet scent one last time. "You're an amazing woman, Jess. And here's one man who likes you a lot."

"Thank you for last night, Cary," she whispered into his ear.

"What did I do?" he asked, surprised, pulling back to look at her.

"You made me realize something my brother's been telling me for years, that there are a lot of good Black men still left out there."

Cary smiled sadly and possessed her lips for the last time. The thought almost made him fall to his knees and beg for her love. He pulled away from her and quickly averted his eyes as her lips glistened and silently called his name.

"Do you need anything, like a ride to your car or money or . . ."

"No. I'll manage."

Cary nodded then stood and walked to the door. He looked at her one last time. "I think you could manage just about anything. Take care of yourself, Jess, okay?"

"Cary?" She slightly hesitated as he stared, hoping, waiting. "Good luck with your job. Don't work too hard."

Cary smiled in acknowledgment and quickly left the lounge. He ran up the stairs to his room and threw his few belongings into his duffel bag. He practically ran out of the house, ignoring the plush greenery that the rain had coaxed out of the forest surrounding the inn. Cary jumped into his Jeep and sped from the inn. He had to stay in constant motion before he ran back to Jessica.

Jessica stood on the front porch of the inn talking on her cellular phone as a local mechanic worked under the hood of her car. The rain had given the trees and flowers surrounding the house a smell of renewal. Birds sang from the treetops, the sun shone, and the sky sparkled a crystal blue as if apologizing for the previous storm. There was still a cold breeze in the air, but Jessica barely noticed as she willed Andy Forester, the mechanic, to hurry on her car. She wanted to get as far away from this place and her memories of Cary as quickly as possible.

In the last few hours since he'd left the lounge, she hadn't been able to forget one second of their time together. She told herself that the pain in every bone and muscle of her body was her own fault. Cary had never promised anything other than that night. He had never pretended to be interested in anything other than company in the storm, but Jessica still hurt. She didn't know what she wanted him to do. Whatever it was, it didn't include him jumping from the couch as soon as the sun shone as if he couldn't wait to escape her presence. She had wanted to yell at him that she had been on the verge of giving herself to him, of making love to him, of feeling that she was certain of him, and he had kissed her senseless then run out the door. Jessica wanted to hate him, she wanted to cry, but she could only stand on the porch and stare at the plush greenery surrounding her. Only she didn't see the nature, she only saw Cary.

She snapped from her daze as the mechanic handed her the ringing cellular phone from her car. Jessica flinched as she heard her mother's screeching voice before she even placed the phone to her ear.

"Where in the hell have you been?" Karin Larson yelled on the other end of the phone in Los Angeles. "There's practically a hurricane up there and you won't answer your phone at the apartment or your cell phone. I made Dave search all over that city for you last night! I've been having a heart attack down here!"

"I'm fine, Mom. I got lost and had to spend the night in a little town called Blue Moon Bay. I'm about an hour and a half away from the city," Jessica said tiredly.

"So you can't call your mother?"

"The phone lines were down from the storm," Jessica explained tiredly. "I didn't even know they were working until I heard the cell phone ring."

"Are you sure you're okay? You sound . . . different. Is something wrong? Are you really being held hostage and you're forced to say everything's okay?"

Jessica wanted to laugh. Karin Larson was a drama teacher at a local community college and lived her own life like a drama. "Mom, I'm not being held hostage or kidnapped or anything exciting like that. I'm just tired."

"If you say so." Karin wasn't convinced but wisely changed the subject. "Call me as soon as you get back to your place. Remember my friend Brenda Presley? You played with her son, Eric, when you were little. Well, Eric's all grown up and back from medical school and asking about you."

Jessica rolled her eyes and sighed. At least once a month, Karin remembered some boy Jessica played with in her youth and tried to create a match. Usually Jessica yelled and gave her mother a speech on how she was focusing on her career and didn't need a man to complicate her life, but today Jessica didn't have the energy. "We'll talk when I get home. I really should go now."

"Are you sure you're okay, Jess?" Karin repeated, sounding more concerned.

"I am, Mom. I love you." Jessica pushed the 'end' button and sat on the porch swing as Jake walked out the front door with two cups of coffee. He handed one to her and sipped from his own.

"Thanks, Jake. This will definitely hit the spot."

"You look like you could use a jolt of caffeine to wake up. You have a long drive ahead of you," Jake said lightly, watching Andy work under the hood of her car.

"I'll be fine. I just had a slow start this morning." The two sat in companionable silence and sipped their coffee. Or Jake sat in companionable silence while every word Cary had spoken and every move he'd made raced through Jessica's mind.

"That Cary Riley was a real nice guy, wasn't he?" Jake began.

Jessica felt her cheeks flush with embarrassment. If Jake could read minds, he had interrupted her memories of their kiss. "Yeah."

"He seemed to think you were something else too," he continued.

Jessica stared at him and he met her eyes. "How do you know?"

"I saw the way he looked at you in the lounge, during dinner. He looked at you like you were the best present he ever got in his whole life." Jake sat next to her on the swing as Jessica's eyesight became blurry from her tears.

"I saw the way you were looking at him too. Are you going to see him again?"

"No," she whispered, quickly wiping away a tear. She wrapped her arms around herself and remembered the vacant look in Cary's eyes when he'd kissed her good-bye. She shook her head and forced a laugh. "I'm a fool to cry over a man."

"Says who?" Jake looked toward the forest as if for confirmation, then abruptly turned to her. "Maybe you should call him. We have his phone number in our guest registry."

Jessica rolled her eyes. "I can already imagine that phone conversation. 'Hi, Cary, this is Jessica.' 'Jessica who?' " She buried her face in her hands. "He didn't even stay until this morning. He just took off at the first sign of light, like a bat out of hell."

Jake considered her statement then shrugged. "Did you ask him to stay?"

Jessica looked at him speechless. "I could not have done that. I don't beg and plead with anyone. If Cary wanted to, he would have stayed. Since he's not here, he must not have wanted to."

"Or maybe he thought you didn't want him to," Jake suggested, and stood with a smile. "I had a hell of a time when I was twenty-six, but I wouldn't be that age again if someone paid me. All the uncertainty and love pains ... gives me a headache just thinking about it. Hell of an age. Call him, Jessica. That man felt something for you, more than a one-night stand. I could tell."

Andy slammed the hood, interrupting their conversation, and walked around to the driver's seat. He turned the key and the engine purred, sounding better than Jessica had ever heard it. "There you go, ma'am."

"Thank you." Jessica beamed, then reached into her purse for her wallet.

"Don't worry about it," Andy said, placing tools back into his tool box.

Jessica stared confused at Jake and Andy, then she grinned and hugged Jake. "You're responsible for this, aren't you?"

"Guilty as charged," he said, grinning.

"You should get going, ma'am. There may be clouds moving in this afternoon," Andy said.

She took one last look at the place that had changed her life, then looked at the old man who knowingly grinned at her. "Jake, thank you for everything. I could never repay your hospitality and generosity."

"Yes, you can. Come back."

Jessica grinned at him and got into her car. As she drove away, she glanced in her rearview mirror to see Jake waving from the porch. Jessica smiled to herself and concentrated on the road, trying to forget Cary's smiles and his warm mouth that had brought her skin to life.

Five

One week later, Jessica stared out the windows of her office building on the twenty-second floor of a high-rise in the Financial District of San Francisco, which displayed a view of the Golden Gate Bridge and the sparkling bay waters. Jessica once had a cubicle in the middle of the floor with the other entry-level consultants until Peter Jannings had spotted her ambition and potential. Now, she had an office the same size as a cubicle, but she could close the door and not whisper on the telephone when she had to allay her mother's fears about the latest controversy.

Usually, Jessica didn't mind the work or the tiny office, but since she'd returned from Hadley's Inn, she could not stand her office or her apartment. She couldn't stand the quiet. Once everything was quiet, she thought of Cary Riley. She thought about his kisses that made her heart melt, his eyes that made her soul soar, and his hands that made her body sing. Before she met Cary, Jessica had enjoyed the silence of her small, comfortable apartment after a hectic day at the office, but now the silence only invited memories of him. She had been comfortable with her single status before Cary, and she vowed to reach that level of comfort again.

"Are you heading home, Jess?" Jessica turned at the sound of her best friend's voice. Erin Hargrove stood in the doorway of the office, holding her briefcase. She and Erin were the only two Black women working at Jannings & Associates and had become instant best friends, because they were the only ones in the office who could completely understand the pressures of being Black and female in the financial consulting world. Jessica relied on Erin's razor-sharp, ruthless attitude, while Erin always said she needed Jessica's precision and composure. Jessica knew that Erin would never cry over any man and that she would probably laugh at Jessica for doing so.

Jessica glanced at her watch and was slightly surprised to realize it was after seven o'clock. "I didn't notice how late it was."

"You haven't noticed much of anything today," Erin observed as she sat in one of the chairs across from Jessica's desk. Erin pushed uncontrollable black curls away from her brown eyes then said bluntly, "Talk, girl."

Jessica ignored Erin's intense gaze and stacked the papers on her desk into meaningless piles. "With the Reimers account taking so much time—"

"Stop stalling and tell me what's bothering you," Erin interrupted, crossing her arms over her chest.

"I have no idea what you're talking about."

"During the meeting today, you didn't even look up when Jannings gave an extra assignment with a big bonus," Erin said, holding up a finger with each point. "You didn't even take the opportunity to insult Jacob Horne when he walked around with a piece of spinach in between his teeth all day. You didn't even blink when a major shareholder walked into the office. You are not the same Jessica Larson that left this office last week for Los Angeles."

Jessica forced a small smile. "I'm not feeling well."

"Obviously," Erin muttered, then stood and glanced at her watch. "Normally, I would cross-examine you until I dragged the information from you, but I have a hair appointment in twenty minutes and if I don't get these locks tamed, I won't be able to drag a brush through them in a few days."

Jessica tried not to smile in relief and said, "I'll see you tomorrow."

"We're having lunch and don't try to get out of it," Erin warned, smiling. "I wanted to talk to you anyway. I have a friend who saw—"

"No more blind dates," Jessica pleaded.

Erin shook her head with a large smile. "This guy is different, Jess. He's kind, sweet—"

"Then why aren't you dating him?"

Erin rolled her eyes and sighed in exasperation. "I'm finished with men for the next fifty years. After Ronald . . . and Ted . . . and Richard, I would rather stick my hand in an electrical socket then deal with another man."

"Why can't I feel the same way?" Jessica asked quietly. "I don't want to go on another blind date."

"Because one of us has to live vicariously through the other, and since I'm hating men right now, that leaves you," Erin replied with a wide grin. She glanced at her watch again. "We'll talk tomorrow." With the threat hanging in the air, Erin left the office.

Jessica pushed the pile of papers aside and switched off the desk lamp. She sat in the darkness for a moment and tried not to cry. Somehow, she would have to find a way to squirm out of that lunch with Erin or she would spend the entire lunch hour crying. Erin would undoubtedly drag the whole story about Cary out of Jessica with one arched eyebrow. Jessica wasn't ready to share her memories of Cary with anyone else, either from embarrassment or fear that she would discover he had been a dream. She wanted to keep Cary and his life-renewing kisses to herself.

Jessica glanced at her tattered running shoes underneath the desk and hesitated. She sighed tiredly then changed into the clean set of running clothes she always kept in the office, hoping the urge to exercise would overcome her during lunch hour. The urge definitely wasn't possessing her now, but she hoped the pain from running would temporarily take her mind off Cary and keep her from an empty apartment.

Jessica snapped from her daze as she realized the telephone on her desk was ringing. "Hi, Mom," she greeted, before the person on the other end could speak.

"How'd you know it was me?" Karin demanded.

"You always call the office around 7:00 to see if I'm still here."

"Then why don't you surprise me and not be there one night?"

Jessica winced. Her mother's remark hit too close to her own questions. "I was just about to leave, Mom. I promise."

"I just got Jenny Abrams's wedding invitation in the mail."

Jessica waited expectantly. She had to remind her friends not to send wedding invitations to Karin, because it gave her too many ideas. "And?" she prodded.

"It says she's marrying Elton Richmond on December twentieth. Isn't that beautiful? A Christmas wedding."

"Mom—"

"I know you want this successful career and I want that for you too, honey. I also want you to be happy, and working fifty hours a week for the rest of your life is not going to make you happy," Karin said passionately. "You and David are going to cause your mother to die from shame. All my friends have grandkids now and they ask me, where are your grandkids? I want them, Jess. I want to spoil them, give them candy when you say not to. I want to walk into the store and be able to browse in the baby department again. I want to have a legitimate reason to watch cartoons again. I want to buy toys and have them waiting when my grandkids visit. I want that, Jessica."

Jessica controlled her laughter, only because she didn't want to listen to more of her mother's soliloquy on the joys of grandparenting. "I didn't know this was causing such trauma in your life," she managed to say.

"Well, it is. So, can you give your dear, old mom a break for once in her long, troubled life?"

Jessica prepared for her run by stretching her arms over her head. "What do you want me to do, Mom? Step into the middle of a bar and announce that my mother is ready to be a grandparent?"

"Don't get smart with your mother," Karin snapped, then said calmly, "David has a friend—"

Jessica abruptly stood and brushed her hair from her face. Her mother always pressured her brother into arranging dates for Jessica with one of his eligible friends. David, a corporate attorney, usually picked the least threatening, dull colleague he knew for his baby sister. "Mom, no."

"Jess—"

"Mom, no!" Jessica repeated firmly.

"Dave's just worried about you. He told me you've lost weight these last few weeks and you never eat a thing. He says you work too much. He just wants you to be happy, we both do, and he thinks this guy will make you very happy. His name is Brian Bross, he's a lawyer with a firm in San Francisco, he's thirty, and David says he's a really nice man," Karin said, finishing her sales pitch.

Jessica looked at her reflection in the shining surface of her desk and remembered her pledge to forget Cary. She wouldn't normally have gone out with David's friend before she met Cary, but now she felt she owed it to herself. Cary was probably dating someone in Virginia, probably beautiful with mile-long legs and huge breasts, she thought bitterly. She knew he hadn't lied to her about anything he'd said. She had seen the sincerity in his eyes, but the harsh light of reality probably reminded him that she was an inexperienced workaholic from San Francisco and he was gorgeous and sexy. The thought made her eyes fill with tears.

"Okay, Mom," Jessica relented, taking a deep breath. "The Bay Area Professional Ball is next week. I'll call Dave when I get home."

Jessica could practically see the smile on her mother's face as she said, "You may even like this one, honey. You never know."

Jessica knew but she didn't want to break her mother's heart.

Jessica jumped over a fallen log without breaking her pace and continued running through the thick foliage of Golden Gate Park. She welcomed the sweat soaking her shirt and dripping from her face, and concentrated on breathing. She had forgotten how much she loved to run, once she passed the initial pain threshold. She loved the solidarity of the trail in the early evening. She usually could finish her entire three-mile run without encountering another person. It gave her time to think, which she couldn't do in an office with telephones constantly ringing, or in her depressingly quiet apartment.

Although Golden Gate Park was located in the middle of the busy streets and loud sounds of San Francisco, the running trails that snaked through the trees were quiet and still. The rocky, green terrain proved slick underneath her running shoes as the early evening, pink-tinted sky peeked through the thick leaves of the trees. The rapidly disappearing sun warmed the sweat on the back of her neck.

Even as she ran, unbidden thoughts of Cary snaked into her mind. She thought of his smile when he talked about his sister, and the way he touched her face as if she were the most perfect woman in the world. As soon as she had driven away from the inn, Jessica knew that she was in love with him. It was the first time she fell in love, and the man was across the country; and he probably didn't even remember her name.

Jessica's thoughts were interrupted as she turned the path and saw a man, laying on the ground, moaning in obvious pain. She ran to him and touched his shoulder, concerned. Runners often underestimated the steepness of the path, not realizing the hilly terrain and long trail. "Are you okay?" she asked.

With lightening speed, the man whirled around, swinging a fist at her. By reflex, Jessica jumped back, feeling the air from his fist brush pass her face. She lost her footing on the damp grass and fell to the ground. The man quickly stood to his feet and Jessica stared in horror. Her mind raced ahead, noticing his short and neat brown hair, his lean build, his high cheekbones and dark brown skin color, but his hazel eyes held her attention. And that's what frightened Jessica; what made her blood chill and her heart momentarily stop. His eyes were a beautiful color, but cold and hard, as if all human emotions had been erased.

Jessica was too frightened to scream. She could scarcely breathe. He seemed to study her for a minute and Jessica felt violated, from her feet to her forehead, as his eyes traveled over her. Then he smiled, a cruel, hard smile and in his left hand appeared a long knife that glistened maliciously in the fading sunlight. Without waiting for him to make his next move, Jessica scrambled to her feet and raced toward the entrance of the park. Branches and leaves whipped across her face, bare arms, and bare legs as she crashed through the trees. Jessica didn't want to look back, but she couldn't resist, and she choked on her scream when she saw him crashing through the trees behind her. Jessica increased her speed, until her lungs emptied and her leg muscles burned.

Her heavy breathing seemed to roar in her ears, blocking out all other sounds. She finally screamed when something tugged on her shirt, but when she whirled around, it was a bush branch tangled in the hem. Her hands shook as she ripped the shirt from the branch's grip and she finally noticed that the man wasn't behind her. Jessica quickly looked above her, expecting the man to fall from the sky, but she only saw more trees and leaves. She knew he still watched her and waited for her somewhere behind the trees.

Jessica abruptly turned off the path and crashed her way through trees that led directly up a hill and overlooked another section of the park, half a mile away. She forced herself to move silently, sacrificing speed for stealth, but she didn't want the man to hear her position. The only advantage she had was that she knew the park like the back of her hand. The problem was, she didn't know how well her attacker knew the park. Questions rolled through her head. Why her? What did he want? Jessica didn't intend to find out.

She moved through the trees, violently shaking and sweating profusely, until she spotted an opening that led directly to an exhibit where a crowd of people stood. Judging from their evening clothes and champagne glasses, they were attending an outdoor reception. She scanned the crowd for a sympathetic face, someone to help her or to scare away her attacker.

Then she saw her attacker crouched by a tree only fifty feet away from her and she bit her bottom lip to keep from screaming. His back was to her but she recognized him. She would see his face in her nightmares for the rest of her life. Jessica whirled around and stumbled down the brambles and bushes toward the people and safety.

She didn't stop running until she burst from the trees,

accidentally knocking over an older man in a dark suit. His champagne glass went flying in one direction and the other guests gasped in shock, as he and Jessica tumbled to the pavement. She cried out as she felt the sharp sting of her knee scraping the gravel.

"Are you—" The man's eyes widened as he saw her face, bloodied from the small cuts from the tree branches, and her wild eyes. "My God, what happened to you?" A small crowd gathered around the two as Jessica placed her face in her hands and began to cry.

Six

"Jess?" David stood in the doorway of Inspector Kerns's office. Jessica smiled at the sight of her brother and threw off the wool blanket that she had been given. She ran into his arms and felt fresh tears fall down her face. She had spent the last two hours telling the San Francisco Police Department detectives everything about the incident, and she had spent the last twenty minutes convinced she had no more tears to spill. Seeing her brother's face quickly destroyed that conviction. She squeezed David closer to her.

She had reached for the phone several times to call Jake Hansot at Hadley's Inn for Cary's home phone number from the guest registry. She needed Cary. She needed to feel his strong arms around her and hear him promise her that everything would be fine. But Jessica wasn't going to call Jake or Cary. She did call her brother, and the concern apparent in his warm brown eyes made her want to cry all over again.

"Jess, what happened?" David asked, concerned, framing her face in his hands.

"I don't know." She broke away from his arms and raked a hand over her sweat-dampened hair. She felt the sudden need to establish her independence. She didn't like feeling helpless and vulnerable, even in front of her older brother. "I was running and this man tried to attack me . . . I just want to get out of here."

"Are you sure you're okay?" David persisted. He grabbed her arm and forced her to look at him. "Don't play this independent, Jessica-against-the-world role with me! I got a call from the police and I thought you were dead . . ." David's face crumpled and Jessica hugged him. He needed her strength now. David and her mother were both emotional people, and Jessica had always been the sensible one in the family. She liked being the logical, calm force, not the one shaking and crying. "God, Jess, I was so scared."

"It's over now, Dave," she assured him.

"What did that bastard want? Did he say anything?"

"No."

"Did he try to . . ." David managed to squeak the word out—"Rape. Did he try to rape you?"

"I didn't give him that opportunity," Jessica replied calmly.

David's expression turned stern once more. "I told you about running in the park alone. If you want to go running, call me. I'll ride my bike or something. You have to be careful, Jess."

Inspector Kerns walked into the office holding a manila folder. The graying hair at his temples and deeply etched laugh lines in his light brown face made Jessica automatically think of her grandfather. As a result, she had instantly trusted him. Or she had until she described her attacker. Then his expression became serious, and he had stopped answering her questions and starting scribbling furiously on the paper in front of him.

"Inspector Kerns, this is my older brother, David," Jessica said with as much calm as she could muster. The two men shook hands.

"I'm glad to see your brother's here, Ms. Larson."

Jessica rubbed his arm and smiled at David's frown. "Me, too."

"Could you two please sit down?" Jessica met David's confused glance and they both sat in the two empty seats in front of his desk. "Are you certain this is the man from the park?"

Jessica looked at the large black-and-white photograph he pushed across the desk. She shuddered as she recognized the man's features. The camera shot had been out of focus and from a distance, but she knew it was him. "I'm positive. I'll remember his eyes for the rest of my life."

"Is there a problem, Inspector?" David demanded. "My sister has been through a horrific experience. She doesn't want to stay in this place to be questioned over and over again!"

Inspector Kerns hesitated, then explained in a soft voice, "If this is the man from the park, then your sister . . . His name is Michael Lyons. He's the leader of a terrorist group in a small country in West Africa called Jubumga. His father led a very corrupt and oppressive regime until he was assassinated two years ago by democratic forces, with rumored American help. Michael and his older brother, Weston, were in Europe when it happened and returned to their country to gain control. They weren't having any success when Weston was killed in a gunfight with the military and, some say, Michael went crazy. He blamed the local government and America, vowing revenge on both. His group was partially disbanded a few months ago, we . . . There's some confidential material involved but I thought you should know this wasn't a run-of-the-mill attacker."

Jessica felt David's hand tighten on hers as she stared at the detective blankly. "What would a terrorist want with me?" she asked softly.

"I don't know; that's what we've been trying to figure

out. It could just involve a case of mistaken identity or maybe a random killing . . ." His voice trailed off as Jessica looked at her brother. His dark brown face grew ashen as he stared at the detective. "Don't worry, Ms. Larson, now that we know he's out there, we'll catch him. I doubt he'll even return. Since you escaped, he knows that we know he's in town. He's not stupid."

Jessica rose to her feet, her legs trembling. "May I go?" she asked, avoiding the man's eyes. She wondered if he could hear the loud pounding of her heart against her chest.

"Yes. Just to be safe, I'll assign a unit to patrol your neighborhood and area where you work every half hour for the next few weeks. If you suspect anything, don't hesitate to call me; that's what I'm here for." Jessica knew her fear was apparent because Inspector Kerns smiled encouragingly and said, "Don't worry, Jessica, our sources say Michael Lyons is probably far away from San Francisco by now."

He stood and shook Jessica's offered hand. Jessica pulled David from his seat and led him from the room.

David didn't speak until the two had walked a block from the police station. He suddenly grabbed her and Jessica couldn't breathe as his powerful arms practically squeezed the breath from her lungs. "Jess, I don't know what I'd do if I ever lost you. I love you, little sis," he whispered emotionally, and kissed her forehead.

"Stop worrying, David. You heard Inspector Kerns; that Lyons character mistook me for someone else. He probably thought I was someone exciting like a *La Femme Nikita*. It's over. Okay?"

David nodded and wiped his eyes with an embarrassed smile. "Isn't this familiar? Me, a basket case, and you, calm and sensible. I've just been worried about you. You've been different these last few months. You don't seem happy anymore. I thought maybe it was my imagination; then when you came back from Mom's last weekend, I knew I wasn't imagining things. I don't know what's going on in your head anymore. Is everything all right?"

Jessica stared at her shoes, then met her brother's worried eyes. She wanted to tell him about Cary, about how she had fallen in love and had her heart broken. But she didn't. David would yell and scream, then he would want to launch a search to find Cary so he could bash his face in for hurting her.

"I'm fine, Dave."

"Why do I have the feeling you're lying to me?" David asked doubtfully.

"I don't know, because I'm telling the truth. There's nothing wrong with me that rest won't cure," she said with what she hoped was a convincing smile.

"Well, I'm taking you home immediately, unless you want to spend the night at my place or maybe you want to go to Erin's."

Jessica quickly shook her head, even as she clung to his hand. "I'm going home."

The two continued to walk toward his car. Jessica thought of being alone in her apartment and her heart raced with fear. She glanced at her brother's strong profile and found him staring at her, as if waiting for her to say something. Jessica muttered a silent curse at her brother's telepathic abilities. Even when they were children, with one glance, he had been able to tell what she thought.

"David—"

He didn't allow her to finish as he squeezed her hand and said, "I'll stay with you tonight." Jessica smiled gratefully and hugged him.

Cary's feet were propped on his desk as he stared out the plated glass, one-way window of his office. He could see the green peaks of the forest only two miles away and the hoods of the hundreds of cars in the parking lot, but no one could see him. From outside the building, the windows looked black and impenetrable, which was exactly how Cary felt inside his heart.

Cary couldn't see the trees or the grass. He saw only Jessica's wide smile and her beautiful brown eyes and the way they had darkened just before he kissed her. Just thinking of her made Cary's insides tighten and harden. One week later, Cary still felt her kisses and smiles, and still took cold showers and nightly runs to forget about the smell of her. He still wanted her. He wanted to feel her smooth skin beneath him. He wanted to hear the sighs of pleasure that he knew he could cause. He wanted her so much that he grew breathless with the need. Then he remembered that she obviously didn't want him.

She hadn't tried to stop him, or asked for an address to reach him. She had used him as a way to pass time in a storm. Cary wasn't stupid. He knew she must've felt some feelings for him or she never would have allowed him to kiss her, but she probably evaluated the situation the next morning, and found Cary lacking in all the areas she deemed important in a man. Cary groaned and closed his eyes. She haunted his dreams and his thoughts. If he went on assignment in this frame of mind, he would get himself killed.

The door to his office opened and Dan Pelstrom walked into the cramped room. Dan was the only agent who actually attempted conversation in an environment where everyone kept his eyes on the floor and his mouth closed and, for that reason, most agents didn't like or trust him. Dan was the same age as Cary and probably had more worry lines than Director Iverson. He had a wife and a seven-month-old baby who he told lies to every day when he left for work. Dan told Cary he was quitting in January to become a cop, a $15,000 annual pay reduction.

Dan placed a folder, marked *Top Secret* on the front in red letters, on Cary's meticulously clean desk. "How are you doing?"

Cary shrugged, not wanting to speak. He found himself not speaking to anyone lately. After leaving Jessica, he couldn't find anyone worth speaking to. "What's this?" He set his feet on the floor and opened the folder.

"SFPD just contacted Iverson. A woman was attacked in Golden Gate Park by a man she identified as Michael Lyons. I thought you should know he was on our side of the world."

"What the hell is he doing in America?" Cary murmured to himself. Michael, twenty-one and a self-confessed psychotic, opened his eyes two years ago to find his entire world destroyed. His father, who had raped their small African country for everything it was worth, was murdered, and four months later Michael's older brother was killed. The Group had information that Michael was preparing to perform terrorism on American soil and Cary, who bared a striking resemblance to Weston Lyons, was assigned to the case.

Cary infiltrated the group of suspected terrorist members in New York over a period of a year and eventually met Michael. Presenting himself as a Black American with a deep interest in African issues—enough interest to kill and die for—Michael embraced him and the two became close. After spending months with him, Cary found himself liking the young man. Cary recognized Michael's loneliness and understood why he was so angry with the world.

Michael returned to his country the day before the Group stormed their New York headquarters. Cary often thought about his betrayal of Michael and he knew the two would meet when the time was right, but his interest was more piqued with the mention of San Francisco. The terrorist was in the same city as Jessica. Then Cary's eyes focused on the name of the woman from the park. Jessica Larson. Cary's hands trembled as he picked up the paper, almost tearing it apart, wanting the words to be wrong.

"What's wrong, Cary?" Dan asked, his voice full of surprise.

"The woman . . . Jessica Larson. I know her." Cary slowly rose to his feet and quickly sat back down as his legs shook. Michael was trying to get to him through Jessica. There were no coincidences in his world, just facts. "He wants to kill her because of me. Is she okay?" Cary poured back over the files and finally read that the "victim" only suffered a few cuts and bruises. Cary breathed a sigh of relief, then stood.

"Where are you going?" Dan asked, exasperated.

"To tell Iverson I'm going to San Francisco," Cary said, without breaking his stride. Two steps down the corridor, he remembered Group policy to always lock doors and turned back to his office. Dan still stood near Cary's desk. Cary impatiently motioned him out the room. "I need to lock up."

Dan nodded then smiled as he walked out the door. "I was wondering if you'd remember. This woman must mean something to you." Cary ignored him, as he locked the door and headed down the hall.

Dan watched Cary round the corner; then he leisurely walked toward the only entrance and exit in the building, past the high clearance and specially trained blind guards, and outside. He walked to his car, turned on the motor, and began a slow drive around the grounds of the unmarked Group building. He picked up the car phone, registered in his dead cousin's name, and dialed a number he memorized months ago.

"What?" came the thick African accent, after one ring.

"He's on his way to San Francisco," Dan said pleasantly,

adding, "You're getting rusty in your old age. You can't even handle one female in a park?" Dan replaced the phone on the console and smiled at himself in the rear-view mirror.

Seven

Jessica looked up from the computer screen as the door to her office swung open and Erin hurried into the office. Jessica could tell from Erin's concerned expression that she knew about the attack. Erin quickly closed the door behind her, and walked around the desk to take her hand. Jessica felt the tears fill her eyes at her friend's concern. Erin immediately hugged her.

"I heard what happened in the park, Jessie," Erin said softly. "Are you okay?"

Jessica pulled away from Erin, carefully wiping away stray tears. "Does everyone in the office know?"

"David called and told me. I haven't told anyone else."

In spite of her own misery, Jessica smiled at her friend. "I thought you and David vowed to not speak to each other again."

"I still refuse to speak to that arrogant pig, but this is different," Erin said, taking her hands. "Are you sure you're all right? That man didn't hurt you, right?"

"Somehow, I managed to get away before he could touch me."

"Maybe I should start running in the park with you." Erin was silent for a few minutes, then said abruptly, "Do you have to run? Couldn't you just ride the stationary bike at the gym like other women?"

Jessica laughed and Erin joined her, squeezing her

hand. "You can put away your sweats because I'm not going running for a while," Jessica finally said.

"What did David say? Did he want to launch a city-wide search so he could kill the man?"

Jessica heard the exasperation in Erin's voice. Since Jessica first introduced David and Erin two years ago, the two had done nothing but argue with each other. Jessica suspected their professed hatred was nothing more than two adults that were too immature to admit an attraction to each other.

"David was pretty calm. I think he wanted to stay calm for my sake."

"David, calm? Are we talking about your brother, David Larson?"

Jessica smiled and said with a laugh, "Anytime you want a date with David, you know where to find me. I can call him and within two minutes, you two—"

"If you say one more word, I'll vomit." Erin's smile disappeared as she studied Jessica. "I love you, Jess."

Jessica smiled and hugged her friend once more. "I love you, too."

"Do you still want to go out to lunch?"

Jessica took a deep breath as an overwhelming fear of walking in public squeezed her heart. She clenched her hands into fists to hide the discomfort from Erin. "Not today, maybe tomorrow."

Erin nodded, then walked to the door. She turned back to Jessica with a teasing smile. "Put my mind at ease and tell me this all wasn't a scheme to get out of that blind date."

Jessica laughed and shook her head. "No, Erin."

"Just checking." Erin winked and walked out of the office. Jessica's smile disappeared as she sat back in her chair. She stared out the window and thought of the cold eyes from the park, of his lunge toward her. She also thought of Cary. She wanted him beside her. She wanted him so much, her body seemed to ache.

Jessica took a deep breath and turned back to the computer screen. There was no use dreaming Cary would suddenly appear like a knight in shining armor. He had a life in Virginia. A life that she knew would never include her.

Jessica quickly unlocked the door to her apartment building and slammed it shut behind her. She had spent the entire day in her office, too frightened to venture past the security desk in the lobby and the locked doors of her company. Jessica had even told Erin to leave work without her, because she didn't want Erin to see her catch a taxi home. She could not handle the idea of standing on a bus, in the middle of a crowd, and dealing with the possibility of Michael Lyons standing beside her.

Jessica told herself every ten minutes that Michael Lyons was in Africa and had simply mistaken her for someone else, but Jessica's hands still shook when she unlocked the door to her apartment building. She trudged up the stairs of the dim hallway with her briefcase and purse slung over one shoulder. This had been one of the longest days of her life. She couldn't wait to slide into an aromatic bubble bath and forget that Michael Lyons or Cary existed.

She unpinned her hair and ran a hand over her aching head. She wouldn't have time to think of Cary tonight, at least. She had a lot of work to complete, not that she would be able to sleep. Before the attack, images of Cary interfered with her dreams and forced her awake at night to think of impossible scenarios wherein he would breeze into her life. Now, she would spend the night awake with all the lights on in the apartment, because a different man had ruined her illusions of safety and invincibility.

Jessica unlocked the door to her apartment and opened it. She felt her jaw drop as Cary Riley stood next to her couch, with his back to her. It was a dream, she decided. But when she stepped into her apartment, she smelled him. The smell, a spine-tingling mixture of cologne and soap, that she had imagined and dreamed about for over seven days. As her eyes drank in the sight of him in khakis and a blue T-shirt, Jessica unconsciously dropped her briefcase and purse against the wall. He'd finally come. She wanted to cry all over again.

Then Cary turned to her and placed a finger to his mouth, conveying quiet. She became puzzled as she noticed the small device in his hands that he swept over his lumpy beige couch, and the preoccupied look in his eyes. Jessica softly closed the door and watched him squat to his knees to look under the couch. He didn't look at her or even acknowledge her appearance except for his initial nod of recognition. Jessica didn't think her heart could tear apart any more, but it did. And along with the hurt came scalding fury as she watched his hands maneuver and caress the instrument. That should be me, Jessica thought, then shook her head. In all her dreams of a reunion with Cary, she definitely didn't imagine him paying more attention to her seven-year-old couch than to her.

She plopped on a nearby chair and crossed her legs. He was obviously here for some reason other than to see her. The anger mounted while Cary carefully continued to move the strange device over the stack of books on her glass coffee table. Jessica snorted in disbelief and he shot her an angry look. She squarely met his gaze, and she rolled her eyes when he looked away. He couldn't even look at her. Jessica vowed not to waste another second mourning over him.

Cary finally stood and pushed a button on the instrument. "I had to complete the sweep first to see if the room was bugged. This machine can detect whether a listening device—"

"What the hell are you doing here?" Jessica demanded, jumping to her feet.

"Is that any way to greet a man you spent a perfect night with?" His sardonic expression and lack of any warmth or greeting, made her anger explode beyond the breaking point. He appeared to consider one of the most important nights of her life a joke.

Enraged and humiliated, she covered the room in four long strides and slapped his face. She instantly wanted to apologize when his shocked eyes met hers, but then his eyes became black and unreadable. "How dare you break into my apartment and act like . . ." Her voice trailed off as she finally noticed the shoulder holster over his shirt and the gun nestled underneath his right arm. She was completely confused as she met his eyes. "What's going on? Why do you have a gun?"

"I'm an undercover agent for a clandestine agency within the government known as the National Intelligence Group. We are an antiterrorist unit within the FBI. I joined the Group straight out of college and I've been there for five years," he said in a calm monotone.

Jessica stared at him in amazement. She had known he wasn't a marketing director the moment the lie slipped from his lips. She wanted to ask him what else was a lie that night. But she knew the answer. Everything that night had been a lie. The Cary Riley she had kissed, shared her secrets with, and fallen in love with didn't exist.

"One year ago, I infiltrated a West African terrorist group with plans to bring their terrorism to America. I bear an uncanny resemblance to the leader's deceased brother and my superiors thought that would give me an edge to gain the group's trust. I became close to the leader, Michael Lyons. Somehow, my cover was blown and the members caught me and planned to kill me. The Group came in and neutralized the American sect to save me. Michael Lyons was in his country when it happened. He wants me dead because he feels I betrayed him."

Jessica quickly looked at her hands as tears blurred her vision. She closed her eyes, imagining the constant pain and loneliness in his life. He could never trust anyone, never engage in casual conversations with anyone without fear or suspicion. She controlled her tears and looked back at him. He had walked to the window and stared out at the street below. "Michael Lyons was the man who attacked me in the park," she whispered.

"I know." She heard the raw emotion in his voice, but when he turned to face her, his expression was composed and blank. "Somehow, Michael found out about you— about us. He wants to get to me through you."

"If you know that's what he wanted, why'd you come?" Jessica wanted him to say he wanted to see her again. She wanted him to smile at her and kiss her, but she could tell from his expression that he would do neither.

"Because Michael and I have to finish this, and I don't want you to be hurt because of me. Michael never should have involved you. He has crossed the line, and he will pay."

Jessica stood and walked to the door. She was suddenly very tired. She wanted to play depressing CDs and keep her fantasies of Cary. In her dreams, he never hurt her like this. In her dreams, violins swelled in the background, Cary wore a tuxedo, and he carried one dozen red roses and a bottle of champagne. "Well, good luck with your duel to the death with Michael Lyons. If you leave your hotel number, I'll be sure to give it to Michael the next time I see him." She opened the door, then noticed the amused gleam in his eyes. Her temper snapped again and she slammed the door. "What, now?"

"I'm not going anywhere." He sat on the couch and placed his hiking boot-encased feet on the table. "If Michael thinks there's something between us, whether in the past or not, he'll stop at nothing to get you. I know Michael. I spent over a year studying how he thinks and operates. I'm the only one who can protect you from him. I have to stay here with you."

"He's after you, not me," she protested.

"He thinks you're a part of me. He's after both of us."

"One night. We spent one night together that meant nothing to either one of us. How could he come away with the impression that I'm a special person in your life?"

Jessica noticed the slight stiffening in his spine, but he replied calmly, "I don't know. I didn't tell anyone about us. Did you?"

Jessica gasped at the pain that coursed through her body with his indirect affirmation that she meant nothing to him. She pretended outrage at his innocent question. "Of course not."

"There's an investigation under way at the Group right now to discover how Michael found out about us. We're also performing background checks on every guest at the inn that night."

"Not Jake or Hadley," Jessica pleaded.

"Don't worry. Those two are fine. I'm concentrating on that man, John Maison, who saw us in the empty room together. I think he was a plant."

Jessica groaned in frustration and demanded, "Can't you spread it around the spy-gossip circles that I was simply a one-night diversion?"

Cary stared at her and asked quietly, "Do you really believe that?"

"It doesn't matter what I believe."

Jessica tried not to tremble as Cary met her eyes. He finally grabbed a magazine from her coffee table and began to lazily flip the pages. "It won't matter. Michael will still come after you."

"Like hell!" Jessica never felt so frustrated and angry

and hurt in her entire life. He was doing exactly what she wanted; he was staying. But there was no interest on his part. She could barely keep herself from running to him, and he talked as if they were two strangers who just met ten minutes ago. "I have rights as an American citizen and I want you out! I want you out of my home this second!"

"You don't mean that, Jess."

Jessica colored slightly at the provocative tone in his suddenly satin voice and his use of her nickname. She kept her glance hard and remained near the door, across the room from him. "Get out right now, Cary!"

Cary rose to his feet and seemed to stalk across the room, effectively pinning her against the door. The heat from his body enveloped her, his essence and smell pulled her against him. Jessica heard her own soft gasps for air as he openly and brazenly assessed her body. He hadn't even touched her and she was ready to offer him anything he wanted. She had hoped her attraction to him would have diminished since she now knew he cared nothing about her or their night together, but the truth was everything about him seemed magnified, more perfect. She could hear her breath fill the room as he tucked loose strands of her hair behind her right ear. Her skin practically sang with the contact from his warm fingers, and she cursed her weak flesh.

"I'm the best agent there is, Jess. You'll be safe with me, and I need to know you're safe." He lightly nipped the lobe of her ear before continuing, "As long as I'm here, Michael will concentrate on me. If he's concentrating on me, then you're safe. I have to stay here. What man wouldn't stay with his woman if she looked like you?" She couldn't hear his words anymore as his eyes traveled to her breasts beneath the black suit jacket. The look in his eyes made Jessica feel as if she were completely nude.

"You're so beautiful, Jess," he whispered, then slowly licked the outer shell of her ear. Jessica's knees trembled and she braced her arms in back of her on the door for support. She looked into his eyes, as dark as the night sea, and knew she was completely lost. As if in slow motion, Cary leaned toward her and touched his tongue to each corner of her mouth, then skimmed along her trembling bottom lip. She knew she could push him away at any second, but she needed him to touch her and comfort her after the events of the last few days.

Slowly, Cary made his way down, and she shuddered as he placed soft, light kisses along the column of her neck. Her head dropped back, giving him better access, and his kisses trailed to the open V of her suit jacket. His tongue darted into her barely visible cleavage and Jessica felt her very soul melt to the floor. He was killing her with his tongue and lips. She knew she would have absolutely no defense when he added his hands.

Then he took her lips, and Jessica moaned with need and desperation. Instead of escaping her dreams, she was stepping right into one as his tongue greedily plundered her mouth. His hands moved under her jacket to rest on her lace-covered breasts, slowly stroking each one as his tongue in her mouth mimicked each movement. Jessica tried to be shocked and outraged, but his hands and lips felt too good for her to do anything more than moan. She was ready to surrender everything to him and she knew that if she did, she'd be back in the same position she was in before. She would be dreaming of a fantasy man who didn't love her, except this time he would walk away with something more precious—her soul.

With every ounce of will power in her body, Jessica pushed against his chest. Cary continued his sweet torture, still cajoling her surrender as his lips suckled on her bottom lip and his hands moved down her back to cup her bottom and pull her closer to him, closing any space she tried to force between them.

Jessica finally freed her mouth and gasped, "Cary, please stop."

With those words, Cary went still and the only sound in the room was their mingled heavy breathing. He finally released her and took several steps back. The look of pure hunger in his eyes was almost as effective as his touch had been. She had never felt so womanly and beautiful in her life as she did at that moment, and she wanted to feel that way forever.

She took several deep breaths and composed herself even as her skin continued to tingle and her blood pulsated. She would not allow herself to make love with him, then have him walk out the door. She had more respect for herself than that, or at least she hoped she did.

"Cary, we can't do this," she said softly.

Cary stared, uncomprehending, then he slowly nodded. "You're right." Jessica didn't want him to agree so quickly, but kept the disappointment to herself. "I promise this will never happen again, but I need to stay here. Do you understand?"

"Of course." Jessica quickly picked up her briefcase and purse, needing to leave his presence. He overwhelmed her, swallowed her completely whole. He made her rely on him and she didn't want to rely on anyone.

"There are several Group agents stationed outside the apartment and around the area, and you'll be watched at work, as well. You can't tell anyone about this, Jess, not your mother, your brother, your friends, or anyone at work. You can never tell who's listening or . . ."

Jessica raised a hand for him to stop talking, and his voice trailed off. She couldn't listen to him any longer or she would burst into tears. She said stiffly, "The couch folds out into a bed. My brother, David, slept there last night so I should change the sheets."

"If you'll just tell me where they are, I can do it."

Jessica nodded, still avoiding his eyes. "The linen closet is down the hall and to the right. You'll find towels and anything else. I . . . I have a lot of work, so I'll be in my room." She turned to leave, but there was something in his eyes, maybe loneliness, that made her stay. She allowed herself one more minute of fantasy as she stared at him. "Was everything that happened that night a lie?" she asked without anger.

Jessica knew Cary wouldn't respond from the blank expression on his face. She quickly turned and walked into her bedroom.

Michael Lyons watched as the lights that shone through the windows flicked off in Jessica Larson's apartment. His fists reflexively clenched as he thought of how close Cary Riley was. Michael could almost smell the murderer. He wanted to burst through the front door and put a bullet between the man's eyes, but he knew Cary wouldn't travel to San Francisco alone. He would have protection with him.

From his position in the back of a stolen van with borrowed license plates, Michael carefully surveyed the street. He spotted two other Group agents in a car parked directly across the street from the apartment. He knew there were probably more agents or undercover police officers around the area, waiting for him to make a false move. But Michael wouldn't. He could imagine his father or brother whispering in his ear, telling him to wait for the right moment to strike.

Michael's vision blurred as he thought of his dead father and brother. He never knew his mother, since she died giving birth to him, but he had spent his whole life with his father and brother. Lionel Lyons was a corrupt politician, stubborn and old-fashioned, but he was Michael's father, and Michael loved him. Michael and his brother, Weston, had been trying to make Lionel see how his corruption had ruined their country. Lionel was beginning to understand when he was ruthlessly gunned down outside the presidential palace, while Weston and Michael were in school in England.

Michael and Weston returned to their country to claim their father's power. They learned their father was murdered by so-called democratic forces in the country, with financial support from America. Michael wanted to campaign against the ruling political party, but Weston wanted to fight, and since Weston was the more charismatic and driven one, they fought. When Weston was murdered, Michael became the leader of the guerrilla movement. His fellow terrorists and gunmen had become his new family, and Cary Riley had them killed. Michael wanted revenge. If he couldn't avenge the deaths of his father and brother, then Michael vowed to punish the murderer of his comrades.

Group Agent Dan Pelstrom suddenly swung open the car door and crawled inside, keeping himself hidden beneath the dashboard. Michael barely glanced at him as he said, "You're late."

"It's hard to get away when you're managing a surveillance team," Dan muttered, unconcerned. "It's not safe for you to be here. There are Group agents crawling all over this street."

"What's Riley's plan to find me?"

"He works alone, but I managed to get out of him that he's visiting African community centers and networks in the Bay Area tomorrow to ask about you," Dan whispered. "What about the woman? She's part of the plan, too."

Michael winced inwardly but kept his face composed. He refused to allow anyone to know how he was feeling. He made that mistake once with Cary Riley and would never make it again, especially with someone like Dan Pelstrom, whom he definitely didn't trust. Even with all his hatred for Cary, Michael could admit that Cary was a decent man, just on the wrong side of the cause. Michael had none of those illusions about Dan.

Michael turned the key in the ignition. "Get out," he ordered.

"Where's my money?" Dan demanded, not moving.

Michael glared at the man, then reached into his coat pocket for the envelope filled with money. "Do you have any pride?" Michael asked bitterly.

Dan snatched the envelope from his hand and opened it to count the bills. Once finished, Dan smiled. "No."

Eight

Cary went to sleep, feeling the need to love Jessica, and he woke eight hours later in the same position. After days of erotic memories, the few minutes against the door with Jessica had set the blood roaring in his ears. He didn't know what had possessed him. When she'd walked into the apartment, he felt more than heard her. His body had hardened instantly. Cary was concerned about the threat Michael Lyons posed, but he couldn't stop thinking about tasting Jessica to compare his memory and dreams to reality. She had tasted better than his dreams, more soft than he remembered from the inn. The need he had felt for her over the last few days was nothing compared to the unquenchable desire he felt as soon as they kissed.

Cary heard the bedroom door open and watched from lowered eyelids as Jessica cautiously walked through the living room in another sexy conservative gray business suit that set his blood on fire. She looked untouchable and forbidden. He wondered what passion would exist if she loosened her hair from the prim ball, and he tangled the golden brown strands in his hands. If her response to his kisses were any indication, then Cary had a feeling she would drive any man insane.

Cary knew it would be more difficult to leave her a second time. But, he owed her that much. As she had told him at Hadley's Inn, she wanted to find her other half; a man who's face Cary would gladly pound in, because whoever he was, Cary knew he wouldn't deserve Jessica.

Cary didn't know what he wanted from Jessica, besides the chance to possess her irresistible body. He didn't want to think of a future. He told lies for a living. He had horrible secrets that he couldn't tell her. He had nothing to offer her besides himself. He had money saved, but . . . Cary stopped himself from thinking about his future finances and Jessica. She obviously didn't want him for the long run or she would not have said their night meant nothing; she would not have walked into the apartment yesterday and demanded he leave, without a smile or any sign of joy at seeing him there. He knew how to make her pant and sigh his name, but he didn't know how to make her look at him like the newlyweds in the dining room at Hadley's Inn.

Cary didn't want to stay with her, mostly to save himself from the sensual torture of being around her, but he had to keep her close to him until Michael was arrested. Michael was an excellent shot. If he wanted Jessica dead, he could have shot her from a distance on her way to work, or in the park. Cary knew the incident in the park was a kidnapping attempt. Cary had often debated with himself about whether he could kill Michael, but now he vowed that if Michael touched a hair on Jessica's head, he would personally slit the young man's throat.

Cary didn't want to, but he stood and pulled on his jeans laying next to the sofa bed. His back ached from the springs that poked through the thin mattress, but he doubted he would have slept well in any bed with Jessica only one room away. Cary replaced the folding bed and rearranged the couch pillows, then walked into the kitchen. He smiled to himself when Jessica jumped slightly at his entrance. He gave her credit for her quick composure.

"I . . . I thought you were asleep," she stammered.

Cary thought she looked more beautiful than she had the night at the inn, even though he had believed that was impossible. Her huge brown eyes stared at his bare chest as if he were part of breakfast, and Cary cleared his throat to hide his smile. He wanted to comment on her hungry eyes, but she looked back at the papers in her hands before he had a chance.

"Is that coffee I smell?" he asked instead.

"Yeah. That's about the only thing I know how to make," she responded stiffly.

"Good thing I know how to cook." He opened the refrigerator and the laughter died on his face. There was a carton of milk, several cartons of cottage cheese, Chinese take-out boxes, and a few apples on the shelves. He opened the freezer door and shook his head at the numerous boxes of frozen dinners stacked precariously on the doors and racks. "You know this is pathetic, don't you?"

He turned to upbraid her but she was laughing hysterically, and he was hypnotized. It was the first time she had smiled at him since she walked into her apartment. He had forgotten what her smile did to him. And he knew without touching her that his dreams were nothing compared to the reality of Jessica.

"I know it's horrible, Cary, honestly," she said, wiping tears from her eyes. "I try to shop but I can't cook and . . ." Her voice trailed off as she fell into laughter.

Cary grinned. "We're going grocery shopping as soon as you get home from work."

Jessica sobered suddenly. "I can't. I have a big presentation to prepare for—"

"And you have to eat," Cary interrupted, then he turned back to the refrigerator away from her huge eyes.

He noticed that the milk expiration date was over a month old and stared at her. "Please tell me you were never planning to drink this."

Jessica shrugged just as Cary heard a scratching sound on the front door. He ran into the living room and grabbed his gun from underneath the couch. Terror leapt into his throat as Jessica casually walked to the front door. He jumped over the coffee table and grabbed her, shoving her behind him just as the door opened. A tall man with black curls, dark brown skin, and brown eyes, and wearing a tailored gray suit, walked into the apartment.

"Jess!" he called, oblivious to Cary standing with Jessica on the other side of the open door.

Cary felt jealousy roar through his body at the thought of another man having a key to Jessica's apartment. He wondered briefly if she had lied to him at the inn, and she was romantically involved with someone. Jessica shoved Cary aside and walked to the man and hugged him. Cary reluctantly tucked his gun in the waistband of his jeans.

"Dave, what are you doing here?" she asked warmly, closing the door.

"I wanted to check on you before work, since you told me not to come over last night—" David abruptly stopped speaking when he noticed Cary. Cary stiffened as the man, with a look of disgust, took in Cary's worn jeans, bare chest, and bare feet. "Who the hell are you?" he growled.

Cary stepped forward to introduce him to his fist just as Jessica stepped between the two men. "Dave, this is Cary Riley, my . . . my boyfriend. Cary, this is my brother, David."

"Brother!" Cary said as David exclaimed, "Boyfriend!"

Cary immediately felt embarrassed as David glared at him. He was never good with family and already her brother, the most important man in her life, hated him.

Then Cary became angry as David placed a hand on Jessica's arm as if to protect her from him. Cary didn't care that David was her brother and had known her twenty-six years longer, he just didn't like the idea of another man touching her. "What the hell are you talking about, Jess? You never mentioned to Mom or me anything about a boyfriend!"

"Well, it's kind of a long story, and I'm late for work—"

"I don't care that you're late for work! Who the hell is this man and what is he doing in your apartment at seven in the morning?" David demanded.

"What are you doing in her apartment at seven in the morning?" Cary pointed out, sounding much calmer than he felt.

David's icy eyes and Jessica's shocked eyes swung to him. David rolled his eyes then looked back at Jessica. "Start talking, Jess."

"Remember when I got caught in that storm and had to stay in Blue Moon Bay, a few weeks ago? Well, I met Cary there. He came to stay with me when I told him about the attack," Jessica explained calmly.

David looked at Cary and Cary stared him down. An overprotective big brother normally would never scare him, but Jessica happened to love this one, so Cary walked to the couch and pulled his shirt over his head. "Jessica's a grown woman," Cary said firmly.

David ignored him and turned to Jessica. "I don't understand, Jess," he said, obviously more calm. "You've been walking around all week like you lost your best friend. You even agreed to go out with Brian." Cary glared at Jessica with this last piece of news. The thought of another man touching her or tasting her smile infuriated him. "If this . . . if this guy is your boyfriend, why were you so unhappy this last week?"

Cary met Jessica's confused expression across the room. She hated lying to her brother, he could tell. She was going to tell David the truth. The less people who knew the truth about Cary's reason for coming to San Francisco, the less people would be in danger. Since he was a professional liar, Cary walked to her side and placed an arm around her shoulders. "We had a misunderstanding before we left each other. As soon as I heard about the attack in the park, I got here as soon as possible and we forgave each other. I care about your sister, David, I only came here to help her."

Jessica smoothly moved from his grasp and grabbed her briefcase. "I have to go, Dave. I'll call you later tonight. You have nothing to worry about. Cary will be here." She smiled at her brother and hugged him. Cary felt another irrational pang of jealousy as her arms wrapped around another man's neck.

Jessica turned to Cary with uncertainty in her eyes. He solved her problem by pulling her into his arms, as if giving her a good-bye hug were a part of their normal routine. And in that brief second, with her hair tickling his nose and her hands rubbing his back, Cary wanted it to be a part of his everyday routine. He quickly pulled away and placed a light kiss on the tip of her nose. He completely forgot about David as he stared into her confused brown eyes that he knew would haunt him for the rest of his life. "Have a good day."

Jessica nodded, and turned to her brother. "I'll walk you to your car," she said in a soft voice.

David shook his head. "You go on. I need to talk to Cary."

Cary withheld his groan of annoyance. He'd planned to spend his day searching for leads on Michael Lyons. He didn't have time for showdowns with big brothers. Jessica seemed to agree with Cary and protested, "Dave, I don't—"

"I just want to talk to him," David interrupted Jessica.

Jessica glanced from one man to the other, and walked

out the door. Cary ignored David and walked to the large living room windows that faced the street. The Group surveillance agents could more easily see her from their position in a car parked nearby, but Cary still watched her walk down the street until she disappeared around the corner to the Muni bus stop. He also watched Tyler Morris, the agent assigned to follow Jessica everywhere, turn the corner a few seconds later. Cary turned to face David and attempt to be civil, but instead he was met by a hard punch to his chin. Cary grunted as he fell to the floor.

He lay on the floor amazed as he realized that an amateur had taken him by surprise. David stood over him, his angry face glaring down at him. Cary knew David wanted nothing more than to stomp on his face. "You hurt my sister again and I'll pound your face in," he warned through clenched teeth. With that, David stormed out of the apartment.

Cary wasn't scared of David—he could have physically handled him in a split second—but he was scared of Jessica. He had been so enthralled in watching her walk, that he hadn't heard David move behind him.

Jessica knocked rapidly on Erin's office door, then swung the door open when she heard the muffled command to enter. Jessica walked into Erin's equally cramped office, trying not to groan in frustration when she realized Erin was on the telephone. Erin glanced at Jessica and concern crossed her face. She held up a finger to Jessica to signal one second, then obligingly laughed at whatever the speaker on the other end of the telephone said.

"It sounds like a fabulous time, James, and I would love to hear more, but another client just stepped into my office," Erin said smoothly. "Should I sign you up for the Trydent Plan?" Erin smiled at his response and said, "You won't regret this, James. Have a nice day and say hello to your wife." Erin replaced the telephone on the desk and rolled her eyes. "How did I get stuck with James McHugh?"

"Erin, I have a problem. A big problem. Can you take a break?"

With a panicked expression on her face, Erin walked around the desk and grabbed her arms. "You didn't see your attacker again, did you?"

"Nothing like that," Jessica assuaged her fears. "Compared to this man, dealing with Michael Lyons would be like taking a stroll around the pier." Erin appeared confused but grabbed her purse and followed Jessica out of the office.

The two women walked out of the office building just as David walked toward the building doors. Jessica groaned and cursed her bad luck. She knew her brother wouldn't simply accept her explanation of meeting Cary at the inn and continue his day, as if everything were fine. She prepared herself for a thorough and painful interrogation.

Erin rolled her eyes when she saw David. David grimaced when he realized Erin stood beside Jessica. Jessica would have laughed at their reactions if she weren't trying to figure out an escape route.

"Don't you have a job?" Erin greeted, crossing her arms over her chest.

"I didn't know you cared," David muttered, reverting to an adolescent sneer that Jessica hadn't seen since high school.

"I don't care," Erin retorted. "Jess and I were on our way to have a cup of coffee. We didn't mean to disturb you from your daily stroll through downtown while everyone else at your company works."

"I don't have time for you, Erin," David snarled; then

he turned to Jessica, with murder brewing in his eyes. "You'd better start explaining yourself, young lady, before I call Mom."

"That's real mature, David," Jessica said, rolling her eyes.

"What does Jessica possibly have to explain to you?" Erin interjected herself into the conversation once more. "If you're trying to figure out what species you belong to, David, I'd be more than happy to take you to the Animal Kingdom section of the library—"

"There was a man in Jessica's apartment this morning," David interrupted Erin.

Erin's mouth dropped open as she turned to Jessica. Jessica avoided both their glances and sighed. "This is why I wanted to talk to you," she finally said to Erin.

"A man?" Erin repeated, amazed.

"I've been known to talk to the opposite sex every once in a while," Jessica muttered, mildly annoyed by the expressions on Erin's and David's faces.

"She gave me some story about meeting him at an inn last week," David told Erin. "Those two want me to believe that they met last week, and he's all ready flying across the country to be with her."

"Who is he really, Jess?" Erin asked in disbelief.

"Don't you think I could make a man fly across the country if I asked him?" Jessica asked indignantly.

"No," Erin and David answered in unison.

"I mean, we both know you could," Erin quickly said, as Jessica's eyes narrowed. "I just can't believe you met this man last week, and you didn't tell David or me, and that he's staying at your apartment. That doesn't sound like you . . . Is this why you've been so upset these last few weeks? You missed him?"

"Don't tell me you're falling for their story." David said, rolling his eyes.

Erin turned to him with an annoyed expression. "Why would Jess lie to us?"

"I could think of one thousand reasons why she would lie to you, but I'm her brother. She has to tell me the truth."

"Why?" Erin demanded.

"It's a proven fact that Jessica can't lie to me."

"I'm surprised your body can even support the weight of that inflated head," Erin said, tossing her hair over her shoulder. Jessica sighed tiredly and steered the arguing couple toward the coffee shop across the street. When the two first began arguing two years ago, Jessica would intervene and attempt to play peacemaker. Then she realized David and Erin wanted to argue, so she accepted her role as the forgotten friend and sister.

"She didn't start acting like this until she started hanging around you," David said, matter-of-factly.

"What are you trying to say, David?" Erin demanded.

"I didn't think I was being too mysterious. You're a bad influence on my sister."

"You are such a chauvinist pig," Erin squealed, as they walked into the coffee shop. Several people glanced at Erin's loud proclamation and Jessica smiled apologetically at them, since Erin and David glared at each other, unmindful of the spectacle they caused.

"I thought we were talking about me," Jessica finally interjected. David and Erin both looked at her, as if suddenly remembering she existed. "In fact, I recall you two just insulted me."

"We didn't insult you," David said, dumbly.

"Erin said I wasn't the type of person to fall in love—"

"That's not what I said," Erin said, shaking her head.

"It's what you implied. You both think I'm a dull, bland, workaholic, and you're probably right," Jessica said angrily, as they both stared at her with wide, innocent eyes. "I'm not the type of woman to make a man fly across the country just to comfort her, but for some reason, Cary's here. And, instead of being happy that I'm actually experiencing something that I'll probably never experience again, you two insult me and accuse me of lying."

For once, Erin and David were completely silent. Several seconds passed, as the three stared at the menu over the counter. David cleared his throat and Jessica glanced at him, expecting an apology.

"This is all your fault, Erin," David said. Erin's mouth dropped open and Jessica rolled her eyes and stepped to the counter to order coffee. No matter what she said, neither Erin or David would believe that Cary had come to San Francisco for her. She didn't blame them, because even she would not have believed the story. Men didn't race across the country for Jessica Larson. Cary would not have been there if Michael Lyons hadn't attacked her.

David finally turned to Jessica and pinned her with an intense glare. "You're not leaving this café until you tell me exactly who this man is. What job does he have that he can fly across the country on a moment's notice? And if you tell me he's unemployed, I'll go back to your apartment right now and throw him out."

"Will you shut up," Erin snapped, as she stared toward the café windows. "I can't look alluring with your big mouth distracting me."

"What are you looking at?" Jessica asked curiously.

"Not what," Erin said with a sly grin. "Who." She pointed toward the front of the café, and Jessica turned to look straight into the eyes of Michael Lyons. He stood outside the café, staring directly at her. Jessica felt all the strength leave her body as the terror from the park screamed through her mind.

"What's wrong, Jess?" David asked, grabbing her arm.

Jessica pointed at Michael and said softly, "That's the man."

"What man?" Erin prompted.

"The man from the park." David didn't wait for the last word to fully leave Jessica's mouth before he ran out of the shop, toward Michael. Michael immediately turned and ran down the street. Jessica screamed after David as she remembered Cary's and the detective's description of Michael as a dangerous man. Jessica ran from the shop after her brother, ignoring Erin's bewildered calls.

Jessica pushed her way through the mass of people on the sidewalk, searching for the top of her brother's head or for Michael Lyons. She turned straight into the broad chest of a man in a dark suit. He grabbed her arms and she wildly struggled from his grip to no avail. Fear and horror at the strength of the grip choked any scream that wanted to leave her throat.

With strength she didn't know she possessed, Jessica rammed her knee into his groin and his hands dropped from her arms, as he staggered to the ground. Jessica pushed past him to run but she suddenly heard what he had been saying all along that she had been too frightened to hear. "Ms. Larson, wait." The man gasped in obvious pain. "Cary Riley assigned me to you."

Jessica stood as far away from him as possible as the late morning crowd streamed around her, shooting strange glances in her direction, but too busy to stop.

"Who are you?" Jessica demanded, staring at the man.

"I'm Agent Tyler Morris. I've been assigned to follow you. I noticed your brother ran out of the cafe and you followed him. Did you see Michael Lyons?" Jessica wordlessly nodded and the man reached into his coat pocket for a cellular phone.

David appeared at Jessica's side, his breath coming in gasps and sweat gleaming on his forehead. "I lost him in the crowd," David said, shaking his head. "Are you all right?"

"I'm fine, David, but you shouldn't have run after him. He's too dangerous."

David wildly glanced at the faces of the people passing by, trying not to stare at their frantic state. "Where's Erin?" David asked, gripping Jessica's hand. Jessica winced from the pain and smiled in relief as Erin ran over to them.

"What happened?" Erin asked, confused.

"Jess saw the man who attacked her in the park," David explained, any concern for Erin completely gone from his expression.

"And you chased after him?" Erin asked, with wide eyes. "Are you stupid, crazy, or both?"

"I must be crazy because I still talk to you," David snapped, then straightened his tie. "I'll walk you to your office."

"You don't have to . . ." Jessica's voice trailed off as she realized Agent Morris was gone. She stared at David and Erin, who expectantly waited for her to finish her sentence. Jessica brushed past them and walked toward the office building. The two followed her.

"I cannot believe you actually chased after that man," Erin said to David. "He could've had a gun or a knife. He could've led you into an alley and killed you."

"Some women would think that was brave," David muttered, rolling his eyes.

"Women on this planet?" Erin asked with a disbelieving laugh. Jessica rolled her eyes and tried to pretend that she didn't know them.

Nine

An hour later Jessica sat in her office, staring at her hands. She had tried to work, but she admitted defeat after staring at the same words on the computer screen for the last forty-five minutes. She hated herself for fearing Michael Lyons, for fearing Cary. She didn't want her thoughts to be occupied by either man. She wanted her life to return to normal, when she thought about stocks and bonds and how to make her brother admit his love for Erin.

Jessica jumped to her feet when the office door flew open. She didn't welcome or question the massive wave of relief that washed over her when she saw Cary. Her assistant, Alice Winchell, trailed behind him into the office.

"Jessica, I tried to stop him at the door. He wouldn't take no for an answer," Alice said breathlessly. "Should I call security?"

Jessica could understand why Alice was nervous. With his dark scowl and thundering eyes, Cary looked like someone Jessica would want to run away from, not cling to with every ounce of strength in her body.

Jessica stared at Cary, but said to Alice, "It's all right, Alice. Please close the door on your way out."

Alice hesitated but walked from the room, closing the door. Immediately, Cary was at her side, his hands on her shoulders. What Jessica originally thought was anger, she now knew was concern. The professional facade fled from her and she wrapped her arms around him.

"Jess, are you okay?" The softness of his voice made tears fill her eyes.

"I'm fine."

"Agent Morris told me what happened."

Jessica turned her face into his solid chest. "It was like being in the park all over again."

She felt his hands clench her shoulders but the pressure was reassuring. Cary pulled away from her, and his hands traveled down her arms to hold her hands. Jessica finally realized that since she saw Michael in the café, she had been waiting for someone or something to be able to stop the nervous flutters in her stomach. She finally realized that she had been waiting for Cary.

"Did he say anything to you?"

"No. He was outside the building."

"Did anyone know you were going to that particular place?"

"It was spur of the moment. No one could have known."

"Then he must've been waiting outside this building for you," Cary muttered, absently placing a kiss on her forehead. In spite of her fear and apprehension, Jessica felt the warmth flood through her body from the feel of his lips. "What time do you leave work?"

"I usually leave about seven."

"Seven?" Cary questioned, amazed. He shook his head. "That's too late."

Jessica bristled at his condescending tone and pulled from his arms. She walked around her desk to sit in the chair. "That's not late for someone in my position. I can't leave before other people in the office; it would look bad."

Cary sighed, clearly exasperated. "Considering the circumstances, I think it would be all right for you to be home before dark."

Jessica gritted her teeth to refrain from yelling at him. If they had not been in her office, she would not have shown the same restraint. She would never understand how he could transform from caring and sweet to a dominating ogre within two seconds. "That's not the point. Besides, what do you think is a decent time?"

"Four-thirty, five o'clock."

"And you leave the office at four-thirty?" Jessica asked doubtfully.

"There's a big difference between you and me, Jess."

"Besides the fact that you're a man, what else is there?" she demanded, jumping to her feet.

Cary raked a hand over his hair, then threw up his hands in exasperation. "Forget it. What was I thinking by even coming here and interrupting your precious work?" Cary pinned her with one last, hard glare then stormed toward the door.

Jessica panicked slightly at the prospect of him leaving. She stood up and said, "We're still going grocery shopping tonight, right?"

Cary paused at the door and turned to look at her. She could see the internal debate raging in his eyes, over whether to walk out of the room or see what her next move would be. He finally sighed and said, "Yes."

"I'll be home by five." She didn't wait for his response and sat in her chair and pretended to read the papers on her desk. She didn't miss Cary's amused expression as he walked from the room.

Cary felt like a caged tiger as he paced the apartment floor, waiting for Jessica. He glanced at his watch, 5:32, five minutes after his last check. Before he was told that Jessica had spotted Michael in downtown San Francisco, Cary had spent the day searching various sections of the city for Michael. After seeing Jessica in her office, and making a fool of himself by treating her like a child, Cary returned to the apartment to wait for her. Cary couldn't handle the fear that cramped his stomach when he thought of Michael within a few feet of Jessica.

Cary rubbed his temples as another headache pounded inside his head. He couldn't remember ever feeling this nervous or apprehensive while on assignment. He would be dead by now if he had allowed these feelings to consume him on a regular basis. He wouldn't be surprised if Jessica stayed at her office until midnight, just to show him she could. He vowed she wouldn't have that opportunity since he planned to leave the apartment in ten minutes and drag her, kicking and screaming if necessary, from the office.

Cary stared out the window then sighed with relief as he noticed Jessica walking toward the building, loaded with folders and papers. He quickly jumped onto the couch and pretended to be involved with the paperwork spread across the coffee table in front of him, and took his first relaxed breath since leaving her office. He heard the key jiggle in the door and calmly looked up when it opened.

"Need some help?" he asked, jumping to his feet. His apathetic attitude was thrown out the window with one look at her haggard face. He quickly took the papers from her arms and noticed her bloodshot eyes. Jessica forced a smile and closed the door.

She squared her shoulders and looked at him. "You win. I'm here. I left the office with a group of people. I took a cab home, instead of the bus. I ran from the cab to the apartment building, looking over my shoulder the entire time. Are you happy?"

Cary nodded, confused and uncertain how to respond. She pursed her lips in annoyance, then walked toward her bedroom. Against his better judgment, Cary followed her. She turned to close the door and surprise filled her eyes when she saw him standing behind her. "Cary, I don't think—"

"You look like you've been crying."

Jessica pulled the restraining pins from her hair and Cary groaned as it tumbled past her shoulders. Whenever her hair was down, he thought of their night at the inn and how her hair had fanned across the couch as he watched over her and convinced himself that he wasn't right for her.

"You really shouldn't be in here—"

He ignored her protests and said gruffly, "Jess, you've been crying. Was it over Michael Lyons?"

She angrily whirled around to face him. "Believe it or not, Cary, I have feelings. Yes, the robot Jessica Larson has feelings. A raving lunatic is chasing me and instead of being the strong woman that I always thought I was, I've become this disgusting little girl who can't even take the bus by herself. Michael Lyons has made me scared of this city, of being alone, and I hate him for it. And I was crying, Cary, because I came to the painful realization that I'm a coward."

Cary wanted to laugh at his initial fears that Jessica was hurt. She was angry because she thought she was a coward, which was about the farthest thing from the truth that Cary had ever heard. "You're the bravest woman I know, Jess."

"You must not know very many brave women if I'm the shining example," she muttered dryly.

"Agent Morris told me how you got past him." A slight flush filled her cheeks and Cary never wanted to touch her more than at that moment.

"I hope he's okay. I didn't know who he was."

"He'll talk in soprano over the next few days, but he's fine."

"I feel so stupid," Jessica muttered, impatiently raking

her hand through her hair. "When I finally find the courage to fight back, it's against the wrong person."

"Let's go over this again," Cary said calmly. "You outran and out thought an international terrorist. Many women and men would have rolled over in the park. They would have been too frightened to run or to fight back, but you did, Jess. You did that and a lot more. If that wasn't enough, you temporarily disabled a trained Group agent. You couldn't be a coward, even if you tried."

"I may have to keep you around," she teased, then abruptly stopped smiling as her words hung in the suddenly heavy air between them.

Cary knew she regretted her last statement, whether she meant it or not, and he prayed she meant it. He meant to lighten the moment with a smile, but at that moment, she took off her suit jacket. Cary's eyes suddenly became glued to her slender fingers as they moved to the top button of her silk blouse, the conversation completely forgotten. The air in the room seemed to fill with the light floral scent she wore that reminded him of the night at the inn. She met his eyes and he noticed they were almost black with desire, the laughter gone, as she slipped the button from the slot. She was going to undress in front of him. She was going to give him the miracle of seeing her naked body, seeing the full breasts he dreamed about at night. That was Cary's one thought.

Then he remembered he was leaving as soon as he caught Michael. He wouldn't be able to fight more memories of her, on top of the ones that already kept him awake at night. Cary ran a hand over his hair and pointed toward the door. "I'll go . . . I have to write the grocery list." Cary stumbled from the room, closing the door behind him. His loins ached as he thought of her undressing behind the door.

* * *

An hour later, Cary placed a package of rice in the shopping cart that Jessica pushed behind him. Cary would admit to only a few people that he liked to cook. His mother always told him, if he liked to eat, he should know how to cook, and she made certain he knew how. He never had the time nor the inclination to cook like he wanted to, but for some reason he felt like creating a lavish meal for Jessica.

He glanced at her as they wandered through the large grocery store that showcased a deli, a bakery, and a fresh produce section. Jessica was obviously one of those types who tried to move in and out of the store as fast as possible. She kept giving pointed looks at her watch then announcing the time to him. Cary shook his head as a pout slowly formed on her face. Even while pouting, the woman had the power to drive him to his knees.

"Cary, I really don't need all this stuff," Jessica protested for the fifth time.

Cary ignored her, but finally looked at her when she bumped the shopping cart into the back of his legs. Jessica smiled innocently, and Cary looked back at the shelves lined with pasta before he laughed. He couldn't believe this was the same woman who left the apartment that morning wearing a suit and holding a briefcase, looking like she could conquer the world with one well-placed phone call. "Watch where you're going with that thing," was his only response.

"Yes, sir," she muttered, then made a show of yawning, drawing his eyes to her graceful, exposed neck. "Do you think we'll have time to actually eat any of this food tonight?"

Cary couldn't stop his grin. "I'm going to make the best lasagna you've ever tasted in your life."

"It better be damn good after ten hours in a grocery store," she threatened, but she was smiling. "I'm sorry I'm so cranky, Cary, I'm just hungry."

Cary tried to concentrate on remembering the exact brand of pasta he wanted, but he couldn't breathe with her eyes on him. He wasn't certain whether she was studying him or watching him, but the effect was unnerving. "Is there a problem?" he finally demanded, pretending annoyance.

Jessica lowered her eyes, ashamed, then looked at him. "Have you come any closer to finding out where Michael Lyons is?"

"We'll catch him, Jess, I promise. I spent the whole day with every African group in the Bay Area," he muttered before he could stop himself. Cary forced a smile to cover his loose lips and the sinking ship in the lower part of his anatomy. "How about I give you money to buy a cupcake at the bakery?"

Jessica stared at him, offended, and Cary wanted her to challenge him, to make him angry at her, but she simply held out her hand. "If you insist," she replied sweetly.

As Cary handed her the money, he saw a blur of red move pass their aisle. His senses seemed to sharpen as Jessica walked toward the bakery. Cary left the shopping cart and deftly moved to the other aisle. He saw a man in a red jacket, wearing a baseball cap and sunglasses, walking quickly down the aisle toward the warehouse in the back of the store. Cary would recognize that walk anywhere. Michael Lyons.

Cary moved down the aisle and followed the suspicious man into the darkness of the receiving warehouse. Inside the cool darkness of the warehouse, Cary saw a few high school students moonlighting as bag boys smoking cigarettes near the door. Cary withdrew his gun as he heard rapidly fading footsteps to his right. He cocked the gun, and walked slowly and carefully in the same direction.

He could feel the sweat on his brow as he gripped the gun in his hand. He didn't have any proof the man in the red jacket was Michael, but Cary knew. He knew by the change in the air and the change in him. If he came face to face with Michael Lyons, he didn't know if he would kill him. Cary would tear Michael apart with his bare hands if Jessica were in danger, but otherwise, Cary wasn't certain he could hurt the man who reminded him so much of himself.

Cary whirled around as a door to his right slammed shut. He raced to the door and threw it open just in time to see a black Volvo speed from the parking lot. He ran diagonally across the parking lot to catch a glimpse of the driver as the Volvo exited the lot, but the car moved too fast.

Cary gulped heavy gasps of air then turned to the grocery store. He noticed a white piece of paper on the windshield of Jessica's car and ran to it. He ripped the note off the window and he cursed as he read, *I see you,* in Michael's familiar scrawl. He wanted to tear the note to shreds and burn it, but he knew it was an important piece of evidence. He carefully folded it and placed it in his shirt pocket.

Cary returned to the inside of the grocery store. He retrieved the shopping cart and pushed it over to Jessica, who sat at a table, eating the cupcake and obviously enjoying every last morsel. "Hey," Cary greeted, regulating his breathing so she wouldn't notice his recent exertion.

"Hey." Jessica pushed another cupcake across the table toward him. "I bought you one."

Cary was speechless as he stared at the cupcake. He didn't know why the gesture meant so much to him, but it did. Another flutter of emotions rocked him. "The last person to buy me a cupcake was my mother," he murmured more to himself than her. Cary finally sank into the chair across from her and met her eyes. "My parents died in a car accident my senior year in college. I haven't spoken to either my brother or sister in four years."

"Why?" Somehow her hand covered his on the table,

and the touch comforted him more than he wanted to admit.

Cary looked around at the fluorescent lights and fresh fruit, and wanted to laugh. He was confessing his innermost secrets to this woman in the middle of a grocery store, with the potential of anyone overhearing. People like him didn't tell anything about themselves in public places. People like him didn't tell anyone anything about themselves, period.

Cary met her concerned brown eyes and almost confessed the real reason for his self-isolation from his brother and sister. He almost told her about the guilt that kept him awake every night for the last five years. The guilt that still tore his life apart and made him the perfect, emotionless employee for the Group. Instead he told her as close to the truth as he could manage, "I graduated from college two weeks after their death and joined the Group. It was just easy to blend in with the work and not remember what happened. If those feelings intruded upon my work, I pushed them away for the sake of the job, or that's what I told myself. The Group gave me a good excuse not to deal with my parents' death or my brother and sister. Now, I've looked up and it's five years later. Five years of my life have passed and I can't tell you what I've done besides work. I haven't talked to my brother or sister, or seen my parents' grave . . ." His voice trailed off as he realized he'd said more than he'd intended.

"Is that why you were at Hadley's Inn that night?" Jessica asked softly. "You were trying to find the five years that passed?"

"Maybe." Cary removed his hand from hers and began to eat his cupcake. She stared at him for a second, then bit into her own cupcake.

Ten

Jessica scanned the sea of plastic, grocery-filled bags covering her kitchen's counters, tabletops, and floor. Cary busily stacked cans of soup on the shelf next to the refrigerator while Jessica sat in a kitchen chair in complete shock. "Cary, this is so much food," she said amazed, looking around the kitchen.

Cary absently glanced at her as he neatly folded an empty paper bag. "You have to eat to survive. Do you eat breakfast?"

"No."

"Do you eat lunch?"

"I never have time at work." Cary stared at her and Jessica felt slightly ashamed. She knew her eating habits were not completely healthy, but she was a busy woman. Jessica suddenly realized how much she used work as an excuse.

"You should really take better care of yourself. I'm going to make dinner tonight and you're going to eat every last morsel. Understood?"

Jessica nodded dumbly. No one, besides her mother or brother or Erin, ever cared if she ate or slept or cried. Cary cared. She saw the anger in his eyes when he came to her job, his shock when he saw her refrigerator, and his true concern over her eating habits. Whether he wanted to or not, Cary cared about her. And Jessica was in love with him.

The phone rang and Jessica picked up the phone on the kitchen wall. "Hello?"

"Is he still there?"

Jessica rolled her eyes at her mother's question. She knew she would hear from Karin Larson after David's daily telephone call to their mother. She only hoped her brother didn't tell Karin about Michael Lyons. The last thing she needed was for her mother to worry about her.

"Who, Mom?" She met Cary's eyes across the kitchen and laughed at his horrified expression.

"This Cary person. Jessica Larson, I can't believe you've been having a relationship and you didn't even tell me! I had to find out from David and he wouldn't even tell me what he looks like!" Jessica could hear her mother's deep breaths over the phone and tried not to laugh. "This man is staying in your apartment? I don't know if I like that. How long does he plan on staying?"

"Not long, Mom."

"Living together is a huge commitment, and you did only just meet him last week."

"We're not living together. He's here to visit," Jessica replied.

"Did David tell you that he hit him?"

"What?!" Jessica looked at Cary. He had turned back to preparing dinner. "Why?"

"Some male thing, but I want to know all about him. David said he couldn't get much out of you."

"Because he was too busy fighting with Erin."

Karin's laugh filtered through the telephone. "I like Erin. She's the only woman, besides you and me, who's not intimidated by him. Now, tell me about Cary."

"I can't talk now, Mom, but he's a nice person and he cares for me," Jessica said quietly, hoping Cary would not hear. He would have thought she was maintaining the ruse to her family about his reason for staying in the apartment, but Jessica hoped she was telling the truth. "And I care for him, a lot."

"Do you love him, Jess?" Karin asked, softly.

Jessica hesitated and glanced at Cary, to make certain he wasn't listening. He continued to stand over the sink and rinse off vegetables. "Yes, Mom."

"Does he love you?"

Jessica bit her bottom lip and raked a hand through her loose hair. She never usually wore her hair down, but she had seen the way Cary's eyes lit with passion in her bedroom when she took her hair down earlier. "I don't know, Mom, but I want him to."

"Oh, sweetie," Karin cried.

Jessica straightened and forced a smile as Cary turned to look at her. He raised a questioning eyebrow. "I have to go now. I'll call you back later. I love you." She didn't wait for her mother's response before she replaced the receiver.

"That was my mother," she said in explanation.

Cary folded the last of the now empty grocery bags and stacked it underneath the sink. "I figured as much when you said 'Mom'."

"She told me David hit you." His face was suddenly flushed and Jessica forced herself to remain in her spot and not throw her arms around him. "I'm sorry."

Cary shrugged. "He's protecting his own. I completely understand about that."

Jessica suddenly wanted him. As she watched him pull pots and pans from the drawers that she'd forgotten existed, she wanted him more than she'd ever wanted anything in her life. She wasn't admitting weakness or dependence, but acceptance of love. As she watched the muscles in his forearm tense and glide under his skin from the weight of a pan, she wanted to tell him. "Cary—"

Cary held up his hands in mock surrender and interrupted her. "I know, I know, you have work to do. I'll call you when dinner's ready." He turned back to the stove. Jessica hesitated, then walked from the room before she made a fool of herself.

Cary stared at Jessica across the table as they ate the food he'd prepared. While setting the table earlier that evening, he barely resisted the urge to light candles or turn on the stereo to a soft music station. There were no candles or soft lights, but Jessica put him in a romantic mood. He barely touched his food as he watched her. He watched her eat; he watched her talk. He wondered what spell she had placed over him to make him think about dinners with her every night for the rest of his life.

Jessica looked at him, then at her empty plate, and laughed. "I feel like I'm going to explode." She groaned. "I'm so impressed with your cooking skills. My brother can't even boil water without calling me for directions."

"Chauvinist," Cary accused, smiling. He wanted to cook for her every night. He wanted to give her love and to protect her. Cary frowned at the direction of his thoughts and began to stack the dirty dishes on the table. "Now, the fun part's over."

"The least I can do is wash dishes." Cary sat back, pleased as Jessica stood and carried stacks of dishes to the kitchen counter. When she turned back to the table, he averted his eyes from her backside, nicely showcased in blue jeans. He had been gawking at her various body parts since he'd seen her yesterday. Cary wanted to control himself but he couldn't. He couldn't handle this new, comfortable feeling between them where they could go grocery shopping together and tease each other like they were friends, like they did at the inn. He didn't act like a complete moron when she was being distant and cold.

He didn't know how to act when she teased him or laughed at his jokes.

Cary finally gave into his need to touch her and stood, stepping between her and the table. Something squeezed his heart when she stared at him, with desire written across her face. "I never told you how much you amaze me," he said, then softly pressed his lips against the palm of each of her hands. "You're an incredible woman, Jess."

If she stared at his lips any longer, Cary knew he would lay her across the table and tear her clothes off. He could imagine her lips opening for him, her tongue competing with his.

"Cary, what is this between us? What do we mean to each other?" Her voice was quiet and tore holes through whatever soul was left in him.

Cary raked a hand through his hair and wished he could give her an answer. "I don't know," he admitted truthfully.

"I know." With those two words Cary knew she loved him. She couldn't hide her feelings from him. He saw it in her eyes and felt it in the hands that touched him. He knew she waited for him to respond but he kept his mouth closed. Jessica smiled sadly, with a hint of regret, then said, "I have work to do."

Cary couldn't allow her to leave the room. He didn't want her to leave his presence any sooner than he would have to leave her. For one night, he wanted to pretend that he could give her everything she should have. His voice sounded awkward as he blurted out, "How's your presentation for work going?"

She seemed surprised by his interest, but she answered, "I'm almost finished. It's been a lot of work, but I think it'll be worth the extra time when it's completed."

She turned for her bedroom again and Cary couldn't resist the panic that filled him at the thought of not seeing her for the rest of the night. He heard himself ask, "Are you going to work all night?"

"I had planned on it." Cary nodded then gathered the remaining dirty dishes on the table as if it were the most important thing in the world at that moment. Jessica touched his arm and he felt the shock from her fingers shoot through his body. "Why?"

"I just thought we could catch a movie, not that it's safe or wise for us to go anywhere. And I don't want to drag you away from your work . . ." His voice trailed off and he felt like he was in ninth grade again, asking Bette Kilrow on his first date. "Forget it. I'll finish cleaning the kitchen."

Her hand remained on his arm and she smiled, making him even more tongue-tied. "I'd love to, Cary."

Cary grinned, embarrassed by the relieved sigh he couldn't prevent from escaping. Jessica shot him a strange look, then walked to the hall closet for her coat. "No foreign films, or subtitles, or chick flicks, or anything where someone dies after a long illness and a lot of crying," he warned her as she pulled on her coat. Cary wanted to pull her hair from the back of the coat; he could still remember how soft her hair was from the inn, but he wisely kept his hands to himself.

"Of course not," she cheerfully responded. "I haven't been to the movies in about two months. I can't believe how excited I am."

Cary stared speechless at her smile then grabbed his sweater off the couch and quickly pulled it over his head.

Jessica stuffed her hands deep in her coat pockets as the two stood in line at the movie theater near her apartment. She stared at the couple in front of her, and felt the irrational pang of jealousy as the man wrapped his arms around the woman to ward off the cold air. She glanced at Cary, who kept darting nervous glances at the street traffic that drove past the theater. She knew he was uncomfortable standing close to the street, without any protection. She could tell from the way his right hand stayed near the gun she knew was underneath his jacket, and the way he practically squashed her in between his body and the wall of the building. She would have thought his concern was sweet, if he didn't look so fierce.

"I don't know what I was thinking. We shouldn't be here," Cary muttered, for the tenth time in the last five minutes. "Why can't we wait inside?"

"It's a beautiful night," Jessica said, unable to contain the happiness that flowed through her body just because she had Cary all to herself. He wasn't exactly hers, but she would deal with reality later.

"What time does this movie start?"

Jessica finally glared at him. "You're ruining this experience for me. Shut up and enjoy the night." She didn't miss Cary's smile or his salute in her direction. Jessica tried not to laugh in return but failed miserably.

A few minutes later, the patrons were allowed into the theater and Cary quickly led Jessica to the last row of seats near the door and against the wall. Jessica didn't protest because she could tell from his predatory expression, that his choice of seats related to his profession. She didn't want him to think about his work tonight, but she also realized she *was* his work. Cary wouldn't be in San Francisco, he wouldn't be sitting next to her in the movie theater, if he didn't feel partially responsible for his job and Michael Lyons. The thought made Jessica's good mood instantly evaporate into thin air.

"What's making you frown?" Cary asked, breaking into her thoughts. Jessica stared around the dimly lit theater to watch the various people walk into the room and pick their seats. She stared at everything but him. Cary loudly sighed then said reluctantly, "We could see the movie about the dying woman and her best friend who adopts her children and dog, if you really want to."

Jessica couldn't help but laugh as she caught the long-suffering expression on his face. "I'm fine, Cary."

"I don't mind."

"Yeah, right," she said in disbelief.

Cary laughed and shrugged innocently as the lights in the room completely dimmed and the large screen at the front of the theater glowed with life. "I tried," Cary whispered in her ear then leaned back in his seat.

Jessica tried to concentrate on the plot of the Wesley Snipes action movie, but after the tenth senseless death, she tuned the movie out and concentrated on being close to Cary. She knew it was adolescent, but she placed her arm on the armrest only for the reason to touch his. His thigh brushed against her leg in the confines of the cramped seat and Jessica could feel the warmth flood her entire body. She glanced around the theater, noticing the other moviegoers' rapt attention to the movie screen. No one would have noticed or cared if Cary took her in his arms and kissed her senseless. She glanced at Cary once more, hoping he would receive her telepathic message to kiss her or touch her, but his attention remained glued to the screen.

Jessica sighed in disappointment and shifted in the seat. She almost jumped from the seat when Cary placed a hand on her arm.

"Are you okay?" he asked, staring at her.

Jessica met his eyes in the dark room and, for a brief second, she was transported in time to the night at the inn. She remembered how dark his eyes had seemed in the stillness of the room when they first kissed, and she noticed how dark his eyes were now. Cary continued to stare at her, waiting for an answer. Jessica abruptly nodded and muttered, "I'm fine. Why?"

"You're fidgeting."

"I don't fidget."

His raised left eyebrow told her he didn't agree, but he wisely chose not to pursue the subject. "Are you feeling guilty about being here and not finishing that presentation?"

Jessica was slightly surprised that he was concerned enough to ask her in the middle of the movie. She tried not to melt in her seat from his intense gaze. She wondered if she would ever be able to have a decent conversation with him without her body going haywire.

"No, I'm glad I'm here," she whispered softly.

Cary lightly caressed her cheek and said, "Then relax." He smiled then turned back to the screen. Jessica forced her eyes away from him and tried not to place a hand on her cheek to capture the warmth from his touch.

Jessica welcomed the cool breeze in the air as they walked from the theater to her apartment. Just when she had thought she wouldn't be able to handle one more second in the dark room with Cary sitting beside her and not being able to touch him, the movie had mercifully ended with a loud explosion. She hadn't been aware the movie ended until she heard the light applause in the theater.

"What did you think of the movie?" she asked, to distract her own thoughts from fixating on the night at the inn. For some reason, she couldn't stop thinking about that night or how he'd made her feel. Her entire body continued to flow with desire from the repeated accidental arm touches in the theater.

"It was okay," he replied noncommittally. They walked in silence a few more feet, passing a Muni stop that would've taken them the half mile to her apartment. Jessica didn't point it out because she wanted to prolong the night.

"Just okay? He was some sort of government agent, right? Was it a realistic portrayal?" Jessica was slightly surprised when he laughed and she smiled. She loved to hear his laugh because she rarely ever heard it.

"I wish it could be that simple," he said once his laughter subsided. "That would be nice if every case was wrapped up, nice and neat, in two hours and the designated bad guys were either dead or in jail. It sure would save us a lot of paperwork."

As they passed directly under a street lamp, she noticed the faraway look in his eyes. She wondered what he thought, but she knew he would never tell her. She abruptly tucked her arm through his, and he glanced at her, surprised. "It's a beautiful night. I love this city. It seems like anything is possible in San Francisco. What's Virginia like?"

"It can be pretty," he said quietly. "The leaves change color in the fall and sometimes it snows. I'm originally from Phoenix and there's not much of a fall in the desert." Jessica privately rejoiced at the small piece of private information he relinquished.

"I didn't know you were from Arizona. I went to the Grand Canyon with friends from college this past spring, but I've never been to Phoenix. Is it a nice city?"

"People move at a different pace there. My parents settled there after my father left the Air Force, and became a police officer in Phoenix." Jessica stared at him as his arm surprisingly tightened around her own arm. "It was hard leaving that environment to go to Harvard."

"Is that why you joined the Group, because your father would've wanted you to?"

"My sister is a career officer in the Navy and my brother is a police officer in Arizona. I guess we all wanted to be like our father."

"You loved him?"

Cary hesitated then said softly, "I worshipped him."

She noticed the shadows cross his face and didn't question him further as they reached her apartment building.

For some reason, Jessica became nervous as he watched her. Every breath she took, every subtle movement, Cary seemed to notice.

Once they reached the door to her apartment, Jessica fumbled for the door keys in her pocket and unlocked the door. By mutual consent, after Cary closed the door the two stood and stared at each other in the darkness of the apartment. Light from the streetlamps sliced through the open mini blinds partially illuminating the dark living room, but neither moved to turn on the light.

Jessica smiled as he simply stared at her. She didn't know where the courage came from but she asked, "Was this a date, Cary?"

She was delighted as he averted eyes in response to her question. He reminded her of a high-school jock trying to figure out how to sweet talk his date. And since Jessica felt like she was sixteen years old and he was the unattainable star football quarterback, she stared at her shoes, too. "What would you say if I said it was?" he suddenly asked, meeting her eyes.

Jessica took another deep breath and her eyes fell on his lips. All she had to do was close her eyes and she could feel those same lips on her. "If this were a date, I'd say you should kiss me good night."

She suddenly realized they were standing in the same position where he'd loved her for a few glorious moments, after she found him in her apartment. The magnitude of how much she wanted that again didn't shock her anymore. Nothing about this man and what he did to her surprised her. His eyes, filled with desire, raked over her, and Jessica felt her mouth slightly part in anticipation as his hands came to rest on either side of her face. Cary slowly leaned toward her and her eyes slid closed. She knew she should've smiled to lighten the mood or turned and ran, but Jessica could only stand and smell his musky cologne.

Then his lips lightly touched hers and Jessica's entire body rioted from the sweet, brief contact. But the next moment, he pulled away and his hands moved from her face. Her eyes flew open as the cool air of the apartment swirled to fill the space around her that Cary had occupied. She noticed his distant expression and wanted to pound the wall in frustration. Whenever she thought they had returned to the same easiness they'd shared at Hadley's Inn, he pulled away.

"It wasn't a date. Good night, Jessica," Cary said firmly. He turned away from her and moved to unfold the couch. "It wasn't a date," he muttered again for his own benefit. Jessica stared at his broad back and forced herself to walk to her room before she attacked him.

Eleven

From across the street, Cary watched Jessica walk into her office building the next morning. He knew it was foolish to follow her every morning. She had three agents assigned to her. One who followed her on foot, and two who followed her by car. Yet every morning, Cary pretended to lounge until she left the apartment, then he threw on his clothes and followed her. He knew his supervisors at the Group would have laughed at the inefficient use of manpower, and rearranged the entire system. Cary would have laughed himself if anyone else had told him about the operation or if anyone but Jessica had been the object of security. Also, Cary liked to watch her long hair glow in the sunshine as she weaved her way through the morning sidewalk traffic toward work.

Cary glanced at his watch. He wanted to interrogate certain people in south San Francisco about connections with Michael, and move farther down the peninsula until he found someone who could tell him about Michael Lyons. Cary turned to catch a taxi when he met eyes with Agent Tyler Morris, who stood fifty feet away from him. Cary groaned as recognition and shock crossed Tyler's face. Tyler had only been an agent for six months, but he was fresh and vigilant, which was why Cary assigned him to foot patrol. Tyler was fresh from graduate school, Black and, for some reason, considered Cary his idol.

Tyler waved slightly, then jogged through the throng of people scurrying to work toward Cary. "Are you checking up on us?" Tyler asked, grinning, once he reached Cary.

Cary shrugged. "You should never abandon your post, Tyler."

Tyler's face immediately fell and he glanced back at the bench in front of Jessica's apartment building where he stood for half the day. "I just wanted to say hi."

"Hi," Cary muttered, rolling his eyes at the ignorance of youth. Although Cary was only a few years older than Tyler, he felt that his experience at the Group made him ancient in comparison to the recent graduate.

"Cary, I know how you feel about her and I want you to know we're all going to keep a good eye on her for you."

A muscle in Cary's left eyelid involuntarily twitched and he stuffed his balled fists into his pants pockets. "And how do I feel about her, Tyler?"

Wariness instantly crossed Tyler's face. "I didn't mean anything—"

"She is an assignment, Agent Morris, and that's all."

"I think she's an amazing woman, Cary. I don't think your loving her is anything to be ashamed of—"

"Get back to your post, Agent Morris," Cary interrupted coldly.

Tyler stared at him for a moment and Cary thought a flash of pity crossed his face. Cary was on the verge of punching him in the face just as the younger man patted his shoulder then promptly jogged back to his position. Cary debated following Tyler and pounding his face into a bloody pulp, but instead turned on his heel and scanned the street for a taxi. He didn't need anyone to pity him because they thought he was in love with Jessica. There was no way he was in love with her. He wasn't capable of love.

"Cary?" said a deep, male voice behind him.

Cary's hand discreetly moved to the gun underneath his jacket before he turned. His hand dropped from the gun, at the same time as his mouth automatically fell open. He stared into the familiar amber-colored eyes of his brother, Logan Riley.

Cary hadn't seen his younger brother in almost five years. He hadn't talked to him in four years. The last time Cary saw Logan, Logan had been nineteen years old and nearing the end of his sophomore year in college. Cary only knew through his sister's frequent letters, which Cary never answered, that Logan had become a police detective in Phoenix.

Logan still looked the same, with a lean, muscular build, laughing brown eyes, the inherited Riley nose, and full lips. He wore an obviously expensive navy blue suit. Logan had always been conscious of his appearance, because he would tell Cary that he always wanted to be prepared to wine and dine a beautiful woman. The two brothers had been as different as night and day, and best friends.

Before he realized what he did, Cary placed his hand on his brother's left cheek. Logan smiled, flashing the dimple in his right cheek that Cary remembered.

"You look just like Dad," Cary said softly.

"Maggie says that all the time," Logan replied.

Cary quickly took a step away from Logan and glanced around the street, to make certain no one watched them. He never told Michael about his brother or sister, and he definitely didn't want Michael to find out about them.

"What are you doing here?" Cary asked, more sharply than he intended.

Logan's smile quickly melted and his eyes narrowed. "I moved to San Francisco three years ago."

"Why?"

"I needed a change. San Francisco police make more money."

"It's also more dangerous," Cary said, annoyed. He glanced around the crowded streets once more. "You should have stayed in Phoenix. This is a dangerous city."

Logan rolled his eyes like he often did when they were children and Cary would make him finish his homework. "I'm a San Francisco inspector, Cary, I think I can take care of myself."

"You were trained in Arizona. It's not exactly the same."

"That's right," Logan said sarcastically, waving his arms in the air. "Why do the rest of us in law enforcement try when the great Cary Riley is around?"

"That's not what I meant," Cary said tiredly.

"What are you doing here?" Logan demanded, then shook his head. "The shadows of the FBI aren't operating in my backyard, are they?"

"I have to go."

Cary turned to leave but Logan grabbed his arm, spinning him around. Cary was surprised by the anger on Logan's face. "I haven't seen you in five years and you have to go?" Logan said in disbelief then laughed bitterly. "You haven't changed at all."

"I'm on assignment, Logan. I don't have time to talk to you right now."

Concern sprung into Logan's eyes and he stepped closer to Cary, as if to protect him from an oncoming bullet. Cary tried not to smile. His brother had never been able to stay angry with him for long.

"Do you need some help?"

"I can't involve local police—"

"Do you need help from your brother, Cary?" Logan interrupted, annoyed.

"No . . . Thank you."

Logan sighed tiredly then shook his head as he muttered, "Have a good life."

He turned to leave and Cary instantly thought of Jessica's expression of disapproval if she found out that he didn't attempt to have one dinner with his brother, while he was in town. Cary quickly called Logan's name and Logan turned to him expectantly.

"Would you like to have dinner with me and my . . ." Cary's voice trailed off as he tried to think of a word to describe Jessica.

"Your woman?" Logan said helpfully.

"She's not my woman," Cary replied too quickly and tried not to notice Logan's wide smile. "She's my friend and I'm staying with her. She can't cook but I could make us dinner."

"All you have to say is free food and I'm there," Logan said cheerfully. Cary wrote down Jessica's address on a piece of paper. He was pleasantly surprised by how much he looked forward to dinner, to talking to his brother after four years of silence.

"I called you last night," Erin accused, as she walked into the employees' lounge, where Jessica sat by herself.

Jessica smiled innocently and stirred the dark liquid in her coffee cup. "I'm sorry. We got back from the movies so late that I didn't think you'd want to be disturbed."

"We? As in you and Cary?" Erin closed the double doors to the small room, then turned to Jessica with pursed lips and hard eyes. "Talk," she said simply.

Jessica couldn't hide her smile as she sat at the round table in the center of the room. Erin sat across from her. "I wasn't lying. I did meet Cary in Blue Moon Bay, the night I drove from LA and got caught in the storm. We spent an amazing night together, talking and laughing. I've never felt so comfortable around a man. When this . . . incident in the park happened, I couldn't think about anything else except that I wanted to see him. And when I called, he came."

"You mean to tell me that you've officially been a non-virgin for over a week and you didn't tell me?" Erin demanded angrily, but her twinkling eyes betrayed her smile.

"I am still a virgin," Jessica whispered fiercely, glancing at the closed door. Erin's eyes grew wide with surprise.

"I thought you said you and Cary spent the night together," she said, confused. "And he's staying at your apartment."

"He's staying on the couch." Jessica smiled at the memory, wishing she could capture their time at the inn and bottle it, to keep for the cold, lonely days that would follow once Cary left. "That night at the inn, we kissed . . . Amazing kisses, but nothing more."

"And a few kisses have you glowing like this?" Erin asked doubtfully, with a raised eyebrow.

Jessica laughed at Erin's expression and nodded. "Our initial meeting was rocky but as soon I sat at dinner with him, everything changed. We talked about anything and everything. He made me feel like the most desirable woman in the world. I've never felt like that before. It was like a dream. I couldn't have imagined a more perfect night, from the food to the conversation to his soul-searching kisses that made me forget who I was."

"You must have made him just as crazy, considering he flew across the country to sleep on your couch."

Jessica felt the embarrassing heat flood her cheeks as Erin looked at her with a sly grin. "You know I would never do anything like that with any other guy. I barely know him, but there's something about Cary. I don't act like myself when I'm around him, or maybe I do. I just know that it feels like I've known him my whole life."

"This isn't your becoming-whole theory, is it?" Erin asked warily.

"Of course not," Jessica lied, then laughed. "Maybe it is. When I'm around him, I can't imagine the possibility of there being anyone else in the world for me."

"You love him, don't you?" Erin said softly.

Jessica hesitated, staring at her hands. "I don't know."

"You wouldn't have allowed that man to come within ten feet of you, if you didn't love him." Erin poured coffee into a Styrofoam cup then returned to the chair across from Jessica. "How long is he going to stay with you?"

"Until he catches . . ." Jessica's voice trailed off as she caught herself. She didn't want to place her best friend in danger and she didn't want Erin to worry about her more than she already did. "Not very long."

"If you love this man, Jess, don't let him get away. No matter what anyone says, including David."

Jessica studied her suspiciously. "What has David been saying?"

"He kept me on the phone until two in the morning, worrying about you and Cary. He said he called you twenty times last night and you never answered the phone. Now I know you were at the movies . . . Stop looking at me like that."

"I definitely wish I could have heard that conversation." Jessica was surprised to see a flush blossom across Erin's vanilla-colored face. Jessica laughed and nudged Erin's arm. "Don't tell me you're going soft on me. My brother is your sworn archenemy, like Batman and the Riddler, Superman and Lex Luthor, Pam and Martin."

"He still is," Erin replied hesitantly, then added with a strange smile, "I just never realized what a nice voice he has."

Jessica faked gagging motions, which made Erin giggle. Erin's smile faded from her face and she placed a hand on Jessica's arm. "You've been so much happier since Cary arrived. Do you feel safe with him here?"

"I do," Jessica said softly. And Jessica knew it had nothing to do with his gun or his training or even the other Group agents. She felt safe because she knew Cary would never allow anything to happen to her. "I know I should be self-sufficient and able to take care of myself. I shouldn't need a man to feel safe, but I do, Erin. He makes me feel like Michael Lyons doesn't matter because he won't allow him to matter."

"He's supposed to make you feel that way."

"What about my independence?"

"You can be independent and still want a pair of strong arms to hold you at night and tell you everything's all right," Erin said.

"I feel like I'm breaking every vow I made to myself."

"Because you love him?" Erin asked, confused.

Jessica forced a smile and shook her head. "In two weeks, I went from a workaholic with career aspirations and goals, to leaving the office at five o'clock and going grocery shopping."

"You went grocery shopping?" Erin repeated, surprised, then shook her head and said, "They're not mutually exclusive, Jess. You can continue to have those same career goals with that same workaholic attitude, and also have a man. If Cary tells you differently, then he's definitely not the man for you or any other woman in the twenty-first century, and he should return to medieval times where he belongs."

"Not to mention the fact that he's living with me," Jessica continued, ignoring Erin's advice.

"He's just here to make you feel safe," Erin dismissed, then abruptly clapped her hands together. "You and Cary should come to dinner at my place. Tomorrow night at seven o'clock?"

Jessica instantly stood and poured the remainder of her

coffee into the sink. "I don't think that's such a good idea. He just arrived—"

"I won't take no for an answer. You and Cary are coming and I'll invite David too, just to even things out."

Jessica saw the unspoken anticipation in her friend's eyes and laughed. "You just want to see David," she teased.

"I do not," Erin protested heatedly as she walked to the door. "Call David and tell him he's invited. Tell him to make certain he's on time. I hate when he's late." Jessica continued to laugh as her friend sauntered out of the room.

Twelve

Cary replaced the lid on the pot of boiling sauce as he heard the front door slam shut. He was almost to the living room before he realized how eager he was to see Jessica after a long day. After another frustrating and endless search for leads on Michael, coming to her apartment, preparing dinner, and thinking about her made him more relaxed than he had a right to be. Cary remained by the stove and tried to think of anything, besides the driving need in his groin that begged to see her, after an entire day apart.

"Hi," Jessica greeted, as she walked in from the kitchen. He watched her take off her suit jacket and resisted the urge to offer to help her take off the rest of her clothes. "Something smells good," she complimented with a smile.

"I'm making fettuccine Alfredo."

"Do you need any help?"

"I have everything under control."

"I'm famished." She stood next to him as she peered inside the various pots and pans on the stove. Cary realized how close she was, how he could smell her, how he could practically taste her lips. He quickly looked at the sauce as Jessica met his eyes with a smile. "How was your day?"

Cary could tell from the interest in her eyes that she

really wanted to know and, even though it contradicted everything he had ever been taught in the Group, he really wanted to tell her.

Instead, he answered, "My brother, Logan, is eating dinner with us tonight. He should be here in a few minutes. I hope that's all right with you."

Surprise filled her eyes but she smiled. "Of course, it's all right. I thought your brother was in Arizona."

"I saw him today near your office building—"

"What were you doing near my office building?" she asked curiously.

"I was in the area," he dismissed quickly then said, "Logan said he moved to the city about three years ago. He's an inspector with the San Francisco police department."

"I'd really like to meet him."

"Why?" he asked suspiciously.

Jessica laughed at his suspicion, brushing past him to walk into the living room. Cary cursed his weak body for reacting to her. For a man who relied on his strength, he didn't like feeling weak, and Jessica made him feel helpless and weak. As if on a magic string attached to her hand, Cary followed her out of the kitchen and watched as she turned on the stereo. The velvet voice of Billie Holiday filled the room and Jessica fell on the couch. She closed her eyes and sighed in contentment. From the soft sigh alone, Cary almost dropped to his knees and begged her to make love to him. Fortunately, at the last moment, he restrained himself.

He abruptly cleared his throat and Jessica opened her eyes and stared at him in surprise.

"Did you want me to help you with dinner?" she asked, confused.

"Why do you want to meet my brother?" he repeated.

"Because he's your brother."

"I told you that I haven't talked to him in four years."

"So?"

"Our relationship isn't like yours with David."

Jessica snapped her fingers and said excitedly, "Speaking of David, Erin invited us to dinner tomorrow night at her apartment."

"I don't know about that," Cary said reluctantly. The last thing he wanted to do was spend the evening with Jessica's brother who hated him, and her best friend who would probably hate him, too.

"Two hours won't kill you."

"If Michael is following you, then we'd lead him straight to your friend's house."

"Don't try to scare me. I promise you the evening will be harmless. You can sit in a corner of the room and not talk to anyone, but Erin wants to meet you, and David has to make certain you're not Jack the Ripper."

"If I were Jack the Ripper, he'd be dead by now," Cary muttered, unconsciously gritting his teeth. Usually, Cary didn't care whether men liked him or not. He didn't need or want friends. For some reason, the fact that David was Jessica's brother made him want to be David's friend or, at least, have David not despise him.

"Cary, please. Erin will never leave me alone until she's met you."

Cary met her eyes and knew he would do whatever she wanted, whether going to dinner or crawling across the city on his knees. "Fine," he murmured. She grinned and Cary tried not to return her smile. "You owe me."

"Thank you. Besides, I can't deal with Erin and David by myself. I guarantee they'll spend the entire evening arguing with each other and ignoring us. You have to come so I'll have someone to talk to."

"Are they a couple?"

"They are, but they don't know it yet."

"What does that mean?"

"Exactly what it sounds like. Sometimes your heart

knows you're in love before your mind wants to admit to it." From the distant corner of his mind, he heard the doorbell ring but he could only stare at Jessica as the word love fell from her lips. She slowly stood and for one insane moment, he thought she would reach for him.

Cary knew he shouldn't have gone to the movies with her or touched her or told her about his family, because now he only wanted more. He definitely shouldn't have invited his brother to her home, involving her further in his life. One moment in time with Jessica Larson would not be enough, no matter how much he tried to convince himself that it would be.

"Are you going to answer the door or move out of the way so that I can?" Jessica asked, with an amused smile.

Cary shook his head to clear his thoughts and moved from her path. She shot him a strange look as she walked past him to the door. Cary cursed himself for his complete lack of composure around her and quickly moved to the door, to neutralize any potential threat that could enter.

Jessica opened the door and smiled warmly as Logan walked into the room. Cary saw the look of surprise in his brother's eyes as he studied Jessica and then Logan shot her the patented Logan smile. The smile that made half the female population of their high school fall under Logan's spell. Jessica returned his smile and offered her hand.

"You must be Cary's brother, Logan. I'm Jessica."

Logan smoothly brought her hand to his lips and kissed it. Cary hadn't realized his fists were clenched until he glanced down at them. He knew he had no right to be jealous because Jessica wasn't his, but he also didn't want another man kissing any part of her body while he was around, even if that other man was his brother.

"It's nice to meet you, Jessica. If Cary had mentioned how gorgeous you were, I would've worn my good suit,"

Logan said with a flirtatious smile that Cary wanted to rub off his face.

"That's because Cary doesn't think I'm gorgeous," Jessica said, with a shrug. Cary stopped glaring at his brother to stare at Jessica in surprise. She didn't know that he thought she was the most beautiful woman on earth. She didn't know that he had to physically fight with himself not to grab her and kiss her each and every time he saw her. He must have been a better actor that he thought. He stared back at his brother, who met his eyes with a strange look.

"Well, if my brother is too stupid to tell you, I will. You're a beautiful woman, Jessica," Logan complimented.

Jessica's face flushed and Cary's jealousy increased another notch. "And you've just become my favorite Riley brother," she told Logan with a grin.

Cary rolled his eyes in disbelief, then muttered, "Logan, do you remember me? Your brother?"

Logan glanced at him as Jessica laughed. "How could I forget your ugly, frowning face?" Logan unbuttoned his suit jacket, obviously prepared to make himself at home, and plopped on the couch. Cary rolled his eyes as Jessica smiled and sat next to Logan. Cary glanced at the kitchen, where the food had probably burned, and sat in a chair next to the couch.

"How do you like living in San Francisco?" Jessica asked Logan.

"With as many beautiful women as this town has, how could I not like living here?" Logan said with another grin that made Cary's head pound with pain. "I love Arizona, but after our parents died and . . . my sister joined the Navy, which coincidentally doesn't exist in Arizona, there was no reason for me to stay there." From the corner of his eye, Cary saw Jessica glance at him. He kept his eyes on Logan, who watched Jessica.

"That must have been a hard decision to make," Jessica said to break the silence.

Cary stood, his need to escape the topic of conversation overruling his reluctance to leave Jessica alone with Logan. "Logan, would you like something to drink?"

"It was a very difficult decision to make." Logan stopped smiling for the first time since he walked into the apartment. "I wanted to stay in Arizona and remember my parents, remember what our family was like, but everyone else moved on. Maggie would visit occasionally, but I could tell that it was too much for her to see our old house and the highway where our parents were killed. And Cary, he never—"

"I think the sauce is burning," Cary muttered, as he escaped into the kitchen. He leaned against the sink and put a hand over his eyes. Even after all these years, he still couldn't handle a conversation about his past life, about his parents. He was a grown man, a hard man, but every time he thought of his parents he knew that everything he had accomplished over the years meant nothing.

Cary heard Jessica walk into the kitchen. He quickly turned to the stove and began to stir the creamy white sauce in the pot. He glanced toward her, since she hadn't spoken, and found her watching him. He forced a smile as he said, "My brother is something else, huh?"

"He's a sweet guy."

"You're probably the only woman in the world to ever call him sweet," Cary said, forcing a laugh. Jessica pulled a bottle of wine from the cabinet and poured three glasses. Cary discreetly watched her, unable to bear the heavy silence in the kitchen. "I'm trying, Jess," he finally muttered.

Jessica looked at him, surprised. "I didn't say a word."

"I know what you're thinking. You're thinking that I shouldn't treat Logan like he's a stranger. I should treat him like my brother and I should apologize for not calling or writing in four years. And all I can say is that I'm trying."

"I know that, Cary." She sent a smile that literally broke his heart. He quickly turned back to the sauce. "If you'd stop being defensive for five minutes, you'd realize that your brother is reaching out to you. He loves you. He wants his big brother."

"You can tell all that from a two-minute conversation where he flirted with you the entire time?" Cary asked gruffly.

"No, I can tell from the way he looks at you."

"Could you pass the salt?" Cary pointedly switched the subject.

"Get the salt yourself," she muttered walking from the kitchen.

For the two hours the three ate dinner, Jessica laughed at Logan's jokes and tried to draw Cary from the shell he'd entered, but she could feel the tense air that hung between the two brothers. Cary had erected an invisible wall between himself and his brother, and there was nothing Logan could do to knock it down. Over coffee, Jessica watched Cary avoid Logan's eyes. He barely mumbled more than three words from the time he served the salad to when he served the slices of cheesecake. He looked miserable. He looked uncomfortable. She wasn't surprised when he put on his coat after dinner, and stood near the door.

"Are you leaving?" Jessica asked alarmed, glancing at Logan. She could see the hurt in Logan's eyes. He pretended to be uncaring and apathetic, but Jessica could see how much his brother's show of disinterest hurt him.

"I have to check a few things," Cary mumbled, then offered his hand to Logan. "It was good seeing you again." Logan shook his hand, with a slight smile.

"You two act as if you'll never see each other again," Jessica said, with a tight smile. Both men looked at her and she swallowed the immediate lump in her throat. They both seemed to silently plead with her to allow the matter to drop, but Jessica refused. She wanted Cary to overcome his insecurities and demons, and she wanted him to have a family that loved him, almost as much as she did.

"Cary, why don't you wait an hour or two?" Jessica said quickly. She flinched when he glared at her, but she continued, "There's a movie coming on cable—"

"I have to go, Jess," Cary finally mumbled. "After Logan leaves, lock the door." He quickly walked out the front door, slamming it behind him.

Jessica turned to Logan and saw him slipping into his suit jacket. When he saw her watching him, he forced a smile. "I don't think Cary would appreciate me staying here too long. He's kind of the jealous type."

"Don't go, Logan. Maybe Cary will return in a little while. He never stays gone long."

"Why is he here?"

"Didn't he tell you?"

Logan snorted in disbelief as he buttoned his jacket. "Were you just here at dinner where he ignored me? My brother doesn't tell me anything."

"He didn't ignore you."

"Don't try to gloss it over, Jess," Logan muttered, shaking his head. "It's been five years. I thought he'd be ready to deal with it."

"With what?"

Logan hesitated, shaking his head. "You'll have to ask him. If you need anything, call me." Logan walked out of the apartment, firmly closing the door behind him.

Jessica paused for only a second before she grabbed a sweater and followed Logan. When she stepped out of the apartment building, she quickly glanced around the

heart&soul's got it all!

Motivation, Inspiration, Exhilaration!
FREE ISSUE RESERVATION CARD

YES! Please send my FREE issue of HEART & SOUL right away and enter my one-year subscription. My special price for 5 more issues (6 in all) is only $10.00. I'll save 44% off the newsstand rate. If I decide that HEART & SOUL is not for me, I'll write "cancel" on the invoice, return it, and owe nothing. The FREE issue will be mine to keep.

Name _____
     (First)   (Last)

Address _____ Apt.#_____

City _____ State _____ Zip _____ | MABQ |

Please allow 6-8 weeks for receipt of first issue. In Canada: CDN $19.97 (includes GST). Payment in U.S. currency must accompany all

BUSINESS REPLY MAIL

FIRST-CLASS MAIL   PERMIT NO. 272   RED OAK, IA

POSTAGE WILL BE PAID BY ADDRESSEE

heart&soul

P O BOX 7423
RED OAK IA 51591-2423

3 QUICK STEPS
TO RECEIVE YOUR "THANK YOU" GIFT
FROM THE EDITOR

Send back this card and you'll receive 4 Arabesque novels!
These books have a combined cover price of $20.00 or more,
but they are yours to keep for a mere $1.99.

There's no catch. You're under no obligation to buy anything.
We charge only $1.99 for the books (plus $1.50 for shipping
and handling, a total of $3.49). And you don't have to make
any minimum number of purchases—not even one!

We hope that after receiving your books you'll want to
remain an Arabesque subscriber. But the choice is yours to
continue or cancel, anytime at all! So why not take us up on
our invitation to receive 4 Arabesque Romance Novels, with
no risk of any kind. You'll be glad you did!

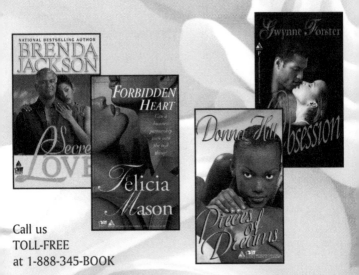

Call us
TOLL-FREE
at 1-888-345-BOOK

THE EDITOR'S "THANK YOU" GIFT INCLUDES:

- 4 books delivered for only $1.99 (plus $1.50 for shipping and handling
- A FREE newsletter, *Arabesque Romance News*, filled with author interviews, book previews, special offers, and more!
- No risks or obligations. You're free to cancel whenever you wish... with no questions asked.

BOOK CERTIFICATE

Yes! Please send me 4 Arabesque books for $1.99 (+ $1.50 for shipping & handling, a total of $3.49). I understand I am under no obligation to purchase any books, as explained on the back of this card.

Name _____

Address _____ Apt. _____

City _____ State _____ Zip _____

Telephone ( ) _____

Signature _____

Offer limited to one per household and not valid to current subscribers. All orders subject to approval. Terms, offer, & price subject to change. Offer valid only in the U.S.

Thank you!

AN090A

Accepting the four introductory books for $1.99 (+ $1.50 for shipping & handling, total of $3.49) places you under no obligation to buy anything. You may keep the books and return the shipping statement marked "cancel". If you do not cancel, about a month later we will send 4 additional Arabesque novels, and bill you a preferred subscriber's price of just $4.00 per title (plus a small shipping and handling fee). That's $16.00 for all 4 books for a savings of 33% off the cover price. You may cancel at any time, but if you choose to continue, every month we'll send you 4 more books, which you may either purchase at the preferred discount price. . . or return to us and cancel your subscription.

THE ARABESQUE ROMANCE CLUB: HERE'S HOW IT WORKS

ARABESQUE ROMANCE BOOK CLUB
P.O. Box 5214
Clifton NJ 07015-5214

PLACE
STAMP
HERE

street for any sign of Cary. When she didn't see him, she ran in the direction that she hoped Logan had gone. She spotted Logan a block away from her apartment building.

"Logan," she called, running to him.

Logan stopped in the middle of the sidewalk and patted his pants pocket. "Did I forget something?"

"What happened with Cary and your parents? Why is he so nervous around you?"

"How could you tell he was nervous and not bored? He—"

"I know him, Logan. Something about you . . . hurts him."

"I look like our father," Logan said quietly, then sighed. "I shouldn't say anything more. Cary wouldn't want me to tell you. He can't talk about it himself."

"Tell me, Logan. What's hurting him?"

Logan appeared to study her, then he nodded. "Let's walk," he said, grabbing her arm. Jessica barely managed to match his long strides. She saw the way he surveyed the street as they walked, looking for any sign of danger. She couldn't help but think how alike he and Cary were. The realization renewed her vow to bring the brothers together. Cary may not have wanted her in his life, but she refused to allow him to shut out his brother. "Cary told you our parents were killed in a car accident."

"Five years ago."

"Did he tell you that he was driving when the accident happened?" Jessica eyes filled with tears as she thought of Cary silently dealing with the guilt and pain of his parents' death. Logan watched her, concerned, and she nodded for him to continue. "It wasn't his fault. It was a drunk driver. Cary's lucky to be alive. He came home from college to visit, and one night he and my parents went to the grocery store. Cary drove on the way home and couldn't avoid a car, heading straight toward him. My parents and the other driver died almost instantly.

Cary walked away without a scratch. Everyone considered him lucky to be alive."

"But, he blames himself," Jessica whispered. She finally understood the guilt she always saw in Cary's eyes; she understood his fear.

"You know my brother well," Logan said, nodding. "There was nothing he could have done to prevent the accident or to save my parents. By the grace of God, his life was spared, and Cary has been questioning that decision ever since."

"He thinks you and your sister blame him, too?"

"He thinks we should blame him, but we don't. We were glad he lived. When we were younger, Cary was like our second father. We both worshipped him. He . . ." Logan's voice trailed off as they stopped next to his car, parked at the curb. Logan stared at the setting sun for a few seconds before he met her eyes. She could see the tears glistening in his eyes and she placed a hand on his arm. "Didn't you ever wonder why he would join an organization like the Group? Why he would willingly place himself in such dangerous situations, every day of every year? He didn't join to protect America or to promote democracy, or whatever reason the federal government gives for the existence of the Group. Cary joined that organization to get himself killed."

"Can't you talk to him and—"

"I've tried, Jess. Maggie and I both talked to him until we were blue in the face. That's why he stopped all contact with us. My sister still writes him, but she doesn't know if he receives the letters because he never writes her back. We don't know what else to do. Cary will only see the truth when he wants to."

"What if that's never?" Jessica asked desperately.

"Then we have to move on with our lives," Logan said firmly, almost as if he knew Jessica asked that same question of herself every day. What if Cary never saw that she loved him? What if he never accepted her love? "I love my brother but I can't live in the past with him."

"He needs you, Logan."

"Cary doesn't need anyone."

"He's hurting inside," Jessica tried again. "He needs his family."

"You can't blame me for this," Logan said defensively. "I called him every day for months, trying to talk sense into him. He never returned my phone calls. He had his number at college changed, Jessica. I'm not the brightest guy in the world, but I can take a hint."

Jessica ignored his excuses and said simply, "He's your brother."

Logan rolled his eyes and snorted in disbelief. "And that means I should allow him to treat me like dirt? I should stand by and watch my little sister become more depressed with each and every letter she sends that Cary won't answer?"

"What would your parents say?" Jessica asked softly. "Would they give up on him?"

"I didn't give up on him," Logan muttered annoyed.

"Well, what do you call it?"

Logan was silent for a moment as he stared at her. She saw the conflict of emotions cross his face before he finally shrugged. "You have to know how frustrating Cary's silence can be."

"Just don't give up on him, Logan. When I first met Cary, I could see the pain in his eyes. He's standing on the edge of a cliff. He only needs one push and we'll lose him forever. He'll become the man that he only thinks he is now."

Logan shook his head and smiled. "Why do you care? He wasn't just ignoring me during dinner."

Jessica glanced at her watch, avoiding his eyes. "I didn't realize how late it was. I enjoyed having you over and, no matter how Cary acted, I could tell he did, too. Don't be a stranger."

Jessica stepped away from Logan as he unlocked the car door. "Hop in and I'll give you a ride home," he said.

"My apartment building is only a few blocks away. I'll walk."

"There's a man following us," Logan said quietly, discreetly indicating a still figure across the street.

Jessica glanced in the direction he pointed and slightly waved to Agent Morris, who hesitated for a brief second then waved back. "That's the man who Cary assigned to follow me."

Comprehension dawned in Logan's eyes as he glanced at Agent Morris, then back to her. "Cary is here because of you?"

"It's complicated."

"Someone is trying to hurt you?" Logan asked, concerned.

"No . . . Logan, please, don't make me say something I shouldn't."

Logan smiled as he said, "On one condition. You accept my ride back to the apartment. If Cary thought he should assign you a security detail, then I'm not allowing you to walk back to the apartment alone."

"You and your brother have a problem seeing women as functional adults, with opinions of their own," Jessica muttered, rolling her eyes.

"You do know my brother," Logan said, laughing.

"Can we give Agent Morris a ride, too?"

Logan groaned and shook his head. "I'm certain that's against protocol—"

"Please, Logan."

Logan glared at her, then reluctantly motioned to Agent Morris, who ran across the street toward them. "I've never been able to say no to a pretty face," Logan mumbled as she grinned from ear to ear. "That's another weakness of the Riley men."

Jessica didn't answer as she sat in the passenger seat and buckled her seat belt.

Thirteen

"Excellent presentation, as usual, Jessica," Peter Jannings complimented as the two walked from the conference room in the office building. Jessica smiled at Peter, surprised by how little the compliment meant to her now, compared to the happiness she would have received from his words a few weeks ago. Their meeting with a multimillion-dollar client had gone extremely well, especially when Jessica had presented options for the expansion of their domestic operations into southern California. Although she remembered the smiles on the clients' faces as they left the room twenty minutes ago, she couldn't remember one word she'd said during her presentation.

She spent the whole time worrying about Cary, worrying about the weight he must carry around each day because he thought he was responsible for his parents' deaths. She had tried to stay awake last night and wait for his return, but she fell asleep at two o'clock in the morning. When she woke up the next morning, Cary had been asleep in the living room and she didn't want to wake him on her way to work.

"You're receiving the Bay Area Professionals award next week, correct?" Peter asked, breaking into her thoughts.

"Yes."

"I plan to attend the ball, Jessica. This is definitely a shining moment for you and Jannings & Associates."

"I wouldn't have won the award without the help and support of you and this company," Jessica said truthfully. She truly appreciated the color-blind, fair chance that Peter gave everyone who walked through his office doors.

Jessica stopped at the door to her office and was surprised when Peter stood with her. Peter was an extremely busy man and believed in not wasting his time with idle conversation. Although Jessica understood his brusque manner, a few of the other employees were frightened of him.

"Is there something else, Peter?" Jessica asked.

"You're aware that Tom Pritchard is retiring as the Senior Consultant Manager of San Francisco projects in a few months?"

"I am," Jessica said calmly, as her heart pounded against her chest.

Peter smiled and Jessica returned his smile, with a grin of her own. "Make an appointment with Eileen sometime within the next few days. You and I need to discuss your very bright future with this company," Peter said, then continued down the hall toward the elevator.

Jessica restrained the unprofessional grin that threatened to take over her face until she walked into her office. She closed the door behind her, then performed a silent dance around her office. She stopped abruptly when there was a knock on the door. Jessica smoothed down the rumpled skirt of her suit and took several deep breaths to calm herself before she opened the door.

She grinned when she saw Erin standing on the other side of the door. Without bothering to glance at Jessica, Erin walked into the office. Jessica's good mood evaporated when she saw the tears glistening in Erin's eyes.

"What's wrong?" Jessica asked, concerned. Jessica didn't think Erin was capable of tears.

"Your brother is a moron," Erin announced.

Jessica sighed with relief that nothing serious had affected Erin, then rolled her eyes in exasperation and sat on her desk. "What happened now?"

"I saw him and his . . . I guess, she was his date, last night at a coffeehouse. You should have seen how David fawned over this woman. You should have seen her. I'm surprised the woman could even walk; her fake breasts defied gravity."

Jessica couldn't withhold her laughter as she said, "You're jealous of David's date?"

"Of course not," she protested vehemently. "I just can't understand how David can be such a skilled and competent businessman but have absolutely no taste when it comes to the women he dates."

"You don't even know the woman, Erin."

"She had a weave down to her waist, fake boobs, and . . . Who knows what was real on that woman? I don't have to know her; I know her type. Men always say they want a real woman, then they pick a Barbie replica. What's even more sickening is that we women allow men to get away with it. We encourage their sexist attitude, every time we wear lipstick or show cleavage or wear a short skirt just to catch some man's attention."

Jessica waited for Erin to finish her tirade, then asked calmly, "Men in general, or David?" Erin's anger seemed to dissipate and she sat next to Jessica on her desk. Jessica had never seen her friend look so utterly dejected. She noticed Erin's tears and her mouth fell open in surprise before she composed herself and placed a comforting hand on Erin's back. "You really do love my brother, don't you?"

"If you say one word to him, I'll never speak to you again," Erin declared immediately, wiping at her tears. "I can't believe I'm crying over David Larson. I've never cried over a man. I've never yelled at a man the way I yell at David."

"When did this happen?" Jessica asked softly.

"I don't know. I don't want to know. I'll still trying not to vomit at the thought," Erin said, obviously annoyed. Jessica grinned then stifled her laughter when Erin glared at her. "This isn't funny, Jess."

"I bet my brand-new sweater that David feels the same way about you."

Erin rolled her eyes in disbelief. "He would laugh, if he knew. I'm not his type. I have a brain and real breasts. Real, small breasts. I actually have hips, unlike the bean pole he was with last night. If that woman represents David's ideal, then I don't have a chance. Not that I care. I'm sure these strange feelings that I have for him are temporary and are being caused by a slight mental lapse on my part."

"Give David more credit than that. He could actually surprise you."

"I start to feel slightly nauseous when I think about this for too long." Erin forced a smile and nudged Jessica's shoulder. "Are you and Cary coming to dinner tonight?"

"Of course. We had dinner with his younger brother last night."

"Cary has a brother? Cary has a family? He seems like one of those men that just spring out of nowhere. They step from the womb, completely grown and not needing anyone."

"He has a family," Jessica said softly, then smiled at Erin. "Should I bring anything tonight?"

"Just you, Cary, and . . . I can't believe I'm about to say this, but really make sure David comes." Jessica tried not to laugh but when Erin groaned in shame, Jessica howled in laughter. "It's not funny," Erin muttered, right before she started giggling.

* * *

David and Erin were either in love or on the verge of starting World War III. After spending an hour listening to their petty arguing and bickering in the comfort of Erin's small apartment, Cary wished they would kill each other and be put out of their misery. He glanced across the dinner table at Jessica, who only smiled at him and stared at her plate. Cary laughed to himself. Jessica must have known David and Erin would spend the entire time arguing with each other instead of interviewing him. Since Cary and Jessica had entered Erin's apartment, neither Erin nor David had said more than three words to them, because they were too preoccupied with insulting each other.

"I can't believe how insensitive to women you are," Erin exclaimed to David. "No wonder you haven't had a woman in the last eight months."

"I've had plenty of women," David shot back.

"I'm not counting the ones you paid."

Cary choked on an abrupt laugh and David glared at him. Cary gave him a sober look of understanding, then quickly gulped down the water in front of him before he laughed again. He glanced at Jessica, who didn't try to hide her own laughter.

"Let's count how many men you've gone out with in the last eight months." David turned back to Erin. "First, there was Ronald, the drug addict."

"He was only addicted to pain killers."

"Then there was Jon, the unemployed actor."

"Painter," Erin weakly corrected.

"Who's next—"

"What about your dates?" Erin interrupted, taking the offensive. "What about Marina? Remember the woman who stole half of your CD collection and several of your credit cards?" David remained silent and suddenly became interested in the food on his plate. Erin grinned triumphantly and continued, "My personal favorite was Hillary, the lovely accountant, with that tiny multiple-per-sonalities problem."

"It's a shame that all five of her personalities were bet-ter than your one," David replied, calmly.

Erin's eyes dangerously narrowed and Jessica held her hands in the air and said, "You two have successfully fought through dinner. Does anyone want coffee?"

"I'll help you." Cary stood, but Erin jumped to her feet and glared at him.

"Sit," she commanded, then followed Jessica into the kitchen.

Cary cleared his throat as David stared at him across the table. The silence lengthened between them and Cary finally said, "Would you like to hit me again, David?"

"I don't know what's going on between you and my sister, but I don't like it."

Cary rolled his eyes and silently agreed with every bad thing Erin had said about David. "Your sister and I are going to be spending a lot of time together over these next few days. You may as well get used to me."

"I don't trust you," David said simply. "I don't think my sister does either."

"Jessica trusts me," Cary said, with more emotion in his voice than he liked.

"That's why she won't look at you, why she jumps every time you talk, why she flinches every time you come within two feet of her."

Cary wanted to protest and deny everything David said, but it was true. Jessica trusted him with her safety, but not with herself. She didn't trust him like she trusted her brother or Erin. Cary met David's eyes and said quietly, "It takes time to build trust between two people."

"That's one thing you don't have, Cary. Any day now,

my sister's going to ask herself why she is wasting her time on you and then you'll be out the door."

Cary tried to ignore the anger that flared through his body. He leaned across the table and said softly, "Only because you're Jessica's brother do you still have all of your teeth."

The two women took that moment to walk back into the dining room with coffee cups and a pie. Jessica took one look at the strained expression on each man's face and said reluctantly, "Now, what's going on?"

"David rubs everyone the wrong way," Erin said simply.

"How do you know I did something wrong?" David demanded innocently.

"Because I know you." Erin smiled at Cary, which made David stiffen in his seat and Jessica accidentally spill coffee onto the table. Cary prayed Erin didn't do anything stupid to make David jealous. Erin grinned at him again then leaned toward him. "Jess was so lucky to find you. Maybe I should get lost in a rainstorm and then I'll find someone just like you."

Cary glanced at Jessica, who stared at him with an unrecognizable expression. Cary didn't know why but he needed to touch her, to reassure her, to reassure himself. Cary brushed a strand of hair from Jessica's face, then softly caressed her cheek. Her eyes darkened and he could feel the sigh that left her mouth caress his hand.

"If anyone's lucky, it's me," Cary said softly, vaguely remembering he and Jessica weren't alone.

Jessica smiled slightly then moved from his reach. Cary tried not to react to the loss and drank his coffee.

"Didn't you meet that saxophonist who eventually stole your car, in a rainstorm?" David asked Erin, with an edge in his voice. Neither he nor Erin had noticed that Cary had almost made love to Jessica on the table. Cary shook his head in disbelief.

"You two sure know a lot about each other's love life,"

Cary finally said. He suddenly wished he had never spoken when David and Erin pinned their heated gazes on him. Cary looked to Jessica for help, but she only shrugged in support.

"What are you implying?" Erin demanded.

"Nothing—"

"You've been in my sister's life for two weeks and you think you can tell us how we feel about each other?" David demanded.

"David, please," Jessica said, sharply.

"I can't believe these words are about to leave my mouth, but I agree with David," Erin said, crossing her arms over her chest. "I want to know exactly what Cary meant by the comment that David and I know a lot about each other's love lives."

"I meant exactly what I said," Cary said, as his irritation rose another notch. He would have gone to hell and back for Jessica, but he was beginning to think that even hell would be more pleasant than listening to Erin and David for another hour.

"Which is what?" David said through clenched teeth. David glanced at Erin, who refused to meet his eyes. "Erin and I are connected through Jessica. Of course, we're going to know about each other's love lives."

"I have never told either of you about the other's dates," Jessica interjected, shaking her head.

"Yes, you have," Erin protested. "Or how else would David know about my dates, and how would I know about his?"

Cary could see the frustration and exasperation written across Jessica's face. He was just glad that David and Erin had stopped looking at him.

"I don't know, Erin," Jessica snapped, rolling her eyes. "Maybe it's because as soon as you and David see each other, you try to make each other jealous with these outrageous tales about the people you date. Then when those dates naturally turn out to be human, you're stuck telling the whole story."

"Jealous," David sputtered as Erin's mouth dropped open. "I am not jealous of any man who dates that woman. If anything, I feel sorry for the poor fools."

"I hate you, David," Erin spat out, glaring at him. She turned to Cary and Cary rolled his eyes. He had grown tired of this conversation as soon as Jessica stopped speaking. "This is all your fault, Cary," Erin told him. "We were having a pleasant dinner until you ruined everything."

"Cary didn't ruin anything," Jessica said, defensively. "Your arguing with David is what ruined this dinner."

"Whose side are you on, Jess?" David said, incredulously.

Cary didn't wait for Jessica to answer the question, because he wasn't certain he would like the answer. "I think I've been very patient with you two since I've had to listen to both of your mouths for the last hour and a half. If it weren't for Jessica, I would've walked out of here about five minutes after I walked in. And after hearing all these insults and put-downs, I only have one piece of advice. Sleep together and get it over with or leave each other alone. You'll never have peace unless you do one or the other." Cary threw his napkin on the table in disgust. "Jess, can we leave now?"

Jessica glanced at Erin and David, who were both speechless with anger. Jessica stood and grabbed her purse from the nearby couch. Cary didn't wait for an acknowledgment from either Erin or David, but led Jessica from the apartment. He noticed her grave expression as they walked down the sidewalk toward her car.

"That was a disaster," Cary muttered. "If your brother didn't hate me before, he definitely hates me now." Jessica didn't answer as Cary held open the driver's door for her. She slid behind the steering wheel without looking at him. Cary closed the door, then ran around the car to the passenger seat. Once he closed his door, Jessica turned the key in the ignition and the motor roared to life. A few seconds passed before he realized neither Jessica nor the car moved.

Cary glanced out the car window at the empty, dark street. "We really shouldn't sit out in the open like this—"

"Is that how you think of sex? As something to get out of the way, so you'll have peace?" she asked abruptly.

Cary heard the strain in her voice. He had the feeling that making love to her would open a whole world of emotions that he had never associated with sex. He wanted to tell her that. He wanted to tell her about his confusion, but he could only answer, "Of course not."

"That's what you said," Jessica said, staring at him. "That's exactly what you said to Erin and David. What if they really are in love with each other? What if they're too scared to allow all the confusing feelings to take over their lives? Then sleeping together wouldn't solve that problem, would it? They still wouldn't have peace."

"I shouldn't have said that—"

"What if they don't want peace?" Her voice cracked and Cary tried to see her clearly in the darkness, but he could only see her profile. "Did you think about that, Cary? Not everyone wants their lives to fit in a neat compartment. Not everyone wants to be able to label and control their feelings."

"You lost me somewhere in between Erin's apartment and the car. I thought you wanted to leave. I thought you were about as annoyed with them as I was."

"Forget it," Jessica muttered as she drove toward her apartment. Cary racked his brain for something to say to make her laugh, to make her forget whatever he had done to irritate her. He stopped himself as he realized what he was doing. That wasn't who he was. He didn't care if someone was happy or not. Every time he was around her, he found himself losing all sense of himself, and he didn't like that.

Jessica bluntly asked, "How much longer do you think you'll be here?"

Cary calmly shrugged and said, "Until we're certain Michael Lyons is no longer a threat to you."

"That'd better be soon, because I can't take much more of this." Cary didn't respond and Jessica didn't elaborate.

Fourteen

Jessica hated feeling like a prisoner in her own bedroom. Without work to hurry to on Saturday morning, she had no legitimate excuse to leave her bedroom. She could have gone shopping or to an art gallery, but she knew Cary would find some reason why it was unsafe for her to go alone and then she would have Agent Morris trailing after her. After seeing Michael at the coffee shop, Jessica also didn't want to go anywhere alone, whether Agent Morris followed her or not.

For some strange reason, she felt safe only around Cary. Unfortunately for her, she would rather walk barefoot on hot coals than ask Cary to accompany her anywhere. She was still annoyed with his virtual confession at Erin's dinner that making love meant nothing to him. With each of his kisses, Jessica had been on the verge of practically begging him to make love to her, of admitting her love for him. She knew that was the real reason why she felt restless. Her heart was breaking and the reason for that heartbreak was only a few walls away.

Jessica glanced out her bedroom window just as a man in running shorts jogged past. Her throat tightened as she realized that she hadn't been to Golden Gate Park since the attack. The immediate thought of Michael Lyons's evil smile snaked into her mind and made her heart race. Michael Lyons had ruined her love of Golden Gate Park and she hated him for that.

Without thinking, Jessica changed into her favorite running clothes. She thought about running through the leaves of Golden Gate Park and feeling the sunshine on her back. She thought about reclaiming her life from Michael Lyons and Cary Riley. If Cary didn't want to admit how special their relationship could be, if they just gave it a chance, then she vowed not to need him either. Jessica had been happy before Cary, and she vowed to be happy again.

She walked cautiously from the bedroom, hoping Cary had already left for the day. She sighed with relief when she encountered the empty living room. Her hand was on the front doorknob when Cary walked from the kitchen with a coffee mug in his hands.

Jessica muttered a curse but met his eyes. Even after her self-lecture only minutes earlier in the bedroom, she still couldn't control the magnitude of yearning she felt for him, for his smiles, his kisses, and his caresses. His blank expression made that yearning turn to fury. She had only to remember his callous remarks about sex in Erin's apartment and her whole body shook with anger.

"Where are you going?" Cary practically accused.

Jessica squared her shoulders and said clearly, "Out."

Cary took several steps closer to her, but she refused to move an inch. "I'll rephrase the question. Where are you going?"

"I'll rephrase the answer. Out," she snapped.

Cary rolled his eyes, exasperated, and slammed the cup on a nearby table. "I'm not in the best of moods this morning, Jessica, especially after that disastrous dinner."

"And somehow that's my fault?"

"I didn't say it was your fault."

"Why did you even have to say anything to Erin and David? The idea of you giving advice to the lovelorn is a sick joke." She regretted the words as soon as they left her mouth, mostly because she knew Cary would be able to tell how completely lovelorn she was.

Cary's eyes narrowed as he glared at her. "I don't want to talk about last night anymore—"

"Imagine that; Cary Riley avoiding a subject," Jessica said, with feigned amazement.

Cary stared at her without speaking, and Jessica almost thought he would walk out of the apartment. Instead, he said in a strained voice, "You said you never went anywhere on Saturday morning. I gave Agent Morris the day off. You cannot go out alone."

"Why?"

"Do you realize there's a man out there trying to hurt you?"

"You seem to forget one important thing. Michael Lyons wants to kill *you*, not me. Why is it safe for you to walk around in the streets of San Francisco but not for me? Is it because I'm a poor, defenseless woman, who must rely on a man for everything?"

"I am trained to deal with someone like Michael Lyons. The fact that you're a woman has nothing to do with it. There are women agents at the Group that I would trust with my life, over some of the men—"

"How enlightened of you," Jessica complimented, dryly.

Cary ignored her sarcasm and continued. "There are procedures you have to follow to help us effectively protect you. You can't just take off without notifying me and you definitely can't—"

"I can do whatever I want!" Jessica practically screeched because she wanted it to be the truth. She was tired of feeling scared and hurt. She crossed the distance between them and poked her index finger into his chest, causing his eyes to widen in shock. "I feel like running in Golden Gate Park and I will go running! There is noth-

ing you, or the FBI, or Michael Lyons can do to stop me!
I will not become a prisoner in this apartment! Do you
understand that?"

Cary simply stared at her and Jessica held her ground.
She ached to tell him that she never wanted to return to
the park and face her nightmares, that she wanted to stay
in her room and eat ice cream, but if she didn't return
to Golden Gate Park then she would probably never return. And Jessica was too stubborn to allow that.

Finally Cary ran a hand over his face and glared at her.
"Would you mind if I tag along?" he asked dryly.

Jessica shrugged casually, as if she hadn't been praying
for that response. She would have forced herself to go
alone, but she wanted Cary, her friend, to come with her.
"If you can keep up," she said lightly, heading for the door.

Cary grabbed his shoes and followed her.

Jessica sat in the passenger seat of his rental car and
shot brief glances at him. She wondered if he'd planned
to exercise anyway since he already wore shorts and a
T-shirt. She decided not to break the taut silence in the
car by asking, but her eyes were drawn to his muscled
legs showcased in the shorts. Jessica didn't think she had
ever seen a more beautiful pair of legs on a man. As the
car cruised closer and closer to the park with the steady
flow of traffic, her thoughts turned from Cary and she
could only see Michael Lyons as he reached for her in
the park. A light sheen of sweat covered her body before
Cary actually parked the car on the outskirts of the park.

Jessica barely looked at him as she climbed from the
car and automatically began her ritual of stretching. She
glanced apprehensively at the running trail, then stared
down at the grass. She was scared, she admitted to herself,
but she would not allow fear to stop her. Jessica finally
noticed that Cary was leaning against the car and watch-

ing her. When he noticed her looking at him, he quickly looked away.

"You should really stretch before you run," she finally said to break the silence.

"Don't worry about me," Cary responded, not meeting her eyes. He glanced at the other people running on the path and the plethora of in-line skaters rolling pass them. Jessica thought he would fall back into his silence, but then he asked quietly, "Is this where it happened?"

Jessica instantly knew he was asking about the attack and her heart momentarily stopped. She thought he had been fooled by her brave front but, as usual, he seemed to read her mind. "A few miles deeper into the trail."

There was a long stretch of silence as Jessica stood and finished her stretches. "I'm sorry," Cary finally said.

Jessica looked at him strangely but he still would not meet her eyes. She touched his arm, needing to feel the muscle and strength beneath, and Cary looked at her. She smiled at the concern and apprehension in his eyes. "It's not your fault, Cary," she said. "I don't know about you, but I'm ready." With that, Jessica sprinted down the path. She laughed as she heard Cary's steps behind her. Within seconds, he was running beside her and easily matching her stride.

The two dodged fallen tree branches and slower runners as they ran along the marked path. Through unspoken consent, they effortlessly maintained a brisk pace. Jessica's anger and fear drifted away with each step as she felt the wind blowing through her hair and heard Cary's heavy breathing beside her. Without speaking, he seemed to comfort her, to make her unafraid of running through the dark shade of the trees, and Jessica loved him even more for that. Their comfortable pace continued through the park until Jessica saw Cary flinch and slow to a stop in the middle of the path. Runners continued around him and she immediately ran back to his side, noticing the strained expression on his face. Her heart seemed to expand in her chest as she realized he was hurt. The idea of Cary hurting made her hurt. She forgot her anger and her hurt over his virtual rejection of her and followed him onto the grass off the trail.

Cary limped off the path and prayed Jessica would not follow him. It was too difficult to stay around her for a long period of time without feeling like his control was strained beyond limitation. He wondered if she enjoyed torturing him. He could not imagine any other explanation for her walking out of her bedroom that morning, wearing tight shorts and a tank top that didn't leave much to his imagination. An imagination that had undressed her three times a day since he'd left her at Hadley's Inn. He welcomed the pain that shot through his left ankle, relieved something would take his mind off Jessica.

Cary fell on the ground beneath a tree and tried not to feel comfort or arousal from Jessica's hand on his left arm. The concern apparent in the depths of her brown eyes made him feel an intense pain in a slightly different region of his body.

"Are you okay?" Jessica asked.

"It's nothing," Cary muttered, untying the laces of his left running shoe. "It's probably a sprain or a slight twist."

"Is it your ankle?" she asked anxiously as her hands moved to his injured ankle.

"Yeah but don't . . ." His voice trailed off as her hands touched his ankle and although he knew the pain was still there, he only felt her soft fingers. Cary stared at the top of her head as she bent over his ankle, caressing and massaging the skin. He wanted to tell her to stop touching him, but he could not speak. He could only clench the grass in his hands and swallow the sudden thick lump in his throat. Finally, Cary cleared his brain long enough to say, "You don't have to do this, Jess."

Jessica glanced up at him but continued to massage his ankle. "This is where I was attacked," she whispered. Cary felt a different emotion squeeze his throat. "I was running down the path and I heard moans. I thought someone was hurt and when I bent down to help him, he tried . . . This always used to be my favorite place in the city, like a small refuge in a city this big and impersonal. And now . . ." Her voice trailed off and she smiled, but he could see the unshed tears in her eyes. "How's your ankle feeling now?" she asked with forced cheerfulness.

"Better." Cary abruptly said. "I bet you can't guess who my mother's favorite singer was."

A smile entered Jessica's eyes. "Who? Luther Vandross? Marvin Gaye?"

"You would think so. My mother's favorite singer and mine, incidentally, is Francis Albert Sinatra."

Jessica collapsed into giggles and Cary couldn't help but smile. "Frank Sinatra?"

"Don't laugh. The rest of my family would make fun of us, but whenever he performed remotely close to Phoenix, my mother and I would pile into the car and go see him."

"The only two Black people in the audience, right?"

Cary grinned at her laughter. "You know what our favorite song was?"

"I couldn't even begin to guess," she replied, still laughing.

"The classic, of course. 'New York, New York.' " Cary didn't know what possessed him because he never sang, not even with the car radio or in the shower, but Cary wanted to sing to Jessica. He began to sing "New York, New York," the rousing, big-band Frank Sinatra way. Cary suddenly realized why he sang, why he'd started the ridiculous thread of conversation; for Jessica. She laughed, and the fact that she obviously no longer thought about Michael Lyons made him sing louder and stronger, caus-

ing people running by and people sitting on the grass
near them to stare and laugh.

Cary stood, mindful of his tender ankle, and sang even
louder to include his new fans. Jessica buried her face in
her hands, and Cary's laughter almost prevented him
from continuing the song. A small part of him protested
the idea of drawing unnecessary attention to them with
Michael Lyons still on the loose, but a larger part of him
was inspired to continue by her laughter. With his un-
steady but loud flourishing last note, Jessica applauded
and cheered along with the other group of twenty listen-
ers. Cary smiled and bowed to his applause then grinned
down at Jessica.

"I didn't know you had such a voice," Jessica said with
barely concealed laughter.

"I try," he responded simply.

Jessica stood and placed her arm around his chest for
support, since he still favored his left ankle. "Are you
ready to go, Pavarotti?" she teased. Cary could have
walked back to the car on his own, but he wanted to feel
her soft skin beneath his fingers. He wanted to touch her.
He made certain not to transfer all his weight onto her
and nodded.

Cary continued to lean on Jessica as they walked from
his parked car to her apartment. He discreetly rubbed
his chin against her silky hair, needing to feel the softness
and hold her close for as long as she allowed. When she
was in his arms, Cary forgot about the numerous reasons
why he should not be with her and thought of ways to
try to explain his confusing feelings to her. Then Cary
remembered her fearful expression when she talked
about Michael Lyons, and he simply kept his thoughts to
himself.

Jessica unlocked the front door and they walked into
her apartment. As soon as Cary stepped into the apartment, the senses that had kept him alive for the last

five years told him something was wrong. Someone had been in her apartment. He didn't want to alarm Jessica but Cary closely followed her to her bedroom to make certain no one waited to hurt her. They saw the message scrawled on the dresser mirror at the same time. Jessica jumped from the mirror and Cary wanted to slam his fist into a wall at the words written in lipstick: *Nice apartment, Jessica.*

Cary grabbed a towel from the linen closet and vigorously scrubbed the mirror clean while Jessica stood motionless in one spot. Procedure called for him to call in a team to dust the apartment for fingerprints and for any clues Michael might have inadvertently left, but Cary knew they would not find anything. Michael Lyons was very smart and careful. There would be no evidence that he had been in the apartment. From the corner of his eye, Cary watched Jessica nervously look around the bedroom. He knew she was seeing Michael Lyons in her bedroom, regardless of whether Michael was physically there or not.

"Don't touch anything," Cary said gruffly when the mirror was finally clean. He balled the towel in his hands. "I'm going to get a team in here to check the rest of the apartment and to make certain Michael didn't leave any other nasty surprises." He left unspoken that he would reprimand whichever one of his colleagues had supposedly protected the apartment while he and Jessica went running.

"I don't want anyone else in here," Jessica replied quietly.

"Jess, I know this is hard, but we—"

She looked at him and the sheer terror in her eyes made him angry with himself more than with Michael for bringing this into her life. "I don't want anyone else in my apartment. Can't you handle this yourself? Please?"

Cary raked a hand through his hair and reluctantly shook his head. He wanted her to feel safe, but he also wanted to know for certain a bomb wouldn't explode in the middle of the night. "I could, but it's not the same as having someone specifically trained—"

"Cary, I can't have . . ." Her voice shook and she rubbed a hand over her eyes, attempting to calm down. Cary wanted to pull her into his arms, but the realization that her pain was his fault stopped him. "I can't explain this to you and I shouldn't have to!"

"Jessica, that's stupid—"

"Don't call me stupid!" Her voice bounced against the walls of the small room. "I could deal with Michael in the park, in the café, on the street . . . but not in my home."

"I'm not calling you stupid," Cary responded calmly. "I just don't want you to be in any danger, Jess. I need to have this place swept by trained professionals before we stay here for another second. Please understand." Jessica remained silent and Cary knew he would relent, before he even admitted it to himself. For some reason, he could never say no to this woman. If she knew what power she held over him, Cary wondered what she would do, besides run from the apartment in horror. "I was trained on all the detection equipment when I first joined the Group; I'll do it myself. I have to leave you here alone for a few seconds to get the equipment. Will you be okay?"

Jessica quickly wiped away several stray tears and Cary averted his eyes. "I'll be fine," she whispered.

Cary turned from the room but then glanced back at her. She stood in the middle of the room with her arms wrapped around her, and his heart crashed to the floor. He hated himself and his job for doing this to her. "Jess, I'm sorry," he said softly.

She glanced at him and he read the confusion on her face. "How is this your fault?"

Cary laughed bitterly then walked from the room. Jessica wanted to delude herself into believing Cary wasn't the cause for her problems, but the facts could not be changed. If Cary had been able to resist Jessica that night in the inn, her biggest worry would be her latest presentation at work and not Michael Lyons.

Fifteen

By early evening, Cary closed the last case of the detection equipment. He had examined every corner of the apartment until his own concern was satisfied. Michael was not the bombing type. Cary knew Michael wanted to make Jessica afraid, to make her afraid of Cary, and Michael's mission had been successful. Before Cary simply wanted Michael to leave America, now Cary wanted to kill him. Three times the man had terrorized Jessica and, to Cary, that was inexcusable.

Cary walked out of the apartment to the building's front door and practically threw the case at Dan Pelstrom, who waited on the steps. Cary wanted to slam his fist into the man's face since Dan was on duty when Michael broke into the apartment.

"I'm finished," Cary spat out angrily.

"I wish you would have allowed me to call in a team to look the—"

"Right now, Pelstrom, I don't care what you want or wish! You're the reason this is necessary in the first place!" Dan's face drained of color and Cary instantly felt remorse for his harsh words. Cary knew he should not blame Dan for his own inability to separate himself from Jessica. He should have allowed Jessica's security detail to run with her in the park, while he searched for Michael himself. "That was uncalled for and I shouldn't have said it. I know from first-hand experience what an expert Lyons is at moving around undetected. Lyons seems to always remain one step ahead of us. It's like he knows what we're going to do before we even do it."

"No offense taken, Cary. You really care about her, don't you?"

"I'd care for anyone who was being harassed by Michael Lyons because of me."

"That's the only reason you're here, then? Because of Michael?" Dan asked doubtfully. "I thought you really had feelings for this woman. I saw your face when you first read the police report about the attack. You would've killed Michael if he had been standing in front of you. Now, you're trying to tell me you don't care for her? That you're staying in her apartment, looking at her with big, puppy-dog eyes, out of some medieval sense of obligation and duty?"

"I've had my head shrunk enough to last me a lifetime," Cary warned in a low voice, mostly because Dan was too close to the truth.

Dan held up his hands defensively, then descended the stairs toward the waiting Group van. Cary walked into the apartment and closed the door, checking and re-checking the locks on the door. He glanced out the living room windows and saw the car with Group surveillance agents parked across the street. He surveyed the other cars lining the street and the light pedestrian traffic before closing the blinds.

Cary turned as he heard Jessica clear her throat from behind him. He cleared his own throat as his manhood instantly hardened at the sight of her in a flannel nightgown that covered her from her neck to the bottom of her toes, but in the light glow of the apartment lamps, was almost seductive. Dan was right. Cary wasn't in San Francisco because of Michael, and he only fooled himself believing that lie.

"Was everything okay?" she asked. Her voice sounded strong and firm. Cary could have imagined the fear earlier if he didn't know her so well.

"Checked out fine."

"Cary . . ." Jessica bit her bottom lip and Cary inwardly groaned from the softness in her words. He could handle her anger or her coldness, but not her softness. "Cary, thanks for understanding about earlier. I know I was a little unreasonable, but I couldn't stand the thought of anyone else in here. I didn't want my privacy to be invaded anymore and . . . Just thank you."

"No problem." The two stared at each other for several long moments, then Cary cleared his throat again. He wanted her to leave before he said anything foolish or lunged for her like he wanted to. "Thank you for earlier, with my ankle."

"Is it still bothering you? I can get you some ice."

"No . . . thank you." He removed pillows from the couch to make his bed as she continued to stare at him. Every time he thoroughly convinced himself the two didn't belong together, he would sniff her perfume or she would smile at him and all his vows of leaving her alone disappeared. Cary may have fooled himself into believing he only lusted after her body while he was in Virginia, but being with her every day was a completely different matter. Face to face with her, Cary could not deny that he was in love with her.

"If we'd met on the street or in a coffee shop," Jessica began abruptly, "if that night at the inn had never happened, what would you think of me?"

Cary met her curious expression and laughed nervously. If he saw her on the street, he probably would have been paralyzed with fear and not said a word because she was everything he ever wished for in a woman. For that simple reason she scared him to death. "What kind of question is that?"

Jessica rolled her eyes and he saw a faint smile. "You can't answer a question with a question. Is that some sort of agent technique?"

"Well, what do you want me to say?" Cary smiled as she started to protest his answer. "Okay, okay, I would think you're an attractive, intelligent woman, and I probably wouldn't say one word to you."

"Attractive, huh?" she prodded.

Cary pulled the folded bed out from the couch and sincerely responded, "Very attractive."

"You would think I was very attractive, but you wouldn't say anything, even if I smiled at you?"

"If you smiled at me, I would think you were smiling at someone else," he replied seriously, still avoiding her eyes.

"How about if I flirted shamelessly with you?" Her voice dropped to a low, husky whisper and Cary felt his manhood respond. Cary occupied himself by carefully smoothing the sheets on the bed. "Even if I approached you and said everything you wanted to hear? You still wouldn't talk to me?"

Cary met her eyes and time in the room seemed to stand still. He could not resist and crossed the room. He expected her to step away from him but when she stood motionless, he touched her face, reveling in the warmth of her brown skin. Then he trailed his fingers over her slightly parted lips as she stared into his eyes. "I wouldn't know what to say," he finally answered, staring at her full lips.

"You knew what to say at the inn," she responded. Her words barely registered as Cary leaned toward her. His one goal in life at that moment was to feel her lips against his, to tangle his hands in her hair, and show her what he could not say. Just when he could practically taste her on his lips, the cellular phone attached to the waistband of his jeans rang. He cursed, then stepped away from her to answer the phone.

"What?" he snapped, after activating the phone. He made the mistake of looking at Jessica and the yearning apparent in her eyes made him walk across the room before he threw the phone on the floor and made better use of his bed.

"I hope I didn't interrupt anything," came Dan's voice over the phone. "We have a hot tip on Lyons. An informant just spotted him in Chinatown."

"I'll be right down," Cary responded quickly. "I want the van to stay here with Jessica and I want a continuous patrol around the building in a five-mile radius. I want this place to be guarded like the Federal Reserve, Dan, understand?"

"Right, Cary. I'll personally talk to the men."

"I'll talk to them myself." Cary pushed the 'end' button then turned back to Jessica. She looked at her bare toes, hiding her face from him. He didn't want to leave her. He knew Jessica could take care of herself but he wanted to do it. "I have to leave," he said, glancing around the apartment. "Do you want me to take you to David's for the night?"

"No. I don't want to have to explain to him."

Cary nodded, realizing she was right. David would love to have his sister visit him, but he would be curious. "You'll be safe. There are Group people all over the neighborhood."

"Like this afternoon when Michael broke into my apartment, or at my job when he followed me to the coffee shop?" Cary didn't know how to answer or apologize. Jessica shook her head with a bitter smile. "I'm sorry, Cary. I'll be fine."

Jessica looked ready to flee back into her bedroom, but he could not leave her just yet. "What's your idea of flirting shamelessly?" Cary abruptly asked.

Jessica looked at him confused. "What?"

"Don't answer a question with a question," he mimicked her then laughed as comprehension dawned in her eyes. "You said if we met in a coffee shop or on the street, you would flirt with me shamelessly. I was just wondering what is your idea of flirting shamelessly?"

Jessica studied his expression to see if he was teasing her, but he looked seriously interested. She thought he would disappear as soon as his phone rang, but he still stood in front of her and she didn't want him to leave, so she answered his question. "I don't know. I've never done it before. I guess I would smile a lot and laugh at everything you said, no matter how stupid it was."

"You'd stroke my ego?" He nodded his approval.

Jessica continued, "I've been told touching a man's arm is a sign of flirting. I guess I would do that."

"Touching is nice."

"Then I'd definitely touch you a lot. I'd also probably compliment you on your eyes."

"My eyes?" Cary asked surprised. Jessica knew Cary didn't realize how handsome he was, which was another reason she loved him as much as she did. She wanted to spend a lifetime convincing him of that fact.

"I like your eyes. And I'd say, 'you have the most gorgeous smile I've ever seen on a man'." His smile disappeared and Jessica laughed. "And then I'd offer to buy you dinner."

"Sounds like flirting shamelessly to me," he confirmed.

Jessica didn't know where her sudden bravado came from, but she asked, "And what would you say?"

"I would probably think I was hallucinating," Cary whispered, then turned to put on his jacket. "You have my cell phone number, right?" he asked, abruptly switching subjects.

"Yes," she replied, nodding.

Cary walked to the door then looked back at her. The

regret on his face made her almost believe he wanted to stay with her and talk. "Lock the door behind me and don't open it for anyone. Okay?"

"This may be a surprise to you, but I've been successfully locking doors on my own for a few years now," Jessica answered sarcastically.

She could see Cary's smile as he walked out of the apartment. Jessica shook her head and walked across the room to lock the door.

Fifteen minutes later, Jessica clicked off the television with the remote as someone knocked on the front door of her apartment. She was paralyzed, as she stared at the closed door, half expecting Michael Lyons to burst into her apartment. She remained in her position on the couch, then flinched when the person knocked again, louder and more persistent.

Jessica cursed herself for being a coward and slowly stood from the couch. She couldn't make herself answer the door, no matter how much she wanted to prove to herself that she wasn't a spineless wimp. She tried to reassure herself that the Group agents outside the apartment would not allow Michael Lyons to simply walk to her front door; then the words on her dresser mirror flashed across her mind.

"Jess, it's Logan," came the muffled voice through the door.

Jessica nearly cried with relief and quickly unlocked the door. Logan walked into the apartment with a suspicious look on his face, and Jessica almost hugged him.

"Are you all right?" Logan demanded.

"I'm fine."

"What took you so long to answer the door? I was about to bust the door in, which is my favorite way to enter a room."

"I was watching television," Jessica responded lamely. "Cary's not here."

Logan took off his jacket. Jessica wanted to protest, but she wanted the company. She didn't want to sit by herself and worry about Cary or think about Michael Lyons.

"Cary called me a few minutes ago and told me to stay with you until he comes back," Logan said.

"Did he tell you why?" she asked carefully.

"He said you needed company. I didn't question."

"And do I have any decision in this?"

"Not really," Logan answered with a shrug. He plopped on the couch, grabbing the remote from the coffee table. "What's on television?"

"Logan, you don't have to stay," Jessica insisted firmly. "I'm a grown woman. I can take care of myself."

Logan looked at her and she could tell he didn't buy her bravery act. "I'll tell Cary I bullied you into allowing me to stay. How's that?"

Jessica tried not to smile but she lost and sat next to him on the couch. "I would've been fine by myself."

"I know that, Jess," Logan said, successfully hiding the doubt from his voice that she saw in his eyes.

"You don't have to stay. I know you're a busy man."

Logan shrugged again, which Jessica found slightly infuriating. "I have nothing better to do. Besides, my cable's on the fritz and I have no food."

"Why didn't you say that you already planned to visit?" Jessica asked, relieved no matter how fragile the distinction was.

Logan wisely didn't laugh as he said, "I meant to ask you if I could come over tonight to watch cable and eat all your food."

Jessica grinned, then after a moment's silence asked, "You said Cary called you?"

"He must really love you to ask me for anything," Logan said, studying her.

"Cary doesn't love me."

"I thought you knew my brother."

"He's worried about me. He feels responsible for me . . ." Her voice trailed off as she realized she'd almost told Logan about Michael Lyons. She blamed it on Logan's eyes. They bore a striking resemblance to Cary's.

"I know about Michael Lyons, Jess," Logan said.

"How?"

"I saw your file at the station. Cary won't allow him to hurt you."

Jessica shook her head. "I'm not worried about me. I'm worried about Cary."

Logan grinned and patted her arm. "I'd worry about Michael Lyons if I were you. Cary doesn't like for people to mess with the people he loves. One of Cary's greatest assets and his greatest fault is his loyalty. He'll kill Lyons if he hurts you."

"Logan, Cary doesn't love me—"

Logan rolled his eyes and made a show of yawning. Jessica laughed and held up her hands in defeat. "Whatever you say, Logan."

Logan grinned and nodded. "I love when women say that. Now, what's on television?"

Cary carefully closed the apartment door and walked silently into the living room. He glanced at his watch. It was close to four in the morning. Even though he knew Jessica had to work in the morning and he knew he shouldn't need to, he wanted to wake her and continue their conversation from earlier. He wanted to forget about the frustration that threatened to overpower him when he and the other agents learned they had missed capturing Michael by fifteen minutes.

Cary also wanted to forget the momentary relief that filled his heart when he learned the news. Once he caught Michael, his reason for staying in San Francisco, for staying with Jessica, would be gone. He would have no choice but to leave or admit he was feeling something for her that he had never felt for anyone else in his life and had no right to feel.

Cary smiled when he saw his brother sprawled across the couch bed. Logan's soft snoring made Cary think of their childhood when they'd shared a room together, when their parents were still alive. Cary clenched his fists against the thought and stared at his brother's peaceful face. Cary missed Logan. He missed the easy acceptance that only a brother could give another brother.

When Cary called Logan to ask him to stay with Jessica, Logan hadn't questioned or made excuses, he had simply agreed. Cary knew Logan had probably discovered Jessica's connection with Michael Lyons, but his brother had been there without question, like in the old days. But he could not ask Logan or Maggie for forgiveness when his stupidity and immaturity had cost them precious years with their parents. He refused to place them in the situation of being forced to forgive him.

Cary noticed the neatly made futon in the corner of the living room. He unconsciously touched the pulled back sheet as he thought of Jessica making the bed for him. Cary didn't like the growing warm feeling inside of him as he noticed the fluffed pillows and the folded blanket at the end of the futon. No one had cared for him or worried about him in such a long time that Jessica's simple acts threatened to unarm him.

Before Cary could understand what he was doing, he moved down the hallway toward her bedroom, almost as if she had called to him. Cary hesitated only a brief second, then pushed the door open until he could see her still form laying in the middle of the large bed. All he had to do was cross the room and slide underneath the sheets. Cary wanted her with a ferocity that surprised him and that he knew would probably hurt her in the long run.

Then she turned in the bed and Cary stared into her wide open eyes. He immediately straightened his shoulders and tried to look like he always stood in her bedroom doorway at four in the morning.

"Did you catch him?" she asked in a soft voice.

"We missed him by a few minutes."

"A few minutes," Jessica repeated. There was a hint of a smile in her voice that Cary knew he imagined.

"I didn't mean to wake you—"

"You didn't. I couldn't sleep."

Cary wondered if she was as confused as he was. "Why?" he finally asked to prolong their conversation. "You weren't frightened with Logan here, were you?"

Jessica sat up in the bed and her long hair fell around her shoulders. Cary wanted to touch her hair, touch her, but he remained in the door frame. "No. Thank you for calling him, but I was worried about you."

He instantly recoiled from her words, violently shaking his head. "You shouldn't worry about me. I can take care of myself."

"I know that." The two continued to stare at each other across the short distance of the bedroom that suddenly seemed like an ocean to Cary. He wished she were an ocean away from him because then he couldn't hurt her like he knew he would have to, like it was in his nature to do.

"You should go to sleep." Desire and longing for a life he could never have made his words sound harsh.

"I'm not sleepy," she replied softly.

Her voice alone tore holes into his soul. Cary knew her touch would break down whatever barriers he had built over the years. He couldn't allow that to happen. "We both have to prepare for the week—"

"I also couldn't sleep because I was scared," Jessica continued, staring at the opposite wall, purposely avoiding his eyes. "Every time I closed my eyes, I would hear a sound or imagine a sound . . . I know Logan wouldn't allow anything to happen to me but I was still scared."

"You're safe here."

"I thought so until he got into my apartment."

"I promise you that won't happen again," Cary said firmly.

Jessica held out her hand and Cary inwardly groaned. She wanted him to do the one thing that his body ached to do. Be with her. "Just for tonight can you sleep in here? I'll think about my lack of bravery in the morning but right now I'm too scared."

Cary crossed the room in two steps, taking off his shirt and shoes on the way. He slid under the covers and Jessica immediately molded her body against his. Cary couldn't stop the groan of pleasure that escaped his lips as her hand rested on his chest over his heart.

"Am I hurting you?" she asked, concerned.

"No." His voice sounded strained to his own ears. "I'm tired."

"This will never end until one of you is dead," she whispered.

Cary stroked her hair as her lips moved against his chest. He couldn't worry about Michael, or the Group, or anything when she was in his arms. He would worry about the ramifications another time, but now he simply enjoyed having her near; he enjoyed being able to touch her. "Michael isn't a bad person. He's confused and alone. He could make a good ruler of his country one day if he ever moves past his need for vengeance," Cary finally said, clinging to the subject of Michael to ignore the longing that raced through his veins.

"You almost sound as if you respect him."

"In a way, I identify with him. I know what it's like to feel responsible for people . . . to let everyone down and to have no one, to have nowhere to belong."

"Logan told me about your parents," Jessica whispered.

Cary muttered a curse and his hand unconsciously tightened around her waist. For some reason, he didn't want Jessica to know how imperfect he was. He didn't want her to know that he'd killed his parents. "So, now you know."

"Cary." She raised her head slightly to look at him. He was surprised to see tears in her eyes. He gently brushed the crystals of water from her cheeks. "Cary, you aren't like Michael. You are a good man, who had something bad happen to him."

Cary gently pushed her head back to his chest, before she saw the guilt on his face. "I killed my parents, Jess. I took them away from Logan and Maggie, when they needed them most. How could they ever forgive me for that? Why would they want to?"

"They can forgive you because they never blamed you. You shouldn't blame yourself either. What makes you think you could have prevented that car accident? What makes you think you could have prevented Michael Lyons's men from dying? What makes you think you could have stopped Michael from attacking me in the park or entering my apartment? You're not God, Cary; you're not even close."

"I'm sure Logan says that but he can't mean it—"

"And you belong somewhere, Cary," she continued, unfazed by his interruption. "You belong wherever someone loves you. You just have to see past all that guilt and pain to believe it."

Cary's hand stilled in her hair as her soft voice tore holes in the shield he had built around himself for the last five years. For the first time since his parents died, he did feel like he belonged somewhere. With her. Anywhere she was, he wanted to be, too. Cary's heart pounded against his chest as he thought of belonging to her, of finding a way to separate his career from his personal life, a way of not being in the shadows. Cary shook his head. He was a murderer. He eventually hurt everyone he loved. He didn't want to hurt her.

"Go to sleep, Jess," he finally said.

Her soft breathing filled the room and Cary shifted in the bed to stare at her. In the pre-dawn light streaming through the room, he saw that she had already fallen asleep.

Cary wrapped an arm around her, protecting her for the night.

Sixteen

Michael and Dan stood across from each other on a large ferry that smoothly traversed the cold waters of the bay in between San Francisco and Oakland. The early morning cold air, combined with the light sprinkle of dew and famous San Francisco fog made Michael think of every postcard of San Francisco he had ever seen. The few passengers on the ferry remained inside the cabin for warmth, leaving Michael and Dan alone on the deck.

"It's five o'clock in the morning and freezing cold on this water. Couldn't this have waited until the sun was out?" Dan grumbled.

"I'm paying you a lot of money to keep me one step ahead of Riley and his investigation. I can't understand why he nearly knocked down my hotel door in Chinatown. Why didn't you warn me?" Michael demanded angrily.

"After that little stunt you pulled in Jessica Larson's apartment, I had to redeem myself," Dan shot back. He reminded Michael of a weasel with beady black eyes and thin lips. "I allowed you to enter her home to look for information to use against Cary; leaving evidence that you were there was never part of our deal! I was the one in charge of surveillance that night. I was the one everyone looked at with questions! Do you even know what sort of position you put me in?"

Michael subconsciously grabbed the handle of the gun in his coat pocket. He hated Dan Pelstrom almost more than he hated Cary. "You should have told me what you were planning. I barely escaped. If I get caught, you go down with me, Dan, remember that."

Dan stared at the Bay Bridge in the distance and asked through clenched teeth, "What do you want me to do?"

"I need to get Riley on neutral ground, away from the other Group agents."

Dan laughed, which wasn't a pleasant sight, as far as Michael was concerned. "You should see the way Riley slobbers over that woman. The poor fool actually has convinced himself that he flew all the way to San Francisco out of some sort of medieval honor code, and not because he's infatuated with Jessica Larson."

"What's your point?" Michael demanded, annoyed.

"My point is the woman is the key. When you get her, you get Riley." Dan stifled a laugh as he added, "I forgot, the woman is too much for you to handle. Do you need me to think of another plan? A plan that doesn't involve her making you look like an idiot?"

Michael glared at him, then said through clenched teeth, "I only wanted to scare her. I wanted her to get away and run to the police."

Dan nodded in disbelief. "Well, she followed your plan perfectly."

"She brought Riley here," Michael said, then shook his head, annoyed with himself for allowing Dan to irritate him. He noticed Dan's chattering teeth from the cold and Michael rolled his eyes in disgust. "Go inside before you catch pneumonia." Dan grinned in relief and quickly walked into the cabin.

Michael released a string of curses directed at Dan's heritage and leaned against the rail of the boat. He never intended to capture Jessica last week. That had never been a part of his plan. He only wanted Cary to come to San Francisco, to be away from the high security of the Virginia area. Unfortunately, Michael overestimated Cary or underestimated Cary's feelings for Jessica. Michael thought Cary would have come alone and would try to track him down like the Lone Ranger he pretended to be, but Cary obviously wanted to protect Jessica, which was why he had dragged half of the Group's agents across the country with him.

Michael suddenly smiled as he stared at the water churning beneath the ferry. For once in his miserable life, Dan was right. Jessica Larson was the key to Michael's final revenge against Cary.

When Jessica woke up the next morning, Cary and Logan were gone. She thought of the pain and self-recrimination she heard in Cary's voice last night when he told her that he'd killed his parents. Her heart had broken at that proclamation. She wanted to hold him until he smiled and laughed like the night at the inn, but she realized that would never happen again, no matter how much she dreamed or wished.

She wanted his smiles because she finally admitted that she not only loved Cary, she liked him. Without asking for explanations or excuses, Cary had simply come to her last night. He must have known how much she needed to feel him beside her after Michael Lyons's invasion of her apartment. Not once did he try to do anything but comfort her. Jessica had not known whether to express gratitude for his chivalry, or to be insulted and wonder why he didn't find her attractive.

Jessica stared out the bedroom window at the charcoal sky. The threatening color of the sky promised rain within the day, and Jessica hoped Cary would be home before the clouds burst. She doubted Cary would appreciate her meeting him at the door with chicken soup, but she wanted to. She wanted to care for him and love him. She liked the image of cuddling on the couch with him and two cups of cocoa and a bowl of popcorn. She wondered if Cary would want to cuddle with her.

The doorbell rang and Jessica glanced at the clock on the nightstand, surprised to realize it was almost noon. Jessica was usually awake on the weekend by seven in the morning to prepare for the next day at work. She couldn't remember sleeping until noon since her high school days. She slid from the bed and slipped on her robe as the doorbell rang again. She ran through the apartment toward the door.

Jessica peered through the peephole in the center of the door and inwardly groaned when Erin's face filled the view. Jessica unlocked the door and Erin walked into the apartment, without even glancing at Jessica. She immediately sat on the couch and crossed her legs, and fixed her expectant stare on Jessica.

Jessica slowly closed the door and glanced at Erin. Neither woman spoke and Jessica finally sighed and asked, "What?"

"You and your boyfriend owe David and I an apology for the other night," Erin said abruptly. Jessica withheld a laugh at the thought of Cary apologizing to anyone. She sat on the couch next to Erin, as Erin continued in a firm tone, "That was very rude and inconsiderate of you and Cary to leave in the middle of dinner. I put a lot of energy into that meal, and I didn't appreciate you two not eating all of it. And I'm more upset because there was no waiting apology from you or Cary on my answering machine."

Jessica's answer stuck in her throat as she noticed the unique gleam in her friend's eyes. Jessica could not place her finger on it, but Erin seemed to glow. Jessica placed a hand over her mouth and shook her head, trying not to laugh.

Erin stopped her tirade to glare at Jessica. "What is your problem?" she demanded.

"What happened between you and David after we left the other night?" Erin stared at her hands and became strangely silent. Jessica screamed and wrapped her arms around Erin's shoulders. Erin laughed and squeezed Jessica's arms. "You and David . . . Did you two . . . ?"

Erin grinned then said slyly, "Let's just say, I got over my nausea."

"You're lying," Jessica accused, grinning. "You and David did not—"

"I know I sound like a hypocrite, but I don't care. It's been the most amazing two days of my entire life. David left my apartment an hour ago for the first time since our dinner."

"David's been at your apartment since we all ate dinner two nights ago?" Jessica repeated, amazed.

"I almost didn't allow him to leave this morning, but he insisted on getting clean clothes for tonight." Erin's eyes twinkled with the joy of a well-loved woman.

"I can't believe this," Jessica said, laughing. "What happened after Cary and I left? Did you two forget you've been arguing and insulting each other for the last two years?"

Erin shrugged, not meeting Jessica's eyes. "After you two left, David and I stopped yelling at each other long enough to talk about what possibly possessed you to date an idiot like Cary. Then David noticed my Billie Holiday CD collection. We put on some of music, drank some wine, and we started laughing because we realized Cary was right."

"About the sleeping together part?"

"We figured that out later, but originally we laughed because we realized that we knew entirely too much about each other's love life. David and I couldn't figure out how we knew so much and then one thing led to another, and suddenly we were actually having a real conversation. I never knew how sweet and funny and wonderful—"

"This is the man that stuck a frog down my shirt in fourth grade," Jessica interrupted dryly.

"He has his faults, he definitely has his faults, but he's all mine and I love him."

"I can't believe I'm hearing this."

"I can't either," Erin admitted, shaking her head. "I was just coming to terms with this strange attraction I had toward him when I realized that night that it wasn't lust, it was love. I never knew why I paid such particular attention to the women he dated, or why his opinion always meant so much to me, or why I automatically compared every loser I ever dated to him. Then that night, as he was droning on about some theory of his, too ridiculous to even repeat, I realized why."

"What happened to your vow about not dealing with men for the next century?"

"There are always exceptions for true love," Erin responded sincerely. "I have to admit that I always thought that becoming-whole theory that you're always sprouting was nonsense and a bunch of rambling."

"But?" Jessica prodded with a grin.

"But, for the first time, I realize that you actually may be right. With David, I think of being whole."

Jessica laughed at the tears of joy in her eyes and said firmly, "He loves you too. I've never seen him look at any woman the way he looks at you. Anyone else he would have dismissed or ignored a long time ago."

"He told me that he loved me about one million times in the last forty-eight hours. I always thought he was a repetitive bore, but now I realize it depends on what he's repeating and what he's doing while he's repeating it."

"A little too much information, Erin, but I'm still happy for both of you," Jessica said sincerely. "I'm happy for me, that I won't have to hear any more of your arguing."

"I've never felt this way before, Jess. With all the men I've dated and all the heartache I've experienced, I assumed it was always love, but it wasn't. What I'm feeling now, I've never felt before—frightened, overwhelmed, and wonderful all at once. Is this how you feel about Cary?"

Jessica's happiness for her brother and Erin instantly disappeared. She wished Cary would say he loved her or even that he cared for her. She wished she could smile when she thought about him, instead of always feeling the need to cry or scream in frustration. Jessica remembered how gentle he had been with her last night, but she also knew it was in his nature to protect. He pretended to be apathetic and uncaring, but Jessica knew if he didn't care about anyone, he would not feel such guilt or pain over his parents' death.

Jessica was horrified as tears came to her eyes. She forced a bright smile for Erin, who suddenly looked concerned. "Would you like some coffee?" Jessica asked abruptly, then walked into the kitchen before Erin answered.

Erin followed her, and Jessica tried to hold back the flood of tears as Erin openly studied her. "Jess, what's going on?" Erin asked, softly.

"Nothing." Jessica filled the coffeepot with water, concentrating on the task to compose herself. "You and David should throw a party for all of our friends who were placing bets on you two finally ending—"

Erin grabbed her arm and forced Jessica to look at her. "I know you too well. You're not happy and I can't figure out why. I know you love Cary; I can tell by how your face changes when you talk about him, but there's something you're not telling me. I'm your best friend, Jess, you're obligated to tell me under the rules of best friends."

"What rules of best friends?" Jessica murmured, smiling in spite of herself.

"The rules that say whenever one of us is hurting, she has to tell the other one. What's wrong, Jess?"

Jessica carefully set the coffeepot on the kitchen counter and said in a choked voice, "I do love Cary. I don't want to, but I do."

"And that's the problem?"

"The problem is, he doesn't love me back." The tears Jessica had been fighting since last night rushed to the surface. Erin immediately pulled her into her arms, and Jessica realized how much she wanted to talk to her friend and share the confusing, strange feelings with her.

"How do you know he doesn't love you?"

"He's leaving. I'll never see him again."

Erin gently pushed Jessica away from her and wiped at the tears on her face. "If he doesn't know what he has in you, then he's not worth it. You don't need him, Jess. You're Jessica Larson, the employee of the decade, the best friend and sister I know. Cary Riley is a fool if he walks away from you."

"I try to tell myself that," Jessica responded. "I try to tell myself that he shouldn't matter this much to me. My life is finally going in the direction that I've wanted all these years. If I keep working like I have been for the past six years, I'll be partner by the time I'm thirty. Everything should be perfect."

"But, it's not," Erin finished.

"I always thought it was until I met Cary. Now, I know exactly what I'm missing in life, and I know what can make my life whole, and the only problem is, he doesn't want me."

Both women turned toward the living room as they heard the front door close. Jessica quickly wiped her face with a dish towel and smoothed down the errant strands of her hair. She prayed it wasn't Cary. She did not want to see him when she felt so weak and defenseless. Cary walked into the kitchen and immediately stopped in his tracks when he saw the two women. Jessica glanced at Erin's fierce expression and discreetly squeezed Erin's hand to beg her not to say anything about their conversation to Cary.

"Did I interrupt something?" Cary asked.

"As a matter of fact—"

"No," Jessica said, interrupting Erin. "We were talking about what an interesting dinner we had the other night."

"That's not what we were talking about, Jess," Erin said, still glaring at Cary.

"I forgot my cell phone," Cary said, apparently deciding not to interrogate the two women.

"You're a pig, Cary," Erin said sharply.

Cary glanced at her, surprised, and Jessica gasped. "Erin . . ."

Erin ignored Jessica. "You had no right to speak to David and me like that the other night." There was a tense silence in the kitchen as Cary stared at Erin and Jessica leaned against the kitchen sink in relief. Erin abruptly smiled, surprising them all. "But, I do have to thank you, too. David and I were united in our hatred of you, and we realized how much we have in common and how much we really do care about each other."

Jessica laughed nervously and Cary glanced at her before smiling at Erin. "I'm glad to be of help," he said, with a strange expression.

There was a knock on the door and Cary reached for his gun, but Erin squealed with glee and ran toward the door. "David said he'd meet me over here," she said excitedly.

Jessica glanced at Cary as Erin swung the door open

and threw her arms around David's shoulders. Cary shook his head at the couple's display then met Jessica's eyes. His amused smile disappeared, and the two stared at each other in silence.

Jessica cleared her throat and forced herself to say, "Thank you for your help last night."

"Stop thanking me for everything," Cary said softly. "If it weren't for me, you wouldn't be in this mess."

"Don't say that, Cary, because it's not true."

Cary stepped closer to her as David's and Erin's loud kisses reached into the kitchen. Jessica noticed the self-loathing and pain in his eyes and tried not to throw her arms around Cary's neck. "If I hadn't bothered you at Hadley's Inn that night, you never would have been a target for Michael, and I wouldn't be here now."

"Is that what really bothers you, Cary?" Jessica whispered, as new tears formed in her eyes. "That you have to be here now? That you have to deal with me, someone you thought you'd never have to see again?"

Confusion crossed his face, then disbelief. "You can't think that, Jess."

"What else am I supposed to think?" she asked desperately. She wanted him to tell her how he felt. She was willing to risk everything and tell him that she loved him, but she needed a sign from him. She needed him to smile or touch her, anything to make her think he cared. Cary only stared at her in speechless disbelief.

"What are you two whispering about?" David asked, as he and Erin walked into the kitchen, arm in arm.

"I forgot my cell phone," Cary mumbled to no one in particular, then walked from the kitchen. A second later, they all heard the front door slam.

"Charming, as usual," David muttered, rolling his eyes. "I'll never understand what you see in that man, Jess." He grunted in pain as Erin gently rammed her elbow into his stomach.

"Maybe what I see in you," Erin retorted. "A big lump of clay that I can mold and shape into a respectable man, with only a few years of hard work."

"You're not funny," David murmured as he placed a hard kiss on Erin's lips, causing her to grin in return.

"Should I leave and give you two privacy?" Jessica asked, noticing the heated glances they exchanged.

David laughed as Erin moved from his arms. "Erin and I wanted to invite you to lunch."

"You really want me to sit across from you two and be ignored?" Jessica asked, shaking her head.

"We don't ignore you," David protested.

"Even when you two proclaimed to hate each other, you ignored me. Now that you're all hands and lips, I have a feeling I could disappear into thin air and neither one of you would notice."

"Well, call back Mr. Personality and we all can go," David suggested.

"Cary's busy," Jessica muttered, turning back to the coffeepot.

"On a Sunday?" David asked in disbelief. "What exactly does he do? You never answered me. He's unemployed, isn't he?"

"Will you leave Jess alone?" Erin demanded. "Cary makes her happy and that should be enough for you."

"Happy?" David cried out incredulously. "Ever since she met him, she walks around as if the world's going to end. If I make you that happy, break up with me."

Erin threw up her hands in frustration, then hugged Jessica. "I hope you feel better, Jess. Call me at David's." She glared at David then announced, "David, you'd better be outside in two minutes." She breezed from the apartment, closing the door behind her.

"I don't want to hear it, David." Jessica sighed, annoyed as David began to protest. "Who I choose to date has nothing to do with you. I'm your sister, not your daughter."

"I want to know what's going on. You can't expect me to believe you met this guy at some cottage in the middle of the woods and now you're allowing him to stay with you. And by the way, exactly how long is he staying?" David demanded, in his usual older-brother tone.

Jessica stared into her brother's warm brown eyes and could not be angry with him. David spent his entire life protecting her. She could not expect him to suddenly stop one day, even when she didn't need him anymore. She smiled obligingly and placed a kiss on his forehead. "I love him, David, that's what's going on. I love him and he doesn't love me."

To her surprise, David didn't tell her all the reasons why she should not love Cary, he only took her in his arms. She smiled as David soothed her like a father would. "He's an idiot if he doesn't realize what he has in you," he finally said.

"He's not an idiot." Jessica pulled away from him angrily. "He has a very difficult job and, yes, he works—that he does very well. He's sweet, considerate . . . The other day, he bought me groceries. Groceries, Dave. No one has ever bought me groceries before. He went running with me in Golden Gate Park and when I started to think about the attack, he sang. He sang 'New York, New York' in the middle of the park and made a complete fool out of himself in front of all these people. He's the only man I've ever trusted in my life, besides you."

"You are in love with him," David said, amazed; then he suddenly began to laugh. Jessica looked at his watering eyes and shaking shoulders, and wondered if Erin had finally driven him insane, like he always claimed she did.

"What is your problem?" she demanded, slightly annoyed.

"You! You're in love with some guy and, for the first

time, you know what the rest of us mortals are like," David said between spasms of laughter. Jessica hit his shoulder and David abruptly sobered or attempted to, but she still saw the laughter in his eyes. "I'm sorry, Jess, I really am. I know you're hurting, but ever since we were young, you've been like a small adult. Since you were eight years old, you've had two goals in life: to be successful and to be rich. You're on your way to achieving both of those goals, and you're finally realizing something the rest of us humans realized a long time ago. It's not enough."

"I'm so happy my misery is your entertainment," she muttered sarcastically.

"You know that's not what I meant." David nudged her until she playfully pushed him back. "You're a beautiful, intelligent Black woman, Jess, and if Cary can't appreciate that then it's his loss. But I think he does."

Jessica rolled her eyes. David would say anything to make her happy. "How do you know? You've never even talked to him."

"I have eyes, Jess. I saw the way he looked at you at dinner, how he could barely meet your eyes. I didn't know how to interpret his reaction to you, but it all makes sense now. That man has feelings for you that run deeper than buying groceries."

"I'm so scared, David. He has this power over me because I love him so much, and I don't like feeling powerless."

"Are you really powerless, Jess?" David questioned.

"I don't know," she replied sincerely then asked hopefully, "You really think Cary loves me?"

"Trust me, a man doesn't sing in front of a woman unless he loves her."

Jessica smiled. "You have about thirty seconds left before Erin storms into this apartment and drags you out by your ear."

David smiled, obviously not concerned with the possibility. "Why didn't you tell me sooner that I could have felt this way being with her?"

"I tried, Dave, and every time I mentioned her, you questioned my sanity."

David laughed, then abruptly sobered. "Don't wait two years like we did, Jess. If you love him, tell him."

Jessica hugged him, and pushed him toward the door. "Have a good lunch."

"Are you sure you don't want to come? What are you going to do around this apartment all day except wait for Cary?"

"Believe me, I have a lot of other things to do besides think about him, including a pile of work."

"Call us later tonight. We could rent a few movies and order a pizza."

"Maybe, Dave." Jessica forced a smile and opened the door. "Don't worry about me." David hugged her, then walked out of the apartment.

Jessica closed the door and tried not to think about what a liar she had become. She knew she would spend the rest of the day thinking about Cary, and probably the rest of her life.

Seventeen

Cary glanced at his watch and groaned. It was only 9:30. Jessica would still be awake, maybe sitting on the living room couch, watching television and twirling her hair around her index finger subconsciously like she always did. With a desire he hadn't known he was capable of, Cary wanted to be sitting on the couch next to her, which was exactly why he sat in a noisy, dark bar a few blocks away from her apartment.

Cary spent the entire day going from one lead to another to find Michael. He finally realized at around two that afternoon that his entire search was useless. He only continued until six because he didn't want to return to the apartment and see Jessica and think about how she fell asleep in his arms. A woman like Jessica wasn't supposed to trust him enough to fall asleep with him. She wasn't supposed to look at him like he was a normal man.

Cary gulped the last few drops of vodka from the shot glass then slammed the glass on the counter, wincing from the strong taste. He hoped if he drank enough alcohol and stayed out late enough that when he finally returned to the apartment Jessica would be asleep. If he was sober, he didn't think the idea of her sleeping would stop him from walking into her bedroom and fulfilling all his fantasies, but Cary reasoned if he was drunk enough he would stumble into the apartment and pass out.

"Agent Riley," came a voice behind him.

Cary's hand went for his gun before he realized Agent Tyler Morris stood next to him. Cary shook his head at his slow reflexes. If Michael found him, he could kill him before Cary even reached for his gun.

"Don't drink," Cary advised Tyler, as Cary signaled to the bartender for another shot of vodka. "It ruins the reflexes."

"You're drunk," Tyler said, amazed.

"Not yet but I'm hoping to get there."

Tyler sat on the stool next to Cary and shook his head in surprise. "I thought it was against Group regulations to become drunk in a host city—"

"It's also against regulations to talk about the Group in a public place," Cary said, laughing at Tyler.

Tyler's face turned red and he stared at his hands. "I'm sorry, sir."

"This isn't the military, Tyler. Stop calling me sir."

"Yes, sir . . . Cary."

Cary downed the contents of his recently refilled glass, then banged the glass on the counter and studied Tyler. "Why did you want to become a Group agent?"

Tyler seemed surprised by the question. "I didn't. I wanted to join the FBI and the Group picked me from the graduating class of FBI—"

"You were picked the second you filled out the application, Tyler, the second you filled out the in-depth character test, which is little more than a moral-aptitude test."

"What are you saying?" Tyler asked, confused.

"We were trained for the Group because we have no morals. We don't feel the same about society's rules that normal people do. We'll never have a normal relationship or kids that love us or even close friends. We're the scum of society that, through some stroke of luck, landed in college, instead of joining the Mafia or a gang."

"That's not true—"

"After your first assignment, you'll realize how right I am." Cary motioned to the bartender again. "A double for me and a beer for him." The bartender stared in concern at Cary, but Tyler nodded and the bartender turned away.

"This is my first assignment," Tyler reminded him. "We're protecting a woman from a monster. What's so amoral about that?"

"Another thing you'll realize after your first assignment is that there are no monsters. There are no good guys. One country's hero is another country's blood enemy."

"You're not making sense."

Cary continued calmly, ignoring Tyler's protests. "The first few months of your employment, the Group sends you on assignments like this. Protection, security detail, escorts. They call them assignments, but they're not. They're testing you. They want you to watch people like me and see what you'll become in a few years. Then if you haven't run away by then, they send you on your first real assignment. Usually, they break us in with a nice assassination. Either a staged car accident or a nice bullet through the head—"

"Cary, you're drunk and talking too much," Tyler interrupted in a firm voice. He quickly glanced around the bar at the laughing and drinking patrons, who paid no attention to the two men. "You could get us both in a lot of trouble."

"What do you think happens to guys like me, Tyler?" Cary asked, staring at the ceiling. He imagined himself alone and old, still sleeping with a gun underneath his pillow. "Do you think I could fade away into the night, not worrying about a Michael Lyons coming to disconnect my oxygen tube?"

"I should take you home."

"To Virginia?" Cary asked hopefully.

"To Jessica's house," Tyler corrected.

Cary groaned and lightly pounded his head on the bar. "That's not my home," Cary finally responded, then he whispered to himself, "Although, I'd like it to be." He tried to cover his admission by gulping down the shot the bartender had placed in front of him.

"Somehow, I knew I'd find you here," came Logan's voice.

Cary rolled his eyes and groaned. "Are you following me around the city?"

"May I help you?" Tyler asked, carefully.

"No," Logan said, sitting on the stool on the other side of Cary.

"Calm down, Tyler," Cary muttered. "This is my brother, Logan. He's one of the locals—a San Francisco Police Department inspector. I've been meaning to ask you, Logan, why aren't you called detectives like every other police department in America? San Francisco always has to be different." Cary thought his question was valid but both men ignored him.

"Brother? I didn't know you had a brother."

"I think he tries to forget," Logan said cheerfully.

"He's pretty drunk. Can you handle him by yourself?" Tyler asked, obviously eager to escape.

"I don't need to be handled by anyone," Cary muttered, but neither man looked at him.

"He could be vulnerable in this state," Tyler said, eyeing Logan.

"He means that I could be too stupid and drunk to notice Michael sticking a knife in my back," Cary told Logan. He laughed as Tyler's face pursed in disapproval. "You act like an eighty-year-old woman, Tyler. Lighten up."

"I know everything, Tyler, and I understand. Nothing's

going to happen to my brother," Logan said, nodding. Tyler quickly walked out of the bar, leaving Cary alone with Logan.

"What are you doing here, Cary?" Logan asked, studying him.

"I'm definitely not here for a lecture from you or Tyler on the bad effects of drinking. I'm twenty-six years old. If I want to wallow in a bottle of vodka, then that's exactly what I will do."

"Why don't you just go back to the apartment and talk to her?"

"Who?" Cary asked blankly.

"Do you think I'm stupid? I know how you feel about Jessica."

"And how could you possibly know how I feel about Jessica? I haven't seen you in five years, I haven't talked to you in four years. You don't know anything about me," Cary retorted. He downed the contents of Tyler's half-full glass, then searched for the bartender. The last thing Cary wanted to do was talk to his brother, especially when he was feeling the effects of the alcohol and could say something he would regret.

"The sad thing is, Cary, you haven't changed at all in the last five years," Logan said with a bitter smile. Cary glared at him and Logan calmly met his gaze as he said, "There are a few changes—you're more guarded, you definitely don't talk as much. And the old Cary would have seen Jessica for what a beautiful woman she is and chained himself to her a long time ago. You have changed in those respects, but I still see the same guilt all over your face. You still blame yourself for Mom and Dad's deaths."

"Where the hell is that bartender?" Cary muttered, frantically scanning the faces of the crowd that blocked his entire view of the long bar.

"How much longer are you going to punish yourself?

How much longer are you going to punish Maggie and me?"

Cary looked at him then, as he felt the familiar hurt roar through his body. "What are you talking about? I'm protecting you and Maggie."

"From what?" Logan asked, confused. "From the possible dangerous consequences of your job? We can take care of ourselves, Cary. I'm a police officer and Maggie's in the Navy—"

"From me, Logan," Cary erupted. "I'm protecting you and Maggie and Jessica from me." Cary saw the comprehension dawn on his brother's face. Cary threw enough dollar bills on the bar to cover his drinks then stumbled away. The cold air hit him in the face like a brick wall as he stepped outside, but he didn't stop to roll down his sleeves. He didn't know where he was going. He just wanted to escape Logan and his questions. He wanted to escape the nightmares about his parents. Most of all, he wanted to escape Jessica, who made him want things that he didn't have a right to want.

"Cary, wait," Logan called after him. Cary continued walking and groaned when his brother fell into stride with him. "Cary, do you really think that? Do you really think that we need protecting from you?"

"Leave me alone, Logan."

"Cary, it's not true—" Cary didn't allow his brother to finish, but grabbed the front of Logan's shirt and pushed him into the wall of a nearby building. Logan grunted in pain as his back hit the building, but he only stared at Cary with the same confusion on his face.

"I said, leave me alone. I never should have invited you to dinner. I never should have talked to you that day on the street—"

"But, you did," Logan shot back, pushing Cary off of him. Cary stumbled a few steps from his brother, surprised by Logan's strength.

"It's for your own good, Logan. Mom and Dad weren't supposed to die that night. If I had paid attention to the road or allowed Dad to drive like he wanted or . . . If it wasn't for me, they would still be alive. I stayed away from you and Maggie because I didn't want to hurt you, like I hurt Mom and Dad."

"The other driver was drunk, Cary," Logan protested.

Cary continued as if his brother had never spoken. "After five years of not allowing myself to love anyone else, to hurt anyone else, I met Jessica. And whether I wanted her to or not, she got to me, Logan. She made me love her. And she was almost killed because of me. Because I love her." Cary noticed the tears in his brother's eyes, or couldn't see past his own. He turned to the building as his stomach threatened to erupt. He wanted to vomit. He wanted to get rid of all the agony and guilt that had haunted him since his parents' death.

"Cary," Logan said softly, standing beside him. "You're my brother and no matter what you think you did or didn't do, I'm going to love you. And if you think Jessica would run away from you because you happened to be driving when some jerk drank too many beers and got behind the wheel, then you don't really know her."

Cary stared at him and shook his head in denial. "Go away, Logan."

"You're not getting rid of me again," Logan said, shrugging. "Like Dad always said, we're brothers, and whether we like it or not, that means we're stuck with each other for the rest of our lives. Somehow over the past five years, I forgot that, but after Jessica reminded me, I'm never going to forget it again."

"I'm not the same person I was, Logan. I can't be like I used to be."

"I have a surprise for you, Cary. You weren't that great a person to begin with," Logan said nonchalantly. "In fact, I remember when I was six and you were eight, you pushed me from the top bunk bed and I broke my arm."

"I didn't push you . . ." Cary's voice trailed off as he saw the smile on Logan's face at their decades-old argument. Cary refused to smile but muttered, "I didn't push you. You lost your balance."

"I bet Jessica would believe that you pushed me."

"Please don't tell her that story," Cary pleaded, shaking his head.

Logan laughed then sobered as he said softly, "Don't you think Mom and Dad would have wanted you to be happy with someone like Jessica? Do you honestly think they'd want you to spend the rest of your life feeling guilty over something you had no control over? You have a chance to be happy with her, Cary. A lot of people never find that."

"She doesn't want me," Cary muttered, shaking his head. "Why would she? She's beautiful and smart—" Cary grunted as his brother pushed him in the chest. Cary barely managed to catch himself before he fell to the street.

"Don't ever insult yourself in front of me again." Cary smiled at the determined expression on his brother's face. Cary could see Logan trying not to laugh, but he eventually did. "Did I just sound like Dad?"

Cary nodded, laughing. "It was almost scary."

"I do that a lot," Logan said, shaking his head. "I find myself saying a lot of things Dad would say, mostly his corny jokes."

"Good," Cary whispered more to himself than to Logan.

"Are you aware that you just admitted you love Jessica Larson?" Logan grinned from ear to ear then said, in the irritating chant of a young brother, "Cary loves Jessica."

"I can still push you around," Cary warned him.

Logan continued to laugh. "Are you ready to return to Jessica's place?"

"I need a few more drinks," he mumbled, making Logan laugh. "What about you, bro? How's your love life?"

Logan groaned and muttered, "Where was that bar?"

"Are you in trouble with some woman?" Cary asked, already knowing the answer.

"Only two or three," Logan said meeting his brother's eyes and laughing. Cary shook his head with a smile, then placed an arm around his brother's shoulders when he realized how good it was to hear his laugh.

Jessica heard Cary walk into the apartment and immediately glanced at the clock. 3:02 A.M. Her stomach churned with anger as she slammed the book that she had been pretending to read for the last two hours on the nightstand. She was so twisted with nerves, fear, and anger that she didn't know whether to throw her arms around Cary's neck or slap his face.

When he hadn't returned home by a decent hour, she'd started to worry. When midnight came and went, she became afraid. She conjured horrible images of Michael Lyons hurting Cary in an unspeakable way. And then there were worse images of Cary meeting a gorgeous woman and giving her the kisses that belonged to Jessica.

Jessica threw back the bedcovers and stormed into the living room. Cary's movements were clumsy as he pulled the bed from the couch. Her relief over his safety and well-being disappeared as she smelled the alcohol on his breath. Anger scalded her entire body. While she had been going prematurely gray over worry for him, he had been drinking and probably flirting with whatever woman threw herself at him, which Jessica knew happened wherever he went.

"Cary," she greeted him coldly.

Cary turned to her and groaned. She crossed her arms over her chest and tried not to react as he unbuttoned his shirt and bared his lean, brown chest. "Can we have this argument tomorrow morning?"

"No." Her voice was low and dangerous, but Cary barely glanced at her. "A simple phone call, Cary. If you had called at any point during the night to say, 'I'm still alive, Jessica,' I could've gone to sleep with peace of mind. It's called common courtesy and respect."

Cary muttered to himself during her speech, then pulled the covers from the bed. "I was busy, Jessica," he slurred.

Jessica walked over to him until she was directly in his face. She winced at the smell of alcohol on his breath. He smelled like he had rolled in a tub of vodka, then consumed it. "You are drunk."

"I always thought you had brilliant powers of perception." His eyes roamed over her body and Jessica remembered she was wearing her usual sleeping attire: a thin, cotton camisole and long, cotton pajama pants. She saw his brown eyes turn to midnight as her nipples beaded against the shirt. "Among other things," he finished, in a soft voice that seemed to caress her.

"I just wish you had called me," she said firmly, but her soul sang from the desire in his eyes. He wanted her almost as much as she wanted him. He wasn't sober enough to conceal his feelings from her or turn away like the other times. "I was worried. I thought you ran into Michael Lyons," she continued hoarsely.

He rubbed a callused finger between her slightly parted lips and Jessica felt the instant heat fill her entire body. She came alive when he touched her; she finally accepted this fact. "I'm more scared of you than of Michael Lyons," he whispered, tasting her lips as if she were the most precious dessert in the world. Jessica clasped her arms around his neck and plunged her tongue into his open mouth. He tasted like vodka and another flavor that was stronger and more addictive: his essence. She ran her fingers through his silky curls as his hands roamed over her back, pressing her closer to him.

Somewhere in the back of her mind, Jessica felt him moving her across the room, but she could only concentrate on his hands and his mouth. She never thought kissing one person would bring such an onslaught of pleasure. She would gladly have spent the entire night kissing him and having him kiss her back. Then Jessica felt him lower her to the bed. His lips never left hers as he pulled his shirt completely off, and he laid on top of her. Every inch of his body pressed into her and Jessica tried to pull him even closer. All of her worry and fear had her frantic and desperate with need for him. She couldn't have stopped him, or herself, even if she'd wanted to.

Cary was going out of his mind with pleasure. She initiated the sweet attack as her tongue swirled in his mouth. Cary pulled the wisp of a T-shirt over her head, and moved from her lips to taste one sweet nipple that had called to him through her shirt when he'd walked into the apartment. He squeezed the softness that was her hips as her hands twined in his hair, pulling him closer to her breasts. Cary moved to the other nipple, wanting to take his time in loving her.

He trembled from the effort of restraining himself. He wanted to plunge himself in her, to lose himself in the safety and comfort and love she willingly offered. He knew she would be angry before he even walked in the door. She was angry because she loved him and she had been worried. And because love entered his mind again, Cary had to find a way to stop. He knew if they made love now, she would expect things from him that he could never give her. And Cary didn't want to hurt Jessica more than he already had to.

"Jess . . ." He couldn't resist meeting her seeking lips as she reached for him. Her hands moved over his chest, causing him to involuntarily suck in his stomach. Cary broke contact with her hungry lips, forcing himself to pull away and roll off of her. She leaned over him, her soft strands of hair brushing his bare chest, and Cary scrambled off the bed. He thought drinking enough vodka in a bar would erase her from his system, but the alcohol only weakened his resolve to stay away from her. "Jess, I—"

"What's wrong, Cary?" she asked, quietly. Cary couldn't look at her until she covered her beautiful breasts. As if reading his mind, Jessica struggled with her disheveled clothing and stood from the bed. "Cary?"

"Here's the truth, Jessica. I want a woman who has, at least, a little experience in bed. Every guy wants to have a virgin, at least once in his life, and I did that in college. I'm too old to break in a twenty-six-year-old virgin; I don't have the patience. How about you buy one of those instructional videos on how to please a man and then we can try this whole thing again?" Cary felt crippled from the pain in her eyes and the tear that rolled down her cheek. He wanted to take his words back, but she loved him and she wasn't supposed to love him. No one was ever supposed to love him. His work was too uncertain and his life wasn't worth it. She needed someone to attend charity balls and business dinners with, someone who had a normal relationship with his family.

"Why would you say something like that?" she whispered.

Cary forced himself to look at her. "I'm here to do a job. Once that job is done, I'm going back to Virginia." Before the last words were out of his mouth, Jessica turned and ran back to her room. Even the closed door couldn't prevent him from hearing her sobs. Cary cursed himself and fell onto the bed.

Eighteen

The next morning, Cary groaned as the sound of clanging pots and plates drummed in unison with the pounding in his head. He rolled off the bed and landed hard on the floor. Cary suddenly remembered why he wasn't supposed to drink while on the job. He also remembered why he didn't like to drink. He didn't like the dullness that followed any all-night drinking binge. Cary knew it wasn't just the drinking that made him feel numb. It was his memory of the pain that ravaged Jessica's face when he'd blurted out those ridiculous words.

Cary opened his eyes and quickly closed them again at the bright sunlight that streamed through the living room windows. He groaned again, then looked toward the kitchen, where Jessica continued noisily to wash dishes. Since Cary had cleaned the kitchen the night before, he knew there were no dirty dishes for her to wash.

"Do you have to do that now?" He groaned, debating whether to chance standing or to remain in bed for the rest of the day.

"Would you like for me to stop?" Jessica asked sweetly.

Cary immediately raised himself on his forearms to meet her eyes. He saw the rage brewing in the dark depths, and he realized she looked more beautiful than he dreamed last night. He moaned at his own stupidity, then forced himself to sit up in the bed. He was a fool.

Any other man would have grabbed the chance to be with a woman like Jessica and he did nothing but push her away. He repeated the refrain that was slowly driving him insane: it was for her own good.

"Jess, about last night—"

"Don't say one word, Cary Riley," she interrupted, coming to stand in front of him. She wore another suit that made him want to tear the clothes from her body. Cary couldn't fool himself. Everything she wore he wanted to tear from her body. "I know you're a brave man or you couldn't be in your line of work. Why can't you be that way about us?"

Cary pretended ignorance and squinted at her. "What are you talking about?"

An intensity entered her eyes that frightened him, as she said, "Relationships are frightening. Don't you think I'm scared? I've never felt this way about anyone, either. I don't like relying on anyone else or feeling vulnerable. But, the more scared I become of all these raging feelings, the more I realize the only time I'm not terrified is when I'm with you. And I want to hang onto you. Can't you hang onto me, too?"

"My parents—"

"Your parents died in a horrible accident and you lived. You lived, Cary. Start acting like it."

Cary stared at her as her words registered in his alcohol-clouded mind. Jessica wasn't crying because she thought he didn't want her. She was crying because she knew exactly what his performance last night meant. Once more, Cary couldn't understand how one woman could see through the numerous masks he had worn for years. "You don't understand," Cary finally responded in a weak voice.

Jessica sighed tiredly, then asked, "Just tell me one thing. If Michael Lyons hadn't attacked me in the park, would you have tried to find me?"

Silence weighed in the apartment as Jessica stared expectantly at him. Cary returned her gaze, then finally stood, wincing at the change in altitude. He saw the determined expression on her face and he realized she wouldn't leave until he answered her question. "Jess, do we have to talk about this now? I can't answer a question like that—"

Jessica interrupted his comment with a bitter laugh and grabbed her briefcase off the kitchen counter. "I want you and all your equipment and all your playmates gone by the time I get home from work. I don't want anyone following me, watching me, or calling me. I don't ever want to see your face again. Do you understand?"

Cary panicked and grabbed her arm. "I know you're angry with me, but this isn't the way to demonstrate it. Michael Lyons is a very dangerous man—"

Jessica yanked her arm from his grip, and Cary recoiled slightly from the hard glare in her eyes. "You keep telling me how dangerous Michael Lyons is, but, of the two of you, you're the only one who's hurt me." She turned on her heel and stormed from the apartment, leaving the door open behind her.

"We can't find her." Cary stared at Tyler and Dan in disbelief, as Dan's words sunk into his brain and heart.

"What are you talking about?" Cary asked carefully. He glanced at his watch for confirmation. Only an hour had passed since Jessica had left for work, and Cary had fallen on the couch to berate himself. Only an hour had passed since he realized he had destroyed the best thing to ever happen to him. The last thing he expected to hear when Dan and Tyler knocked on the apartment door was that Jessica was missing.

"We have no idea where Jessica is," Dan repeated, with an uneasy glance at Tyler.

"Jessica's at work," Cary replied calmly, as something akin to fear threatened to consume him.

"We checked her office at work," Tyler muttered, avoiding Cary's eyes. "She's not there."

"What happened, Agent Morris?" Cary clenched his fists to prevent from slamming them into the younger man's face. He also noticed the same attempt at restraint in Dan's expression.

"She took the bus to work," Tyler murmured, finally meeting Cary's eyes. "I was only separated from her by two people. Two people, Cary. But she didn't get off at the usual spot. At the last minute before the doors closed, she jumped off the bus in Union Square. There was no way I could follow her. I called for backup, but by the time they got there, she was gone."

"Gone?"

"Will you stop repeating every word he says?" Dan snapped at Cary, raking a hand over his hair. Dan paced the length of the living room, then abruptly stopped and looked at the two men. "We are trained agents. We can find one civilian woman in San Francisco."

"One woman who knows the area and who doesn't want to be found," Tyler interjected, flinching slightly when Cary glared at him.

"What are you talking about? Why wouldn't Jessica want to be found?" Cary demanded.

"I've been following her for almost a week and I can tell when she's happy or upset, and this morning . . . I've never seen her like that. Did something happen this morning . . . here?"

"That's none of your damn business," Cary snapped, tiredly rubbing his eyes. He wanted to burst from the apartment and scour every inch of the city until he found Jessica. He wanted to apologize. He wanted to love her. If Michael knew she was alone in the city, Cary didn't want to think about what could possibly happen. "I want her found. I want that woman back in this apartment by the end of the day. Do you two understand?"

"What if Michael Lyons has her?" Tyler articulated what they all thought.

"Michael doesn't have her," Dan said shaking his head. "If he had her, we would have heard from him by now."

Fear squeezed Cary's heart but he forced his expression to remain neutral and turned to Tyler. "Take Williams and Owens with you and scour every inch of this city. Start at Union Square then branch out, including the lower peninsula." Tyler nodded, obviously glad to receive instructions, and ran from the apartment.

Cary grabbed his jacket from the back of a chair and headed toward the door. "Where are you going?" Dan asked, following him.

"I need to follow a few leads."

"Where will you be?"

"I don't know," Cary said, giving him a warning glare.

"How am I supposed to get in touch with you if we find her?"

"I have my cell phone."

Cary moved to the door but Dan grabbed his arm. Cary stared at the man's hand and Dan slowly removed it. "You're too close to this, Cary. You're going to get yourself, and maybe one of our agents, killed. Let me come with you."

"For the last time, Jessica Larson means nothing to me," Cary said through clenched teeth. "The Group taught us to have no weaknesses and I don't, especially not Jessica." Cary walked from the apartment, wondering if Dan saw through his lie.

Twenty minutes later, Cary scanned the contents of David's plush corner office in a large building in the financial district, while he waited for David to return. Cary hadn't bothered to announce himself to David through receptionists and secretaries. He had simply utilized his

Group knowledge to reach David's office undetected. Cary was almost glad David hadn't been in his office when he'd first arrived. In Cary's current state of mind, he knew he would have said or done something that he might later regret. The few minutes of quiet in David's office gave Cary time to compose himself and control his shaking hands. He wouldn't admit it to anyone but he was a nervous wreck. For a man who prided himself on complete control, the panic and helplessness were strange and unwelcome feelings.

David walked into the office concentrating intently on a piece of paper in his hand. Cary remained in the plush leather chair behind the desk and waited for David to notice him. David moved to sit in the chair and nearly screamed when he saw Cary. Cary gave him credit for regaining his composure quickly.

"What the hell are you doing here?" David demanded angrily.

"Nice office," Cary complimented, picking up David's stress balls from the corner of the desk. "Where is she, David?"

"Where is who?" David asked, blankly.

"I'm not in the mood for games. Where is Jessica?"

David continued to stare at Cary as he sat in one of the wing chairs on the other side of the desk. "What are you talking about? Jessica's at work, the same place she's been every Monday morning for the past five years."

"She's not there."

"Maybe she's late or out of the office at a meeting."

"She's not there and they don't know where she is." Cary could feel the anger spread through his body as David continued to shake his head in disbelief. Cary smiled, the same smile he'd used on countless informants over the years. David shifted in the chair but his expression remained wary. "Did you know there are over sixty bones in the human hand?"

"So what," David snorted.

Cary leaned across the desk, the same smile frozen on his face. "Because you're Jessica's brother, I would only break fifty-nine of those bones in your left hand."

David laughed but Cary could hear the nerves jangling in his voice. "Are you threatening me?"

"Not if you tell me where Jessica is."

"I don't know where Jessica is and, even if I did, I still wouldn't tell you."

Cary regarded David for a second and realized, with disappointment, that David was telling the truth. He didn't know where Jessica was, which meant Jessica was either in trouble or, like Tyler had guessed, she didn't want to be found. Cary stood with a tired sigh and headed for the door.

David jumped from his seat and grabbed Cary's arm. "What the hell is going on here?"

"Your sister and I had a disagreement." David still didn't release his arm.

"Tell me the truth, Cary. I'm not as dumb as I look."

"I don't have time for this—"

"Make time."

"Jessica could be in danger." Cary saw the concern instantly cross David's face as his hand fell from his arm. He knew that whatever differences existed between him and David, they would both be united in their concern for Jessica. For some reason, that made Cary feel not completely alone.

"The man from the park?"

"Michael Lyons. I'm not certain if he has her, but it's a strong possibility. I'll find her either way, David, I promise."

"Why would he want her?" David asked, confused. David didn't wait for Cary to answer as he asked softly, "Who are you, Cary?"

"I'm someone who loves Jessica."

"She never told me what you did for a living," David whispered more to himself than to Cary. Comprehension dawned in David's eyes as he said, "Michael wants her because of you."

"David, you can't tell anyone, not even Erin."

"Who are you? What are you?"

"I work for a government-intelligence agency. Michael has a score to settle with me, and he thinks Jessica is a way to get to me."

"Is she?"

Cary hesitated, then replied, "Michael knew how I felt about her before I did."

David appeared to digest all the news and he sagged against the edge of his desk. "What can I do?" he finally asked.

"Stay by the phone; wait for her call. Men are all over this city, searching for her. We'll find her, whether Michael has her or not."

"You said Michael holding her captive was only one possibility. What did you mean?"

Cary felt his face flush as David stared intently at him. "This morning she told me she never wanted to see me again. She told me to leave and since she knows I can't do that while Michael Lyons is still out there, it's a possibility that she left."

David smiled for the first time since he entered the office. "Jessica didn't go to work because of you?"

"I didn't mean—"

"This is terrific," David interrupted with a huge grin. "All this time, I thought maybe she was confused about her feelings for you, but if she missed work to avoid you then she really does love you."

Cary was too confused and worried about Jessica to attempt to understand David's rantings. He opened the office door. "I'll be in touch."

Cary doubted David heard him since he continued to

mutter to himself about Jessica's work-absenteeism rate. Cary closed the door and noticed the window at the end of the hallway, with a view of the lush, green hills that separated San Francisco from the peninsula. He imagined Hadley's Inn shaded among the trees on the coast. He wished he could freeze the night he spent with Jessica at the inn.

Cary suddenly smiled as he thought of the possibility. Jessica wouldn't return to Hadley's Inn, he told himself, but then he laughed because it made perfect sense. It would be the one place he never would suspect her of going.

"Where is she?" Michael demanded, as soon as Dan stood next to him at the wooden railing of the pier. Both men stared at the seals laying on the planks in the water, and pretended to ignore each other as numerous people walked behind them.

"We don't know."

Michael rolled his eyes beneath the sunglasses he wore. He was growing tired of this country. He longed for his home, for his friends, for his family. He wished he could return to his country and place flowers on his mother's grave, but the orders to police in his country were to shoot him on sight. Michael realized killing Cary was the other thing that motivated him to wake up in the morning. He laughed at how pathetic that was and how pathetic he was to rely on a man like Dan Pelstrom.

"How could an entire regiment of Group agents lose one woman?"

"We're working on it, Michael," Dan snapped, his nerves obviously frayed. "She gave one of our agents the slip."

"Why?"

"I don't know. Do I look like a mind reader?"

Michael counted to ten for patience, then gripped the wooden rail when that didn't work. Counting to ten never worked for him. He tried to remember who taught him that and he squeezed the rail tighter. Cary had taught him the trick. "If you don't tell me where that woman is within the next forty-eight hours, you won't receive your final payment."

Dan coughed into his hands. His eyes frantically searched the water, as if he'd find Jessica there. "She's being honored at a ball tomorrow night. She has to return for that."

Michael smiled and patted the man's shoulder. "That wasn't so hard, was it?"

"I forgot about that. Some organization in the city honors young, successful men and women in business. It's supposed to be a black-tie event. Some of the guys were complaining about having to rent a tuxedo—"

"Get me in there."

Dan glanced at him uneasily. "That could be impossible—"

"Ten thousand dollars, Dan." Michael shuddered in disgust as Dan's eyes lit with anticipation of the money. "I'll find a way."

"I knew you would." Michael watched Dan walk away and blend into the crowd, then he turned back to the water. He tried to remember how satisfied he would feel when Cary was dead, but all he felt was loneliness.

Nineteen

Jessica parked her brother's car in front of Hadley's Inn and wiped at the tears that filled her eyes. She had done it. She had escaped Cary, his Group agents, her brother, and Erin. She knew even Michael Lyons couldn't know where she was. David never drove his car during the week. Jessica knew it would be sitting in the parking garage of his apartment building. That morning, she'd used her key to his apartment to find the car keys to his navy blue BMW. After leaving David a note to tell him she had his car, she drove straight toward Hadley's Inn.

Jessica didn't know why she was drawn to the place where she'd met Cary. She left San Francisco because of him. She hadn't meant to return to Hadley's Inn. She didn't have any specific destination in mind, since she had never thought she would be able to allude Agent Morris or the other agents assigned to watch her. She had, and now she sat in front of the one place that reminded her of Cary more than staying in San Francisco.

Jessica screamed at the hard tap on the car window. She placed a hand over her racing heart as she stared at Jake's smiling face on the other side of the window.

"Jessica Larson?" he said uncertainly.

Jessica got out of the car and forced a smile. "I couldn't stay away."

Jake didn't return her smile, but he studied her face. "Don't you have work?"

"I needed a vacation."

"I thought your career was important to you."

"My career means everything to me," Jessica responded quickly, then laughed too loud. "Am I not welcome here?"

Jake laughed at his own behavior, then hugged her. Jessica clung to his stooped shoulders for the comfort for a second too long, then stepped away from him. "I'm sorry, Jessica, I just didn't expect to see you here. A lot of people pass through and promise to come back but they never do."

"This is the only place I want to be right now," she told him truthfully. "Is there any room?"

"For you, always," Jake assured her, taking the briefcase from her hands. He led her toward the house as the wind swirled around their legs, shifting the leaves on the ground. "How long do you think you'll be staying with us?"

"I don't know."

Jake stopped on the steps of the porch and stared at her. Jessica couldn't meet his eyes. She didn't want to cry in front of him or tell him what a fool she had been. "Running away is not the answer, Jessica," he said simply.

"I'm not running away."

"I've seen the look before," Jake said. "You think you'll spend a few days on the coast with the fresh air, the water, the trees. You think it'll clear your head and by the time you get home, whatever the problem is will have gone away. That's not how life works. We have to face our problems head-on."

"I'm not running away," she repeated.

Jake continued to study her, then he smiled gently. "I like you, Jessica. I don't want to see you hurt. If he's hurting you, he's not worth it."

Jessica wiped at the tears that instantly filled her eyes at the thought of Cary. She forced a laugh and shook her head. "He's not hurting me, Jake. I'm hurting myself. I allowed him to make me feel things that I can't deal with if I want to be a strong, independent—"

Jake snorted in frustration and grabbed her shoulders. "Haven't you learned by now, girl, that the right man doesn't want to take away your independence or your career? He'll want all that for you and more. Loving someone and being loved by someone does not mean you can't be successful or hungry for your career. The two can exist together."

Jessica paused for a moment as Jake's words sunk into her heart. She tried to respond but, instead, walked past him into the house.

That evening, Jessica entered the dining room wearing the comfortable skirt and sweater she had stuffed into her briefcase before she'd left for work that morning. She was fairly surprised by the crowded room. Eight of the ten small tables in the room were filled with glowing and laughing people. Jessica had expected to be alone, able to wallow in her misery, but the laughing families and couples around her would make that difficult.

Jessica picked a table in the corner and placed the cloth napkin on her lap. She planned to eat as fast as possible, then return to her room and go to sleep, hopefully free of dreams about Cary. Jessica debated calling her brother or Erin and assuring them that she was safe, but she also imagined their numerous questions. She knew Erin had probably called her house ten times when she'd heard through the rumor grapevine at work that Jessica had taken her first day off in five years.

"Do you mind if I join you?" came a familiar male voice that sent shivers down her spine.

Jessica stared straight into Cary's beautiful brown eyes. She knew her mouth dropped open, which was why she told herself she couldn't stop him from sitting in the seat across the table from her. Anger quickly replaced shock as she noticed the smug expression on his face.

"What are you doing here?" she demanded angrily.

"Making sure you're safe," he replied simply, then glanced at the plates of food on the tables around them. "I think we're having veal tonight. I like veal."

"Go away," Jessica hissed through clenched teeth.

"Where am I supposed to go, Jessica?" Cary asked innocently.

He was entirely too calm for her sanity. Her entire body came alive because he sat across the table from her, yet he had no idea.

"I don't care where you go, as long as it's away from me."

"You're drawing attention to yourself," Cary said nonchalantly, then smiled at the couple at the next table, who were staring at them.

"How did you find me?"

"I find people for a living, Jessica. Besides that, I know you."

"You don't know me."

"I know you like old movies, I know you like opera music, I know you like to dance." Jessica's anger melted away as his voice grew softer. "I know when you're scared or nervous, you play with your hair. I know you love your brother and mother. I know you don't like pickles. I know you like your coffee strong. I know you wear your hair in a ball because you hate having it in your face. I know you like the color blue. I know you truly do love your job, almost to the point of it being unnatural. I know you cry at the end of sad movies and try to hide it. And I know you can never stay angry with one person for long."

Jessica stared at him when he finally finished. She could feel the usual tears rushing to the surface, not from misery or pain, but from the sweetness of his words. Whether he wanted to be sweet to her or not, he was. Jessica shook her head as she realized she was falling into his trap once more.

"What do you want from me?" she said helplessly.

"Dinner," Cary replied simply, then smiled as Hadley walked toward them. "Hadley, how are you?"

"Cary," Hadley greeted with a bright grin. "I was wondering when you'd arrive to keep your young woman company."

"I had a little delay, but better late than never, right?" Cary said cheerfully. Jessica stared at him in speechless disbelief. She had the insane urge to laugh with him and Hadley, and hated herself for it.

Cary couldn't remember the last time he had enjoyed himself as much as this night, except when he was at Hadley's Inn two weeks ago. He couldn't believe it took only two weeks to turn his life upside down, to hope that maybe he could have what everyone else had, that he could love someone and have her love him back. Maybe Logan was right. Maybe he did have a chance with Jessica, a chance to live and love like his parents would have wanted him to.

Cary glanced across the table at Jessica, who hadn't said more than six words since their food had arrived. He couldn't wait to love her. If he had to talk all night until she made love to him just to shut him up then he would. If he had to wait the next five years and wear her down with his pleading then he would, as long as he was in her life. Somewhere during the two-hour drive from San Francisco, Cary realized he loved Jessica. He didn't know if he could admit his feelings to her, but they were there and they were real. They meant he was normal. The Group hadn't stolen everything from him and, as long as he had Jessica, the Group would never be able to take what they had away from him.

"That was delicious," Cary announced as he wiped his

mouth with the cloth napkin. "I wonder what we're having for dessert."

"Have you thought about where you're going to sleep tonight?" Jessica asked, fully meeting his eyes for the first time in half an hour.

"Yes." Silence followed his answer and her eyes considerably narrowed. Cary tried not to smile for fear that he would be wearing her glass of wine on his face.

"Where exactly is that, Cary?" she asked slowly.

"With you," he answered simply.

"If you think—"

"You look gorgeous," he blurted out. He wanted to impress her with soft words and a sonnet or two, but Cary could only think about how gorgeous she was and how she was his. She may not have wanted that, but the moment they kissed in that empty room two weeks ago, she became his.

"Cary—"

"You're so beautiful, Jess."

Jessica jumped from the table and ran from the room, leaving a room of bewildered diners. Cary stood with an apologetic smile and walked to her room on the third floor. He knocked on the door and waited patiently. He heard her on the other side of the door, trying to be silent.

"Jess, open the door," he said.

"Go away."

"Jess—" The door swung open and he saw the fury on her face. He thought she was gorgeous when she was angry, sad, happy, and whatever emotions came in between.

"I want you to leave me alone, Cary. Do you understand?" she said desperately. "I specifically came here to get away from you. How did that point escape your notice?"

"We need to talk."

"We have nothing to talk about."

"You have to come back to San Francisco at some
point, and we'll just have to talk there. You have that Bay
Area Professional's Ball to attend. You can't miss that.
We'll have to go to that—"

"I'm not going to the ball with you," Jessica interrupted, shaking her head.

Cary froze and the good mood he was in disappeared.
"You're going with David?" he asked carefully.

"I'm not going with David either. I'm going with a
friend of his, not that it's any of your business," she announced, then walked inside the room.

Cary followed her into the room and slammed the door
behind him. His patience and composure snapped at the
idea of Jessica with another man. Another man having
the smiles and laughs that belonged to him. "If you think
I would allow you to go to that ball with another man,
then you don't know me very well," he said, still able to
control some of his anger.

Cary almost retreated when he saw the violent look in
Jessica's eyes. "Allow me," she repeated in a strange voice.
"Since when do you have the right to allow me to do
anything?"

"Since I drove all the way to Hadley's Inn to find you,"
Cary practically shouted.

"I didn't ask you to." Jessica matched the volume of
his voice.

"And I sure as hell did not fly all the way from Virginia
to watch you ride off into the sunset with another man."

Jessica's expression turned deadly. "As you've reminded me every day since you've been here, you flew
to San Francisco to catch Michael Lyons, not to associate
with me," she responded coolly.

Cary crossed the room to tower over her but she didn't
move. His anger didn't prevent his stomach from clench-
ing with desire at being so close to her and smelling her
light perfume. After worrying about her for the entire

day, all he wanted to do was take her in his arms and make certain she was fine. But, somehow they were in an argument that involved Jessica going some place with another man.

Cary would literally go insane if he had to watch Jessica walk out of the apartment with another man. Cary knew he was being illogical, but he was in love for the first time in his life and had a right to be illogical. He bellowed, "There is no way in hell you are going to that ball with any man besides me. If you'd rather not go then fine, but you will not take any friend of your brother's or anyone else for that matter."

"Who's going to stop me?" Her eyes practically dared him to touch her.

"Me."

"You and how many of your Group agents?"

Cary cleared his throat as his desire increased to an almost painful level. He finally realized that he loved Jessica and she looked like she would rather walk on a bed of nails than allow him to touch her.

"Besides, why do you even care?" Jessica continued in that same silky voice that he knew she purposely used to drive him insane with lust. "Last night you made yourself abundantly clear about how you felt about me. What I do is none of your business."

"I'll sleep in the lounge," Cary muttered, purposely ignoring her question.

Jessica advanced on him and Cary took several steps away from her until he bumped against the door behind him. He didn't want to touch her or he knew he wouldn't be able to control what little restraint he had left. Just smelling her and being close enough to touch her at dinner made him nearly insane. "I guess you didn't hear me in San Francisco, so I'll tell you again. I want you out of my life. I never want to see you again. Just go back to your pathetic life in Virginia where you don't have to love anyone and no one will love you. Isn't that what you want, Cary? Well, I'm letting you go, with no strings attached."

"Just the other night, you were begging me to stay with you," he said, in a dangerously low voice.

There was complete silence as her expression hardened. Cary almost apologized but then she covered the remaining distance between them, and her bare feet touched the tips of his shoes. He had never seen her walk that way before, as if purposely to arouse a man's interest. Her voice whispered across his skin like fine silk as she practically purred, "Believe me, Cary, I won't ever make that mistake again. If I need anything from a man in the near future, I'll find a real one."

Cary growled at the insult and dragged her to him, crushing his mouth against hers. He welcomed her struggles and increased the pressure on her lips. He wanted to hurt her for hurting him. He wanted to make her pay for capturing his heart weeks ago.

Then Cary felt the softness of her hair brush his hands and whatever anger he imagined he felt disappeared. He gentled his attack on her lips but couldn't release her. He didn't have to because Jessica suddenly surrendered, opening her mouth for him and him only. His tongue plunged into her mouth, exploring and soothing the moist depths.

Cary couldn't contain himself anymore and ran his hands up her bare legs and underneath her skirt. She gasped softly into his mouth and dug her fingernails into his shoulders as he massaged her bottom through her thin cotton underwear. Cary finally pulled away from her to clear his head, and he met her passion-clouded eyes. "Jess, I do want you, more than I've ever wanted anything or anyone in my entire life. I don't know what any of this means, except that I need you."

His mouth found her neck as his hands roamed over her body, trying to touch everywhere at once. The need

o touch her skin nearly drove him mad and he lifted
er sweater over her head to feel her against him. She
elt like silk and satin, he remembered. The sight of her
ull breasts encased in the navy blue satin bra made his
hest constrict even more. Unlike the other times when
hey had almost made love, Cary didn't think of reasons
o stop. He wanted to be inside of her and to feel her
are body against his.

Cary trailed kisses along her neck, then placed his
nouth over hers. She instinctively welcomed him and
Cary moaned as her tongue forayed into his mouth. She
troked his mouth, her teeth nipping at his lips, and Cary
vent over the edge he had been clinging to for the past
wo weeks. This woman would never escape his thoughts,
r his mind, or his senses, and he didn't want her to.
Her hands moved underneath his shirt and began to skim
ver his bare chest. Cary wanted to scream from desire,
ut instead he pulled her even closer, not wanting to
reak the contact of her lips on his.

As his hands became more insistent, Jessica's head bean to swim with desire, love, and fear. She had known
s soon as he sat across from her at dinner that they
vould make love tonight, but now in the darkness of the
oom, hearing her own breath raging in her ears, inse-
urities plagued her. He was beautiful and perfect, and
he had a feeling that she would disappoint him. She
new he would never tell her, but Jessica still feared the
ncertainty, feared that she had waited too long. Even as
er body ached to continue in response to his hands
kimming over her bare stomach, her mind screamed at
er all the doubts and fears.

Cary seemed to sense her hesitation, because he slowly
ulled from her. She couldn't help her smile in response
o the slow, lazy look that he sent her. With one look, he
nade her feel comfortable and loved and sexy. Without
ne word, he made her realize that she could never dis-

appoint him. He gently pulled individual strands of her hair, causing the strains of pleasure-pain to race through her body.

"Don't be scared, Jess. If you want to stop, say so, okay. It'll be hard to stop, but I don't want to hurt you. I could never hurt you." He began to nuzzle her neck and her ears, sending roaring heat through her body at warp speed as her skin rejoiced at the contact. She couldn't resist her curiosity any longer, and nervously pulled his T-shirt over his head. His bare, muscled chest gleamed in the candlelight that Hadley had left burning on the windowsill. Jessica eagerly roamed her hands over his brown chest, amazed by the solid, hard feel of him compared to her softness. Her nerves melted to the floor and she kissed first one dark chocolate nipple then the other, loving the grainy, unfamiliar texture beneath her tongue. Cary muttered incoherently and abruptly pushed her down on the bed.

"Just show me, Cary," Jessica whispered, her dark eyes boring holes into his.

"Don't think, Jess. Just do whatever comes naturally." Cary finally unhooked her bra and thought he'd found heaven when he tasted one luscious breast. He watched in fascination as the berry red nipples beaded before his eyes, puckering to offer him more sweetness. Cary could have spent the whole night, tasting and memorizing the sweetness of her breasts, but he needed to see her entire body. He tore himself away from her breasts, smiling at her protesting gasps, and slid the thin skirt down her long legs, followed by her sensible underwear. He inhaled deeply as he viewed her body—the long legs, proud breasts, and flat stomach, all molded in cinnamon brown. "You're perfect, Jess," he whispered, meeting her eyes in the candlelight. The passion screaming from her eyes drove him to the edge that he thought he could hold on to for a while longer. He attacked her with his burning eyes, hot mouth, and slightly trembling hands.

His mouth tugged on one perfectly formed nipple that begged for his attention, then her shoulder called to him. Cary supported his weight on either side of her writhing body as he suckled and nipped every visible place on her body. He could already feel the sweat forming on his back as her soft sighs and moans drove him higher and higher, but, he restrained himself because he wanted this to be special for her. He wanted her to tremble like he was, before he would take what she willingly offered.

Jessica reveled in his touch, his eyes. She could barely form a coherent thought; she was experiencing more pleasure than she thought possible. She felt in her soul every place his hands touched, and when his tongue touched her stomach, she thought she would explode. She was imprisoned by his lips tracing her body, and his tongue leaving a wet trail across her. His callused hands on her body and the feel of his rough khakis against her soft legs were the only thoughts she wanted to think. She was beginning to feel out of control, and as much as it scared her, she would not have stopped him for all the money in the world.

"Your pants," Jessica panted, fumbling with the button.

Cary grinned and helped her with his pants, then threw them and his briefs onto the floor. Jessica wanted to shrink when she saw him. She wasn't sure if she would be able to accept him or even pleasure him. But when Cary kissed her with so much desire and she felt his pulsating manhood on her thigh, all doubts were erased.

When Jessica touched his manhood with her incredibly soft, uncertain hand, Cary almost came on the spot. She arched brazenly as his hands and mouth wandered down her body to her heat, where he longed to touch her. Jessica opened her eyes in shock as his hands traveled past her belly button and toward her center.

Cary noticed her shocked expression and immediately returned to gather her soul into his as he slanted an open, exploring kiss on her lips. He felt her body relax again as her hands roamed over his back and she matched the passion in his kiss. "I just want to be sure you're ready, sweetie," he whispered as he slipped one finger inside of her. Jessica went completely still and his heart plummeted as her eyes slid closed. He feared she was going to tell him to stop and get the hell off of her and Cary didn't think he could. He flexed his finger inside of her, finding her hot center, and he grew harder than he thought possible when he felt how tight and ready she was for him. Then Jessica's hips began to match the motion of his finger and he saw the lazy smile on her face. She wasn't going to tell him to stop and his heart soared.

Jessica moaned in protest when Cary removed his torturing fingers. She opened her eyes and saw the concern and desire in his eyes as he stared down at her. He abruptly reached beside the bed and removed a package from his pants pocket. Her heart soared as she watched him put on the condom, and she realized the precautions he took for them both.

He settled on top of her and stared directly into her eyes, as if waiting for a signal from her. She placed a hand on his cheek and tried to think of the words to tell him how much she needed to feel him, how much she wanted to feel him.

He kissed her hand, then leaned down to her ear and whispered, "It'll only hurt once, sweetie, I promise. I'll go as slow as I can." Then he slipped inside her and Jessica didn't know if there was pain or not, she just felt an incredible sensation begin in her and travel like light through her body. Jessica had no doubt this was her other half, because she was now whole.

Twenty

Jessica snuggled against Cary's side as her breathing became even once more. She knew she would never be the same again, she would never look at actors kissing on the movie screen and dismiss it. She would never turn with disgust from kissing couples in public. She would always see Cary's brown eyes gazing into hers as his hands played her body to a beautiful sonata he created. She was glad that she had waited twenty-six years for him, for this moment.

She could barely comprehend what had just happened between them. She could only feel the pleasant, erotic tremors that still vibrated through her body. She could only feel his closeness and smell his scent that now clung to her body. And she realized, with surprise, that she already wanted him again.

"A penny for your thoughts," Cary whispered, as his hands gently stroked her hair.

"I just didn't expect . . . It was beautiful, Cary." She felt foolish for the tears in her eyes and turned her head to stare out the window. Then she realized that of everyone in the world, Cary was the one person who would never think she was foolish for crying.

"For me, too," he said softly, gently wiping at her fallen tears. "I never knew it could be this way."

She wanted to tell him that she loved him, that she

needed him, but she was scared. She placed a kiss in the middle of his chest then closed her eyes and snuggled into the warmth of his arms.

Cary groggily opened his eyes and glanced at the clock on the nightstand. He had been asleep for two hours. He couldn't remember the last time he had slept so well. Then he realized the reason why he had awakened. Jessica's fingers flirted across his chest, as she watched his face with a smile. He couldn't resist smiling in return. From his sleep-induced haze, with her slight smile and shining eyes, she seemed like an angel sent to administer to his soul.

"I was wondering if you'd ever wake up," she mumbled, as she licked both his nipples, provoking an internal riot of pleasure. "You're a modern-day version of Sleeping Beauty; you need a kiss from a princess to wake you up."

"Then kiss me, Jess" Cary responded, not feeling the slighest bit foolish for liking her comparison. Jessica didn't disappoint him as she placed her searching mouth over his. Cary tangled his hands in her hair, pulling her mouth even closer, fusing it to his.

Jessica pulled away from him, her mouth glistening in the soft moonlight of the room. "I don't remember Sleeping Beauty being that active in the fairy tale."

"Maybe if her prince kissed like you, she would have been." Jessica giggled and Cary grinned in response. Only with Jessica would he discuss fairy tales as if they ther down. Cary's mouth suddenly grew dry as her eyes traveled down his body to the part of him that had grown uncomfortably hard as her hands and lips moved over his body.

He tried to respond to her teasing, but he could only watch as she trailed a path of kisses down his stomach toward his navel and lower still. He had officially lost all powers of intelligent speech.

"Jess?" he inquired uncertainly. She smiled up the length of his body at him but slowly continued on her journey. Cary reached for her but she evaded his arms and placed her searching mouth on the part of him that painfully ached for her. Cary moaned her name as she tortured him over and over, her tongue swirling around and around, until he was rendered speechless when her mouth inhaled him whole. Cary meant to control himself, but couldn't as the intensity built from her devastating mouth and radiated to every part of his body. His fingers clenched her hair as he felt the release finally explode throughout his body in one wave after another.

Jessica slid back up his body, placing open-mouthed kisses across his chest as he tried to breathe after the powerful experience. He couldn't believe he could instantly grow hard again, just from one look into her eyes. She became his undoing when she hovered over him and sent him another sexy smile. He could only stare at the siren as her eyes traveled over his nude body, branding every inch.

"I've created a monster," he murmured, resisting the urge to laugh at her and Cary heart. He tell her the sorry about of it. I just

Jessica sm

Remember . . .

kiss. "I know." Cary groaned from passion then flipped her over so quickly that she grunted when her back hit the mattress.

Jessica laughed when she saw concern etched across Cary's face. All her worries and fears were erased in his arms. She didn't care if a million terrorists were outside the door, she was in here alone with Cary and he was touching her like she had dreamed for weeks. She wasn't going to stop him anymore or allow him to stop her. She wasn't going to deny herself the pleasure.

Jessica knew she portrayed a sense of power and independence at her job, but the feelings she experienced when pleasing Cary made her realize what absolute power was. She felt like she could command him to do anything for her and he would do it unquestioningly. The other side was, she knew she would do whatever he asked of her. Just as she could make him feel out of control with a kiss or stroke, he did the same to her. And the surprising thing was, she didn't care which one was in control and neither did Cary; they both gained pleasure either way. She wasn't powerless with him; together they were stronger than she could ever be alone.

"Did I hurt you?" Cary asked, concerned.

Jessica grinned and ran a finger along his shining lips. "No, but you can kiss me to make it better."

Cary placed a light kiss on one breast then shot a smile at her as she groaned in pleasure from the feel of his lips on her sensitive skin. "How 'bout there?" He then moved to touch the very tip of his tongue to the other bead-hard nipple. "And here?" Jessica couldn't hear any more of his teasing as his mouth stroked every inch of her body. When his hot tongue dipped into her navel, Jessica's hips roared off the bed of their own volition. She couldn't control her body's reactions anymore as she responded uncontrollably to Cary's caresses.

Jessica felt heaven when his hands began a slow exploration of her body, following his mouth. She loved his hands on her and inside her. Then his mouth traveled pass her stomach and kissed the insides of her thighs. Her legs came farther apart of their own will. She bit her bottom lip in pleasure as she felt the tip of his tongue on the place where her ache for him began. Cary quickly slipped on protection while Jessica closed her eyes, not wanting an ounce of pleasure to escape. As she ran her hands over his smooth back, she could feel the muscles straining under his warm skin and reveled in the strength that was apparent there. Intense waves of heat rolled through her body as his tongue stroked and caressed her. Finally, the heat became unbearable and she screamed his name in ecstasy.

Cary hovered above her with a satisfied smile on his lips. Jessica wanted to return his smile but she could only whisper his name. His hands fully cupped her breasts then ran over her arms and down to link their fingers. Then he flipped her again, and she found herself straddling his hips as he lay on the bed. Jessica's eyes widened at the new position, but he had one breast in his mouth and she lost her train of thought. She couldn't stop her body from writhing, in pleasure and anticipation. She knew after the first time, only hours before, that she should have been prepared for their reaction to each other, but nothing could prepare her for making love with him.

"Please, Cary," she begged in the stillness of the bedroom. She wasn't embarrassed to beg him, not tonight or ever.

"Bring me home, Jess. Make us whole again," he whispered.

Jessica didn't know if he purposely chose those words but she opened herself and brought him into the depths of her body, her soul, and her heart. Jessica didn't really believe in the Fates, but at that moment as they raced each other toward blinding completion, Jessica believed the Fates drew her to Hadley's Inn two weeks ago. They gave her a chance to find her other half and to become whole.

Twenty-one

Jessica woke to the bright rays of sunlight streaming into the room. She stretched like a large contented cat and realized that everything in her life was finally right. Although there had been no words of love spoken last night, Jessica knew there was something between them. Something more than just sex for peace of mind. Even if he didn't love her, she loved him enough to last them both a lifetime. As weak and helpless as that sounded to Jessica, she held on to that for now.

Jessica rolled over to wake Cary and a ball of fear instantly lodged in her throat at the empty sheets. In disbelief, she touched the sheets still warm from his body. Tears fell from her eyes and she flew from the bed, wrapping a blanket around herself. He had already returned to San Francisco.

Jessica ran to the closed bedroom door and swung it open. She almost screamed in surprise when she saw Cary, carrying a tray filled with plates and food, on the other side of the door. He looked surprised to see her out of bed as he walked into the room.

Jessica took several deep breaths and quickly wiped away the tears that had surfaced at the thought of him gone, as he turned his back to set the tray on the table. She forced a smile and tried to smooth down errant strands of hair, as Cary looked at her.

"Where were you going like that?" he asked with a laugh, noticing the blanket she wore. "Are you aware that this place is filled with people?"

Jessica avoided his eyes and stared at the tray. She gasped in surprise at the elaborate breakfast—an omelet, waffles, fresh-squeezed orange juice, and strawberries. Jessica quickly gulped down the orange juice to give her something to do since Cary continued to stare at her.

"How did you arrange this? Hadley and Jake?"

"You were crying," Cary said softly. He took the glass from her hands and set it on the tray. She forced herself to look at him. "What's wrong, Jess? Are you regretting last night?"

"No. Are you?"

"No." Cary continued to watch her and Jessica nervously tucked the blanket tighter around her body. "Are you going to answer me? Why were you crying? Were you trying to run to another room just now so you wouldn't have to face me? Did I ruin your escape route?"

Jessica shook her head in disbelief as she saw the suspicion mixed with pain in his eyes. She instantly took his hands. "No, Cary. I was going to find you. I thought you left and . . ."

"And that made you cry," Cary finished her sentence with a pained expression. "I would never leave you like that, Jess. Don't you know me by now?"

Jessica nodded without meeting his eyes and stared at the breakfast tray again. She couldn't look at him or she knew he would see the love in her eyes and although she embraced her feelings, she didn't know if she wanted him to know just yet.

"I'm starving."

Cary pulled her into his arms and softly kissed her forehead. "I'm starving too." His hands fluttered around the knot of the blanket.

"For food, Cary, for food."

"There's that," he murmured as he nuzzled her neck. Jessica smiled as the unshaven morning growth of beard on his face lightly scratched her soft skin.

"We need nourishment," she tried again.

Cary finally looked at her with a large grin. "Especially after you wore me out last night."

Jessica couldn't prevent the laugh that escaped her throat and she met his teasing gaze. "Did I scare you last night?"

"Did I act scared?"

Jessica's face flushed as she remembered his enthusiastic response. She shook her head and said, "I think I scared myself."

Cary pulled her closer and Jessica could feel the proof against her right thigh that she could never frighten him in bed. "You have my permission to frighten me any time you want."

"I really am hungry." Cary groaned in disappointment, smiling as he arranged the tray on the table in the corner. Jessica sat in one of the chairs and attacked the food on the tray. Cary sat in the other chair and grabbed his own plate. "I guess we have to return to San Francisco at some point," she said, breaking the comfortable silence.

"Unfortunately."

"Do the others know we're here?"

"I haven't called anyone. You had me so crazy with worry last night that I'm surprised I didn't drive off a mountain." Jessica smiled happily and Cary laughed. "Don't look so smug," he warned her, then said seriously, "Do you know how dangerous your disappearing act was? What if Michael Lyons had found you?"

With a serious expression, Jessica set the plate on the tray and moved into his lap. Cary eagerly wrapped his arms around her. "He didn't find me, Cary. I can't worry about him every second of every day and neither can you."

Jessica winced slightly as Cary's arms tightened around her waist. She could tell from the faraway look in his eyes that he had no idea what he was doing. "I never thought I would be able to kill Michael, but if he hurts you, I'll rip his heart out."

Jessica slightly shuddered as she heard the promise in his voice. "I don't want you to kill anyone for me."

Cary smiled at her but she saw the smile didn't quite reach his eyes. "I should probably call Dan and tell him where we are."

"Not yet," Jessica protested as she slowly unbuttoned his shirt. "I don't want reality to intrude yet."

Cary grinned as her hands moved over his chest. He pulled on the knot in the blanket and it fell to her waist in one heap. "Have I told you how beautiful you are?"

"I could always hear it again."

Cary laughed as he placed a kiss on her shoulder. "You're beautiful, Jessica."

Jessica couldn't resist and traced his smiling lips with her fingers. "You should smile more often," she whispered.

"I always do when I'm around you," he said before dulling her senses with a hard kiss that curled her toes.

"Make love to me, Cary," she whispered against his lips.

"I thought you'd never ask," Cary said as his lips settled against hers.

Cary took Jessica's hand as the two walked from David's parked car on the street to her apartment building in San Francisco. Cary could tell from her expression that she dreaded the return to the city, almost as much as he did. Being at Hadley's Inn was like living a different life where there was no Michael Lyons or Group work. Cary liked that world. He didn't want to have to think about safety or regrets, or to question his ability to feel love.

Cary glanced at the van parked across from Jessica's apartment building. Dan stood outside the van, watching him with an angry expression. Cary definitely wasn't looking forward to whatever Dan would have to say about his breach of Group regulations. As soon as Cary found Jessica, he should have contacted the rest of his team and waited in a safe location until reinforcements arrived. Instead, Cary acted like a high school teenager and he didn't regret one second.

"I'll meet you in the apartment," Cary said to Jessica, placing a kiss on her forehead.

"What's wrong?"

"I have some explaining to do."

"I hope I didn't get you in trouble."

Cary smiled at the worry in her voice. He hugged her to him, uncaring that all the agents in the van saw them and probably laughed. "It was worth every second."

Jessica grinned and tugged on his shirt. "Don't take too long. We have to christen the apartment." Before Cary could comment, she walked into the apartment building. Cary grinned after her. If it took the rest of his life, he would never understand how one woman could make him so happy that he forgot years of pain and loneliness.

Cary wiped the smile from his face as he glanced across the street at Dan's stony countenance. Cary crossed the street, trying not to feel embarrassed or ashamed. He was a grown man. He didn't owe Dan or the other agents anything. Cary knew that was a lie. He owed them his life because they protected Jessica.

"Where was she?" Dan asked in a cold voice.

"I should have contacted you."

"Damn straight," Dan retorted angrily. "We spent the past forty-eight hours searching every inch of this dirty city for her. Then when we didn't hear from you, we figured Michael had gotten to you, too. I was on the verge of calling headquarters and requesting a full search-and-rescue team."

"I appreciate the concern, Dan, but I'm fine and Jessica's fine—"

"Do you want our help or not?" Dan interrupted. "If you want to play the Black Lone Ranger, we can pack up all the equipment and head back to Virginia within five minutes. There's no reason for these men to be away from their friends and families, if you're not going to include us in the investigation."

"I apologize, Dan," Cary said in a low, warning tone. He would not apologize again.

Dan finally sighed and raked a hand over his hair. "I guess you and Jessica worked out your problems."

"I guess so," Cary said nonchalantly.

"Is she still planning to attend the Bay Area Professionals Ball this evening?"

"Yes."

"Are you escorting her?"

Cary glanced across the street at the light shining through the windows of Jessica's apartment. The thought that she was in there, waiting for him, made his heart pound against his chest in anticipation. He refrained the urge to run across the street like a lovesick puppy, and focused his attention on Dan, who stared at him expectantly.

"Yes. I'll go over the specifics of security with you later this evening." Cary turned to leave, but Dan cleared his throat. Cary rolled his eyes in frustration and turned to him.

"The ball would be a perfect opportunity for Michael to try something. Maybe she shouldn't attend."

"She's going. I won't allow Michael to take this away from her, too."

"There's nothing I can say to talk you out—"

"I'll see you later tonight, Dan." Cary quickly turned from the man and walked across the street.

In a small corner of his mind he knew Dan was right. Michael could use the ball as a chance to attempt to kidnap Jessica again. It would be like Michael to test his fate at the most public event Jessica would attend. Cary vowed simply to be prepared for whatever situations arose, rather than to make Jessica more frightened than she already was. He wouldn't allow Jessica to leave his sight the entire evening, not that he needed the threat of Michael to stay close to her.

Cary opened the door to Jessica's apartment and froze in the doorway when he saw David, Erin, Jessica, and an older woman, sitting and talking in the living room. When Jessica saw him, she quickly jumped to her feet and moved across the room to grab his hand. Cary knew the older caramel skinned woman was Jessica's mother from the pictures on the mantelpiece. The pictures hadn't done much justice to her. Karin Larson was beautiful with a large smile that made Cary smile back. Her wild black curls radiated from her head in every direction and Cary noticed the brightly colored clothes and the abundance of jewelry she wore. Karin obviously liked bright things and happy colors. Cary couldn't reconcile the sight of Karin with her two straight-laced, conservative children.

Karin stood as she said with a smile, "You must be Cary."

Cary glanced at Jessica, who only shrugged in confusion. Cary crossed the room to shake hands with the older woman. He hadn't met a woman's mother since high school. He didn't know what to say or do. For the first time, Cary wished he had his brother's easy manner with women of all ages, shapes, and sizes.

"It's nice to meet you, Mrs. Larson."

"You're making me feel like my grandmother. Please, call me Karin."

"It's nice to meet you, Karin," he repeated awkwardly.

"Where did you two lovebirds disappear to?" Karin asked. "I decided to surprise Jess at her job. After I took the most frightening taxi ride of my life from the airport to Jessica's office, Erin told me you weren't there."

"Then we called David, who let us into your apartment," Erin concluded.

"Tell us, Jess, Cary," David prodded, his eyes twinkling with amusement. "Where did you two disappear to?"

Cary met Jessica's stricken glance and he almost remained silent in order to watch her squirm. Instead, Cary squeezed her hand and said, "Jess needed to get away. We went to the inn where we first met."

"How romantic." Karin sighed. "Cary, I want to know everything about you. My Jessie never brings home a man for her mother to meet. You must be extremely special to her."

"I didn't bring him home to meet you, Mom," Jessica reminded her in a strained tone.

"Home is wherever we all are," Karin dismissed, with a wave of a heavily jeweled hand. She pinned Cary with a hard gaze that made him realize Karin Larson wasn't as carefree as she wanted her children to believe. The steel glint in her eyes reminded Cary of a mother bear, circling him to protect one of her baby cubs. "Cary, sit right next to me on the couch and tell me about yourself."

"That's our cue to exit," David said, taking Erin's hand. "Both Erin and I have to return to work. Mom, we'll see you for dinner tonight. Have fun, Jess, Cary."

"Thanks, Dave," Jessica muttered, glaring at him.

Erin hugged Jessica and Cary saw her whisper something in Jessica's ear, which made Jessica smile and glance at him. Cary wondered what exactly Erin said. He glanced at Karin Larson and found her staring at him, like a trained Group agent would.

"Where are you from, Cary?" Karin asked politely.

"Originally Arizona, but I live in Virginia now."

"What do you do?"

Cary glanced at Jessica, who turned to them with a panicked expression. He looked back at Karin and answered truthfully, "I work for the government."

"What exactly do you do for the government?" Karin pressed.

"Mom, Cary and I are really tired. We had to rush back here in time for the ball tonight," Jessica interrupted, sitting on the couch next to her mother. "You are coming to the ball with us, aren't you?"

"That was the other reason I came," Karin said excitedly, then briefly hugged Jessica. "I'm so proud of you, Honey."

"It's not that big of a deal, Mom."

"Yes, it is, Jess," Cary blurted out. "You should be very proud of yourself. They pick the top ten promising professionals in the city out of hundreds of referrals. That's a big accomplishment, to stand out enough to be referred for the award, much less to actually win it." Cary almost missed the unreadable look Karin directed toward him.

"Have you been doing research?" Jessica asked, with a small smile at him.

Cary lost all thought of Karin Larson in the room as he met Jessica's soft eyes. Karin abruptly cleared her throat as the silence lengthened in the room. Jessica broke Cary's stare and glanced at her mother. "I'm tired from the long flight. Could you fix me a cup of hot cocoa; then I could take a nap in the bedroom?"

"Of course, Mom." Jessica stood, obviously uneasy about leaving Cary alone with her mother. Cary tried to give her an encouraging smile but even he wasn't certain why Karin obviously wanted to be alone with him. Jessica hesitated for a second longer before walking into the kitchen.

"Now, you were telling me what you did for a living in Virginia," Karin said, with a sweet smile and a firm tone.

"I work for the FBI." Cary gave the legitimate answer that the Group allowed for family members. He didn't find it strange at all that he already thought of Karin Larson as family.

"And why did my daughter run from you?" Karin asked bluntly. "David and Erin tried to hide it from me, but I knew before David did that Jessica took his car."

"We had an argument."

"And you two made up?"

"I hope so."

"And will you be having very many arguments?"

Cary couldn't resist the smile that covered his face as he said, "I hope so."

Karin grinned in return and Cary wondered if he passed whatever test she had prepared for him. "My Jessie is a strong woman. She has a lot of dreams and hopes. I want her to fulfill all of them."

"I do too, Karin."

"I know Jessica and David aren't telling me the complete truth about what's been going on these last few weeks and I don't think I want to know, but I know you'll help her." Karin stood with a bright smile and stretched her arms over her head. "I need my beauty sleep if I'm going to be any company during the ball tonight. You will be joining us, won't you, Cary?"

Cary smiled as he stood. "I wouldn't miss it for the world."

Karin patted his cheek and walked into Jessica's bedroom, closing the door. Jessica walked out of the kitchen with a cup in her hands and stopped in her tracks when she noticed that her mother was not on the couch.

"Where'd she go?" she asked Cary.

Cary wrapped his arms around her waist and led her back into the kitchen. Jessica smiled and set the cup on the counter as he moved her against the wall. She was trapped, but Cary could tell from the bright look in her eyes that the position didn't particularly concern her.

"I have to give her the cocoa before it gets cold," she said, in the breathless voice he loved to hear.

"Your mother wanted cocoa about as much as I wanted to eat breakfast this morning," he murmured, running his tongue along the swirl of her ear. He didn't know how he could possibly feel amorous with her mother in the next room, but he did. He wanted her with a fierceness that he would have understood if they hadn't spent the previous night and morning making love to each other.

"She didn't grill you, did she?" Jessica asked in that same breathless voice that had him reaching for the buttons of her sweater.

"I've suffered through worse," he muttered, bending to kiss each expanse of skin that was revealed with the open sweater.

Jessica tried to push him away from her. "Cary, we can't do this with my mother in the house. What if she comes to the kitchen for a drink of water or she opens the bedroom door—"

"I'll be quiet," Cary promised as his lips brushed across her flat stomach, causing her to inhale sharply. Cary grinned at her response and slowly began to pull up the hem of her skirt until the material was draped around her waist. He saw the passion in her eyes mix with indecision. To help her decide, Cary gently stuck his hand inside her underwear and stroked her center. He closed his own eyes at her first soft tortured sigh.

Cary pressed his lips against hers, stroking the inside of her mouth with his tongue. He would never grow tired of kissing her. He would never grow tired of feeling the shudders of desire race through her body.

"Cary, we shouldn't—" she murmured against his lips.

"We should," he responded.

"I have to find a dress for tonight and I should check my messages at work and . . ." Her voice trailed off as he unbuttoned his own pants. She became silent and her hands battled with his to release the final buttons.

"A few more minutes and then I'll stop." Cary laughed silently as she kissed him. His laughter stopped when one of her cool hands wrapped around his length and he swallowed a loud groan of pleasure. He realized she was right. He shouldn't have started this in the kitchen with her mother in the next room. He started to pull away from her but Jessica grabbed his arms and pulled him back to her.

"Where do you think you're going?" she asked, nipping his ear.

"I shouldn't have—"

"I will kill you myself if you try to walk out of here," she fiercely whispered, then she plunged her tongue into his mouth.

Her blatant possession made Cary moan and enter her with a delicious ease that had them both biting their lower lips to withhold their screams of passion. Cary stared into her eyes as their bodies matched rhythm in the time-old dance. His love for her was on the tip of his tongue but then she unbuttoned his shirt and licked both his nipples and Cary was lost in his own world of passion, desire, and love. A world where only Jessica could take him.

Twenty-two

Jessica felt slightly guilty for not going back to work when she and Cary returned to San Francisco, but she wanted to find a dress for the ball that evening. Once Cary finally left the apartment that afternoon after making her practically bite a hole in her lip from not screaming at the pleasure he gave her, she had gone through the dresses in her closet at home. Immediately, she rejected the conservative, ankle-length blue dress she'd originally bought for the ball. She wanted a dress that was sexy, and alluring, and that would drive Cary crazy. She wanted a dress that the normal Jessica Larson would never wear. Unfortunately, it was hard to shop for that dress with her mother.

Jessica and her mother had been in the majority of the stores in Union Square, the major shopping district in San Francisco, before Karin pleaded weariness and sat at a café to wait for Jessica. She walked into one of the major department stores and grinned to herself when she saw a short, form-clinging maroon dress on a mannequin in the formal dress department. She rubbed the sheer material between her fingers, then forced herself to look at the price. Jessica inwardly flinched. The dress was expensive, beyond what she was prepared to spend, but then she imagined Cary's surprised expression when he saw her in it, and she went to find the dress on the rack.

"I think it's store policy to approve all purchases with Cary Riley," came Cary's deep voice in her left ear.

Jessica turned around and threw her arms around his neck. He seemed like a woman's every fantasy, surrounded by the feminine ballroom dresses. Jessica felt slightly embarrassed by her exuberant greeting, but couldn't control the surprised grin that followed.

"What are you doing here?" she asked, barely giving him room to breathe.

He actually seemed to blush. "I called the agent assigned to watch you, and he said you were here."

Jessica glanced around the store, seeing several other customers milling around the dresses. "Agent Morris follows me everywhere?"

Cary turned her shoulders to look toward the bottom floor, visible through the glass railing, and pointed to Tyler Morris, who watched them from the men's shoe section on the bottom floor. Cary waved and the man nodded in acknowledgment. "He's like a two-hundred-thirty-pound shadow," Cary told her.

Jessica didn't want to think about why Agent Morris had to follow her and instead busied herself by straightening the slightly askew tie Cary wore with a navy blue suit. "I'm glad you're here. We can go around the corner to the tuxedo rental place."

Cary rolled his eyes and groaned. "Suddenly this doesn't seem like a good idea."

Jessica laughed, then placed the maroon dress against her body and was satisfied when Cary's eyes narrowed with desire. She could already feel his hands running over her body and his soft kisses on the inside of her knee. "What do you think?" she asked innocently.

"I think if you wear that dress, I'll have more trouble than I do now keeping my hands off of you," Cary said as he pulled her close.

"My mother is here," Jessica said softly.

"Outside the store. I saw her on my way inside."

"I want to spend the day with you," she said, surprising herself with her honesty.

Cary grinned and rewarded her with a long, thorough kiss that had her crushing the dress between them. "I want to spend the day with you, too. You and your mother."

"Mom's going to have to take a taxi home." Without any notion of others in the store, Jessica leaned into him for a kiss.

As Agent Tyler Morris milled around the shoes, Dan and Michael Lyons, from their position in the men's clothing department, watched the couple kiss. The two could see the back of Jessica's head and Cary's hands roam over her back.

"That's sickening," Michael spat out angrily. "That pig doesn't deserve that woman." He was more jealous that Cary Riley could have a normal life with a beautiful woman who loved him than for any of the past wrongs he attributed to Cary.

Dan shrugged, then forced Michael to turn away from the couple and look at him. "The charity ball is tonight and I've arranged for you to enter as a waiter with the hotel."

"I can't wait to erase his traitorous face off the earth."

"Don't screw this up, Michael. My ass is on the line."

"I don't screw up," Michael said loudly, causing a woman holding a shirt to her husband's back to look at him. Michael smiled apologetically then turned back to Dan with a vicious scowl. "Just keep your end of the bargain. You bring Riley to me and I get to kill him."

"What about the woman?"

Michael studied Dan's excited expression. Dan was obviously anticipating the death of Cary Riley. "What about her? Do you have plans for her?"

"I could," Dan answered quickly then looked back at

the couple still kissing on the floor above them. "She's very beautiful."

Michael grabbed Dan's shirtfront, causing Dan to look at him with wide eyes. "I am warning you to stay out of this. Jessica Larson has one purpose: to bring Riley to me. Otherwise she remains unharmed." Michael abruptly released his shirt and Dan stumbled to his feet.

Dan's eyes glimmered with anger but he nodded and quickly walked away. Michael shook his head and turned back to the happy couple.

Cary leaned against the wooden railing of the pier and watched the dark gray ocean waves crash against the beams beneath him. The sharp, cold breeze from the bay awakened him to his behavior over the past few hours. He had been acting like a lovesick puppy as he and Jessica explored the city. He followed her wherever she went, oblivious to the sights she pointed to or the other tourists who milled around them. He couldn't keep his hands off her and had embarrassed her several times with a surprise kiss in the middle of the streets.

Cary vowed to control himself from this point forward, which he could do with Jessica nowhere near him. She stood a few feet away at a café window to buy a bread bowl of clam chowder, but Cary knew as soon as she returned any promise or vow to himself would be destroyed. Not only was he scaring them both with his intense emotions, he was also making them an easy target for Michael Lyons. Several times that day, Cary bumped into people he hadn't seen because he was too busy watching Jessica.

Cary rubbed a hand across his eyes as Jessica walked toward him. He took one look at her bright smile and his entire pep talk floated off the pier with the breeze. He swept her windblown hair from her eyes and tucked

it behind her ears. "You have to taste this, Cary, it's delicious," she said, offering him the bread bowl.

He wanted to tell her she was the most delicious thing
he ever tasted and he didn't have an appetite for anything
else, but instead, he asked, "Are you cold?"

Jessica shook her head, smiling. "No. I love this place—"
She turned abruptly as the loud wails of a young boy caught
her attention. Cary had spotted the child wandering
around the pier earlier, obviously searching for the adult
that brought him to the pier. With a crop of black curls,
brown eyes, and chocolate brown skin, the little boy looked
the picture of six-year-old innocence and Jessica was apparently touched. With concern written across her face, she
started immediately for the boy. Cary grabbed her arm, his
other hand touching the holstered gun underneath his
jacket.

Jessica turned to him, surprise in her eyes. "What's
wrong?"

"It may be a trap," Cary said silently, keeping his face
impassive.

To his surprise, Jessica yanked her arm from his grip
with a look of disbelief on her face. "That child is scared,
Cary. I'm going to help him." She walked to the little
boy and squatted to his height, softly speaking words of
comfort. The boy's cries became soft sniffles as he looked
trustingly into Jessica's eyes. Cary couldn't blame the little
boy; Jessica soothed him, too. She made him feel safe.
Cary reluctantly walked over to join them.

Jessica looked at Cary and the anger in her eyes almost
made him turn and walk away. He'd never had to answer
questions or explain himself before he met her. He didn't
know if he wanted the responsibility or the worries that
came with her expectations. But, as the sun slowly descended into the horizon and the medley of colors from
the sun's rays played against her hair, Cary knew he

wanted to try. He kneeled beside her and stared at the little boy.

"Eric, this is Cary, my friend," Jessica said to the small child.

Cary stuck his hand out awkwardly as Eric stepped even closer to Jessica. Eric looked at Jessica for confirmation, then hesitantly placed his hand in Cary's. Jessica felt tears well in her eyes as Eric's small hand disappeared into Cary's much larger one. "Is your mommy lost?" Cary asked with a gentle smile that Jessica had never seen.

Eric nodded with big eyes at Cary's question. "Mommies have a way of doing that sometimes," Cary said sympathetically. Eric apparently had begun to trust him, because he no longer stood as close to Jessica. "I bet she was walking right behind you, then you turned around and she got lost, somehow."

"Yeah," Eric agreed.

"I bet your mommy is looking all over for you right now. To make things easy on her, you and Jessica stay right here while I buy us some ice cream to make the time go faster. How does that sound?"

Jessica stood as Cary looked to her for approval. If she hadn't been certain of her love for him before that moment, she was now. Since he could usually read every expression on her face, she didn't want him to see the love and the future she wanted from him. She loved children and wanted several of her own, and she now knew Cary would make a perfect father, whether he thought he would or not.

"I like chocolate," Eric said, his tears forgotten. Then he added, "Your name's Cary. Isn't that a girl's name?" He looked at Jessica for support.

Jessica laughed as Cary looked up at her, rolling his eyes in amusement. "That's exactly what I said when I first met him," she told Eric.

Cary stood, just as a woman ran to Eric, with frantic

tears in her eyes. Jessica watched with a smile as she scooped Eric in her arms. His thin arms eagerly tightened around her neck. Jessica marveled at the resemblance between the mother and son, the same nose and similar shaped eyes. She wondered if her children would closely resemble her or look more like Cary. Her heart turned at the idea of holding a little boy with the same brown eyes as Cary's. She erased thoughts of children with Cary from her head; he had never mentioned a future with her. Even though their relationship had changed since last night, there were still no promises or obligations. As soon as Michael Lyons was gone, Jessica knew Cary would be gone, too.

"Eric! Are you okay?" Eric's mother asked, setting him back on the ground. Eric nodded excitedly as she wiped her wet eyes. "I'm glad you're fine, honey, but mommy is very upset with you. I told you about wandering away from me."

"I'm sorry, Mommy," Eric said without any trace of remorse. He pointed at Cary. "He promised to buy me an ice cream while we waited for you."

Eric's mother looked at Cary and Jessica with relief in her eyes. "I can't thank you both enough for watching him. But, I don't think Eric deserves an ice cream for disobedience."

"I promised," Cary said with an apologetic shrug.

"Please, Mommy," Eric begged, practically on his two, bony knees.

The beleaguered woman looked to Jessica for support and Jessica pointedly looked at the sky. "Okay, but one scoop. Thank you both once more."

Cary touched her arm and Jessica looked at him, trying to mask her deep feelings at that second. She forced a smile for his sake, then tousled Eric's hair. "Do you want ice cream?" Cary asked.

Jessica shook her head and indicated the bread bowl,

dripping with clam chowder, in her hand. "No. I'll sit over there and wait for you." She quickly walked toward a bench and sat. She closed her eyes and tried to rein in the emotions treading through her stomach like a hurricane. She had truthfully only known this man a few days and she was ready to pledge her undying love to him. Jessica wanted to laugh at herself, but the thought of loving a man who didn't love her wasn't funny.

A few minutes later, Cary joined her on the bench. They sat in heavy silence as she finished eating the chowder, without offering him any. Jessica didn't trust herself to speak at that moment. She stole several glances at his gorgeous profile as he stared at the raging bay water. She envied the wind for moving through his hair with ease, while she didn't know if he would want her to touch him.

"I finished all the chowder." She broke the silence in an overly cheerful voice. "Do you want me to get more?"

Cary wordlessly took the bread bowl from her hands and threw it in the nearby trash can. "I can't apologize for what I originally said about that little boy," he said in a flat voice. Cary looked at her for her reaction and wasn't surprised when she shook her head in confusion.

"I'm not asking for any apologies, I just want to understand."

Cary stared into her beautiful brown eyes and wanted to touch her, but he balled his hands into fists in his lap. Once she heard what he wanted to say, he wondered if she would want him anywhere near her. That thought alone made him almost drop the subject, but he wanted her to know who he really was.

"I've heard stories about children carrying explosives for terrorists or assassins. A child offers no threat, adults implicitly trust children, and terrorists use that. A Group agent was killed in that manner. In the middle of England, a little boy was crying, pretending to be lost. The agent went over to comfort him, like you just did, and the little boy placed a bomb in her purse and ran away. They say she never even knew what hit her."

Cary ignored Jessica's horrified gasp and stared at the disappearing sun. "I can't afford to offer comfort to little kids or be the generic friendly stranger. I have to be very careful. That's the kind of world I live in, Jessica, where little kids can be just as evil and deadly as adults. I'm not supposed to trust anyone or care about anyone. Maybe I needed that barrier between other people and myself after my parents' death, or maybe that's who I am, but it's too late for me to change. That's how I am and how I'll be for the rest of my life."

Cary was surprised when Jessica placed her arms around his neck and squeezed, almost painfully. He couldn't resist wrapping his arms around her and burying his face into her hair. She pulled away, but Cary kept his arms around her waist. Pain and sorrow were written across her face and Cary wondered if she would tell him that he disgusted her.

"I'm sorry you have to be in a world like that," she whispered, placing her hands on either side of his face. Cary drew strength from the contact and ran a finger across her soft lips. "But, you can't go through life like that, Cary. You can't live the rest of your life never trusting anyone, never loving anyone. Maybe other people can, and we all probably need them to protect us, but that's not who you are."

"How can you care about me, Jess?" Cary asked, shaking his head. "I've done nothing to be worthy of your trust. I've hurt you."

"You hurt me, but not for the reasons you think. All that matters is that whenever I need you most, you're there," she said softly.

"Is that all it takes for you?"

Jessica brought their entwined hands to her mouth and

placed a kiss on his. "Yes," she finally said, with a small smile. "What will it take for you to trust me?"

Cary caressed her right cheek for a second, then stood from the bench, ignoring her last question. She had seen in a few weeks what had taken Cary five years to discover; that he couldn't be a Group agent without sacrificing a part of himself. A part of himself that longed for love and family, a part of himself that he tried to bury after his parents' death, but that he could no longer ignore.

Cary pointedly looked at his watch as Jessica continued to watch him. "We should head back to your place. The ball will start in a few hours and we don't want to be late."

Jessica appeared to hesitate, then stood and took his hand. His fingers automatically entwined with hers and they walked home.

Twenty-three

"You look gorgeous, Jess," Karin complimented as the two women stood in Jessica's bedroom, preparing for the ball. "Cary isn't going to know what to do with himself when he sees you."

Jessica turned to her mother with a huge smile. She smoothed down the front of the expensive dress and glanced at the mirror one last time. "Do you think I should wear my hair up or—"

"Stop fussing, Jessica."

"I can't help it, Mom. I want to look beautiful tonight."

"You do."

Jessica studied her reflection and the sexy dress. She almost didn't have the nerve to leave her bedroom with the dress on, or with what little the dress hid of her body, but she also wanted to see Cary's expression. She wanted to see the desire and passion. She also prayed that maybe she would even see a hint of love.

"Are you sure I should wear these shoes?" Jessica asked uncertainly. She was surprised when her mother placed a hand on Jessica's chin and forced her to look at her. Jessica blushed when she saw the amusement in her mother's eyes.

"You could wear a trash bag and Cary would think you were the most beautiful woman in the world."

"I seriously doubt that, Mom."

"I don't."

"He's had such a hard life these last few years. I want to wipe away all those painful memories and make him smile again." Jessica flushed slightly and laughed nervously. "I must sound like a love-struck teenager."

"He does smile when he's around you." Karin caressed Jessica's cheek and whirled around, modeling the ankle-length black dress that flattered her trim figure. "How do I look for a mother of one of the award recipients?"

"Beautiful," Jessica said truthfully. She hugged her mother because she knew Karin, who normally would have worn a bright pink and orange outfit with a sun hat, had purposely chosen the more sedate dress to blend in for Jessica's sake.

Karin grinned proudly, turning to the mirror to finish applying lipstick. "Where does Cary run off to every few hours? I thought he was on vacation."

"He has friends in the area," Jessica said, carefully.

"And he has to talk to them twenty minutes before we're supposed to leave for the ball?" Karin asked, confused.

Jessica knew Cary went across the street to talk to the other agents to make certain security would be flawless tonight. She wanted to tell her mother that, but that would entail telling her mother about the attack in the park and Michael Lyons. Jessica didn't want anything to ruin this night, especially her mother worrying about her.

The brief knock on the bedroom door saved Jessica from answering. "Come in," she called eagerly.

Cary opened the door and whatever he was about to say froze on his lips as he stared at her, completely awestruck. Jessica decided at that moment the dress was worth every penny. He continued to stare at her, from head to toe, completely speechless. Jessica had never felt so beautiful in her entire life. She met his burning eyes and suddenly felt shy. She stared at her shoes, while her mother laughed silently at the both of them.

"You look very handsome, Cary," Karin said to break the silence in the room. She crossed the room to straighten the black bow tie of his tuxedo. Jessica never thought her mother was prone to understatement, but Karin definitely missed in her description of Cary. He looked more than handsome. In the perfectly fitted black tuxedo, he looked like a walking poster for a clothes advertisement. Jessica had never considered the allure of a tuxedo on a man until that very moment when Cary stood in her bedroom, wearing one. His comfort in the tuxedo made him look exactly like the mysterious, dangerous man he was.

"Thank you, Karin. You both look breathtaking," he recovered quickly.

Karin rolled her eyes in amusement. "I may be old, but I'm not senile. You weren't looking at me a few seconds ago when you were trying to breathe." Jessica wanted to drag Cary to her bed and kick her mother out of the room when she saw his cheeks flush slightly at her mother's words.

Cary cleared his throat nervously and said, "I saw David and Erin driving around the neighborhood for a parking place. They should be here in a few minutes." As if on cue, the doorbell rang.

"I'll answer that," Karin said to no one in particular, since Cary and Jessica only stared at each other. Karin shook her head and left the room. Cary softly closed the door behind her, and Jessica felt the rhythm of her heart increase as he turned to look at her.

She didn't protest when he crossed the room and pulled her into his arms. Without a word, their lips and tongues met in a contest for passion and love. Jessica wrapped her arms around his neck and tried to pull him even closer into her. His hands moved down her back, bared by the dress, and she inhaled sharply.

"We don't have to go tonight," Jessica murmured when he pulled away from her. He smiled slightly and nipped her bottom lip. She ran her hands over the line of his broad shoulders encased by the black jacket. "I could tell my mother I'm sick and we could send her with David and Erin. We could stay here and . . ." Her voice trailed off as he nibbled her ear, sending delicious shivers through her body with the feel of his hot, moist tongue.

"And what?" Cary prodded gently.

"Jess, come out here, I want to see your dress." Erin's voice floated from the living room.

"You two aren't supposed to be alone anyway," David yelled after Erin. Jessica rolled her eyes and rested her forehead against Cary's chest as he laughed.

"I don't think we have a choice about going tonight," Cary said, shaking his head. "David would drag you to the ball. Plus, I want to see you walk onstage and receive the award so I can take the picture. I even bought one of those disposable cameras from the grocery store."

"You didn't," Jessica pleaded.

"Face it, Jess. You're going to be embarrassed tonight."

Jessica groaned, then couldn't hide her smile any longer as she kissed his lips. "As long as you're with me, I can handle anything," she said, before he captured her lips in one, last hungry kiss.

Cary and Jessica, followed by her mother, David, and Erin, walked into the glittering ballroom of the large hotel in the heart of downtown San Francisco. A large band onstage played soft music, while a dance floor contained a throng of couples, spinning around the floor. Women, in flowing dresses, sauntered around the room, accompanied by men in crisp black tuxedos. The smell of expensive cologne and perfume mingled with money, to give the room a vibrant feel that made Jessica smile.

"Everything looks so beautiful." Karin sighed, glancing around the room.

"There are a lot of handsome, older men here, Karin," Erin said with a grin.

"Why are you telling Mom that?" David asked blankly.

Erin rolled her eyes in exasperation and said, "Maybe your mother would like to meet a nice man to dance with—"

"That's enough," David interrupted, shaking his head. "Mom's not interested in any men."

"She's a woman, David. Of course, she's interested in men."

Jessica noticed with a laugh that while David and Erin argued, her mother was being led onto the dance floor by a smiling older man. Cary grinned with her then looked at David and Erin.

"I don't think you two have to worry about Karin," Cary interrupted their bickering. They both glared at him then noticed Karin on the dance floor, amid the throng of dancing couples.

"I told you," Erin said with a smug smile.

"He dragged her out there," David protested.

Jessica sighed in exasperation and grabbed Cary's hand, leading him farther into the ballroom. Cary laughed as he walked beside her.

"How did you tolerate them for two years?" Cary asked, shaking his head.

"I have no idea." Jessica waved to several business acquaintances across the ballroom and squeezed his hand. "Would you like to meet some of my colleagues?"

"Anything you want to do, Jess," Cary said gently. He placed a kiss on the tip of her nose then smiled. Jessica didn't think she could ever love him more than at that moment. "Are you ready?" he asked uncertainly, as she continued to stare at him.

Jessica shook herself from her trance and nodded with a smile. For the next hour, she introduced Cary to various acquaintances and friends around the room. After watching Cary charm every person he came into contact with, Jessica no longer gawked at his ability to connect with anyone on any given subject. From the mail clerks at her company to board members, from man to woman, Cary left each person with a smile and a congratulatory look at Jessica.

Then Jessica realized as Cary talked to Peter Jannings, that she was seeing a different side of him. He was relaxed and comfortable. He didn't look over his shoulder every five minutes, as if expecting a man with a gun to burst into the room. He didn't have the usual fierce expression on his face. There were no frown lines around his mouth and no dark gleam in his eyes. He looked happy. Jessica hoped and prayed that she was a small part of the change in him. She wanted him to be happy and free from worry. She wanted him to laugh and smile.

The two finally broke from the crowd and hid behind several large plants in the corner of the room.

"Exciting crowd," Cary noted dryly.

Jessica laughed and slipped her hand into his, which he squeezed. That assurance from him made her knees weaken. Independent, self-assured Jessica Larson was melting because of a tall, perfect man in a tuxedo. Cary Riley was far from perfect, she knew, but he was all hers.

"I thought you were having the time of your life to hear you talk to everyone."

"They don't call Group agents chameleons for nothing," Cary said, adding, "Your boss and coworkers seem to have a very high opinion of you."

"They were just being nice in front of you," she said, dismissing his compliment.

"Why do you do that?" Cary asked, seriously. "Why do you brush aside your accomplishments and skills? You're an intelligent woman and your boss and coworkers recognize that. You should be proud of that. I am."

Jessica felt her eyes water then forced a smile to lighten his serious mood. "Let's dance."

Cary shook his head with a twinkle in his eyes. "I can't dance. It's against Group policy, something about distracting and—"

Jessica ignored his protests and pulled him onto the dance floor. Cary gathered her into his arms and moved to the slow tempo of the band's music. Jessica closed her eyes and leaned against his shoulder, inhaling his familiar cologne, which beckoned to her with sensual promises of later that night.

Cary discreetly smelled her hair, tightening his hold on her. No matter how long he lived, he would never forget her smell. It wasn't her citrus shampoo or her tantalizing perfume; it was her. Cary tried to restrain himself but his hands had a mind of their own and began to explore her velvety back, bare in the dress. Jessica looked like his every secret fantasy in the impossibly tight dress. Cary wanted to snarl at all the men who dared to look at her. Then halfway into the hotel, Cary realized Jessica was only looking at him and he stopped caring who else noticed her.

"You had nothing to worry about. You dance well," she said, breaking the silence between them.

Cary traced the line of her spine down her back and smiled when she shivered slightly. "I think I just do everything naturally well," he teased. Jessica laughed loudly, causing several people to glance their way. Cary usually would have turned his face to avoid attention, but with Jessica his only reaction was to laugh. With Jessica, he sang in the park.

"Did I ever mention how modest you are?" Jessica asked, giving him a dry look. Cary pulled her back into his arms and placed a hard kiss on her lips, then met her surprised eyes. She grinned suddenly and Cary drew her into his arms, melding her body into his. He couldn't resist her any longer. The dress, her smell, her shining eyes all combined to drive him completely out of his mind with lust and need. And love.

Cary attacked her mouth with his teeth, his lips and his tongue. He nipped her bottom lip, then lightly soothed by running his tongue across it. He drew her bottom lip into his mouth and suckled and comforted, while his hands had a mind of their own, massaging her bare back. He was in love with her and he tried to show her through this kiss in the middle of the ballroom. In the back of his mind, Cary knew he shouldn't be kissing her like this in such a public place, inviting attention, but he didn't care. He would probably have her on her back in the middle of the dance floor if he wasn't careful.

Cary finally released her and couldn't resist placing another quick kiss on her lips, loving the dazed expression on her face. She was as stunned by him as he was by her. He loved her. The thought resonated in his head as they stood among the throng, her confused eyes still glued to his.

Cary grinned and grabbed her hands. He probably didn't deserve her but he definitely wanted to take the time to find out. He wanted finally to tell her his true feelings, but not in the middle of a hotel ballroom filled with people. He wanted to tell her as he undressed her and could visibly demonstrate his love.

"How much longer until they present your award?" he pleaded. "I want to go home and make love to you until we both can't move any more and it's all your fault, because of that damn dress."

Jessica laughed, feeling unreasonably happy. He kissed her senseless, made her feel like she was a blazing, free star in the sky, and then blamed her. She could barely remember the names of her various acquaintances surrounding her; she certainly didn't want to stay at the ball when he promised her another blissful night in his arms. She needed to tell him how deep her feelings ran before anything more happened between them. She vowed to herself she would tell him she loved him before the night was over.

"We could leave now," she said softly.

"What are you two whispering about?" Logan stood next to Cary. Jessica grinned at him while Cary only groaned and tried to pull her closer. She moved from his grip and hugged Logan.

"You're easily the most attractive woman in here, Jess," Logan complimented, glancing at his brother before he added, "Of course, I'm the most attractive man in here."

"Shouldn't you be outside, patrolling the hotel?" Cary muttered, although Jessica could see the laughter in his eyes.

"Are you here on business?" Jessica asked, curiously.

"We're trying to show Cary's spy company how things are supposed to be done," Logan said, nonchalantly. Jessica laughed while Cary shook his head.

"Well, I'm glad you're here," Jessica said, grinning.

"Save me a dance, Jess, and we'll show these people how to really do it," Logan said, then shrugged at Cary's suddenly stern expression. "I can't help it if your woman finds me irresistible."

"Excuse me," came a male voice. The three turned to see one of the Group agents, Dan Pelstrom. Jessica could feel Cary instantly tense and his hand moved from hers.

"Is something wrong?" Cary asked Dan.

"The chairperson is gathering all the award recipients and I wanted to personally escort Ms. Larson myself."

"I'll take her—"

Dan interrupted Cary in a quiet voice, "They spotted Michael in the area."

Jessica's heart squeezed with fear and she glanced at Cary, who's expression remained carefully neutral.

"Where?" Cary demanded.

"In an underground parking garage in the area. They lost him, but he's nearby. You know him better than anyone. You should lead the search."

"Cary, stay with me," Jessica whispered, ignoring Dan. "Someone else can look for Michael."

"I'll go, Cary. You stay with Jess," Logan said, quickly.

"You stay with Jessica," Cary said to his brother, then he met her eyes and she knew he would leave. She tried not to plead and grab his jacket. "I'll only be a few minutes; I don't want to miss you receiving the award. I didn't buy that camera for nothing." He slowly brought her hand to his lips and placed a soft kiss on the palm. Her palm burned from the brief contact with his soft lips, as the electricity traveled throughout her body. Even a simple kiss from him on the palm of her hand made her shiver.

Jessica watched him weave smoothly through the crowd and bit her bottom lip to refrain from running after him. She didn't care about any stupid award. Jessica smiled at her own thinking. It was true. She didn't care about the award or her colleagues' opinions. She wanted to be with Cary.

Jessica started after him but Dan grabbed her arm. She turned to him and tried to return his friendly smile.

"Cary would be very upset if he thought he caused you to miss your award," Dan said, with a firm smile.

Jessica hesitated then glanced at Logan, who nodded in agreement. She nodded in resignation. "Where am I supposed to go?"

"Follow me." Dan led her through the crowd and up the stairs toward the second-floor hotel terrace. Since the majority of the guests stood in the lobby on the main floor or in the ballroom, the farther they walked from the ballroom, the more quiet and deserted the hotel became. Soon Jessica, Dan, and Logan were the only people in the hallway.

"Why would they have you all meet back here in the dark?" Logan asked, glancing around the hallway.

"I don't know," Jessica answered.

"Are you certain this is the meeting point, Agent Pelstrom?" Logan asked.

"I was definitely told to bring Jessica to the second-floor terrace," Dan said, nodding.

The three stopped in front of the closed glass doors of the enclosed terrace. Jessica didn't see anyone inside the dimly lit terrace and briefly met Logan's worried eyes. He smiled for her and squeezed her arm but Jessica was confused. She didn't have time to question him since Agent Tyler Morris ran toward them.

"Dan, where are you going?" Tyler asked. "The award recipients are meeting in the front of the ballroom."

"Are they?" Dan asked, then he shook his head, laughing. "Maybe I'm too old for this spy stuff, huh?" Jessica didn't miss Logan roll his eyes in annoyance. She discreetly jabbed him in the stomach.

Tyler smiled shyly at Jessica and she flushed when she remembered their first encounter. "Good evening, Ms. Larson. You look very beautiful."

"I did want to apologize to you about the other day," Jessica said haltingly. "I didn't know who you were or I never would have—"

Tyler shook his head quickly and glanced nervously at Dan. "It's really all right, Ms. Larson." He motioned toward the closed doors of the ballroom. "We should return to the ballroom before we miss the festivities."

Jessica smiled and turned toward the ballroom when she saw a movement from the corner of her eye. She whirled around in time to see Dan pound his fist onto the back of Tyler's head. Tyler crumpled to the floor, unconscious.

Logan whirled around toward Dan, reaching for the gun inside his coat at the same time. In a whirl of movement, Dan knocked the gun from Logan's hand then kicked him in the face. Logan fell to the floor, with blood flowing from the side of his mouth. Dan pulled a gun from his coat and pointed it at Logan. Without thinking, Jessica screamed Logan's name and pushed Dan's arms toward the ceiling, just as he fired the gun. Logan scrambled to his feet and dove behind a large table as Dan's missed shot lodged in the ceiling.

Dan grabbed her arm and twisted it behind her back. She gritted her teeth and struggled against him, but he only pulled her arm harder, making her scream in pain. Dan pulled her against his body and sticking the gun under her chin.

"Don't give me an excuse, Riley," Dan called to Logan.

"You'll never get out of here, Pelstrom," Logan called, from behind the safety of the table.

Dan smiled and said, "Watch me."

Jessica screamed as Michael came to stand behind Logan and the table. He brought his fist on the back of Logan's head and Logan fell from behind the table, unconscious.

Jessica squeezed the tears back as Dan flung open the glass door of the terrace. He dragged her into the dark room and Michael followed, closing the door behind him and blocking the light from the hallway that would have lit the dark room. Jessica stared at Michael Lyons, unable to take her eyes off him. He was her living nightmare, her bogeyman. She tried to prevent the panic that threatened to consume her, but her body began to tremble.

Michael walked toward her and Jessica forced herself to act. She bit down on Dan's hand, which was covering her mouth. He cursed and abruptly released her. Jessica pushed Dan, with all her strength, and he tumbled into Michael. She ran to the door, screaming Cary's name. Michael pushed Dan to the floor and, with incredible speed, jumped in between her and the door, with a gun pointed directly at her head. She stopped in her tracks and met his crazed eyes.

"I see you remember me." His thick accent confirmed her worst fears. Jessica barely nodded as Dan suddenly grabbed her arm again and raised his arm to strike her. Jessica flinched and prepared herself for the blow. "Hit her and I'll shoot you," Michael warned calmly.

Dan muttered a curse but pushed her away from him. "She broke the skin on my hand," Dan said angrily. "How am I going to explain this to Riley and the others?"

Michael ignored Dan and turned to Jessica. "I don't want to hurt you, Jessica. Do as I say and you'll have a nice, exciting tale for all your friends and family. I'm after your boyfriend, not you."

Thick terror settled in her throat as she thought of Michael harming Cary. "Leave him alone," she whispered hoarsely, surprised her voice sounded strong when her entire body trembled with fear.

"Don't waste your breath on him. He wouldn't think twice about blowing your brains out if you got in the way of his job. That's what he does, Jessica Larson. He uses people, he lies, and he deceives."

"You don't know what you're talking about—"

"Cary has you believing he's one of the wonderful defenders of American democracy, but he's not. He's no different than me, Jessica. We both have goals and we'll do whatever is necessary to meet them. If you compare us, Cary may be even worse than me. At least, I'm a known murderer. I'm known for doing what I must for my beliefs, but men like Cary Riley, they slip into your head and you never know what hit you."

Jessica shook her head, her anger overruling her fear. "Cary is nothing like you."

"You can argue about this later, Michael," Dan said frantically. "You have to get away from here before Tyler and Logan wake up and bring the entire Group to this room. Maybe I should kill them both."

"No," Jessica protested hoarsely.

"We have to give you a legitimate excuse for being in here," Michael said in a strange tone. Before Dan could respond, Michael rammed his fist into Dan's face. Dan fell to the floor unconscious, blood flowing from his nose. Jessica noticed the small smile on Michael's face as he stared at Dan on the floor. "I've been waiting to do that for a long time." His smile disappeared and he turned to Jessica. "Let's go."

Jessica stared at the gun in his hands then walked out the door.

Twenty-four

Cary searched the numerous faces of the ballroom for Jessica or his brother. Panic slowly replaced the confusion when he noticed the nine other award recipients standing at the front of the ballroom, preparing to walk onstage. Jessica was not in the ballroom. Cary finally saw David and Erin, dancing in each other's arms on the dance floor, oblivious to anyone or anything around them.

Cary grabbed David's arm and David stared at him surprised, as if he just realized there were other people in the room. David frowned when he looked at Cary.

"What's wrong?" David asked.

"Have either of you seen Jessica?" Cary asked, trying to keep the frantic tone from his voice.

"No," Erin said, shaking her head. "It's almost time for the awards presentation. Where could she be?"

David stared at Cary and Cary knew they both thought the same thing: Michael Lyons. Karin joined the group, as the host of the ball stepped onto the stage and the band stopped playing. People in the room stopped dancing and talking, and streamed around Cary and the others, toward the podium.

"Where's Jessica?" Karin asked worriedly. "She's going to miss her award."

Cary pulled the earpiece that connected him to the other Group agents, from the collar of his shirt and stuck it in his ear. He ignored the wide eyes of Erin and Karin when he also pulled his shirt lapel to his mouth, where he attached the transistor that he needed in order to communicate.

"This is Agent Riley. Can you give me a location on Jessica Larson, Agent Pelstrom, or San Francisco Inspector Riley?" Cary said quietly into the transistor.

"That's a negative, Agent Riley," came the reply in his ear piece.

"Any last known locations?" Cary asked, as fear seized his heart.

"Inspector Riley reported a previous location near the hotel terrace on the second floor. Is there a problem, Agent Riley?"

"Maybe." Cary glanced at David, then at the confused expressions on the two women's faces. "I'm going to check something out."

"I'll come with you," David said quickly.

"You stay here with your mother and Erin," Cary said firmly. He didn't wait for David's response as he ran from the ballroom toward the second floor.

Cary knew he aged ten years when he saw the unmoving lump at the end of the hallway. He quickened his pace and slid across the carpet to Tyler. Cary felt the side of Tyler's neck for a pulse and released the breath he hadn't known he'd held when he felt the strong, steady rhythm. Cary used the radio to call for reinforcements, then shook Tyler's shoulders.

Tyler moaned in pain as his eyes fluttered open. He winced and placed a hand on the back of his head. "What happened?"

"Where's Jessica?"

"I don't know. Dan, Logan, and I were about to lead Jessica back to the ballroom when I was hit from behind," Tyler whispered, rubbing his head.

Cary glanced around the empty hallway. "Where are an and my brother?"

"I don't know. Maybe they woke up before me . . . Mi-hael did this, didn't he?" Tyler briefly met Cary's eyes, s he muttered, "Cary, I'm sorry. I shouldn't have turned y back."

"Nothing's going to happen to her for you to be sorry out," Cary said firmly. "Don't move. Paramedics are n the way. I'm going to check inside the terrace." Cary n inside the terrace and heard a moan of pain. He unded a corner of trees and saw Dan, laying on the oor, holding a white handkerchief to his profusely bleed-g nose.

"Where's Jessica?" Cary asked immediately, running to s side.

"I don't know, Cary," Dan said, as he struggled to and. Cary stood with him. "Somehow, Michael got into e hotel. He has her."

Cary's heart momentarily stopped and he staggered to nearby bench to regain his breath. He took several deep reaths to clear his head. He needed to think clearly. He uldn't. All he could think about was his Jessica with ichael. He would go out of his mind with rage if Mi-hael hurt Jessica.

"What does he want from me?" Cary said desperately.

"He wants you to know what it's like to lose someone ose to you," Dan said with a shrug. "Who knows? He's sane, Cary."

"Are you okay?" Cary asked, finally noticing the blood-aked handkerchief in Dan's hands.

"This isn't my first bloody nose and it definitely won't e my last. How is Tyler?"

"He's awake."

"Did he see anything?" Dan asked. Cary stared at Dan, most on the verge of answering. He remembered the lood on the back of Tyler's head. Tyler told Cary he

had been hit from behind. Cary and Tyler both had a
sumed that Dan had been hit from behind too, but Car
didn't see any blood on the back of Dan's head, onl
Dan's nosebleed.

"No. Tyler didn't see anything," Cary said automa
ically, as he studied Dan. Someone from Michael's organ
zation obviously had seen him at the inn to know abou
Jessica. Only Dr. Myers and Director Iverson had know
Cary would go to Hadley's Inn. Then Cary remembere
leaving the brochure on his desk one afternoon befor
he left for California. He remembered Dan walking int
his office and seeing the brochure before Cary placed
in a drawer.

"Why are you in here, Dan, when Tyler was blindside
and you were the only one standing behind him?" Car
asked, softly. Dan met his gaze and they both knew Car
had discovered who Dan really was.

"My wife left me, Cary! Sheila left because of the jol
because I was gone all the time and too distant. Becaus
I couldn't play with my daughter without seeing bomb
and guns!" Anger suddenly crossed Dan's face, erasin
the tenderness that existed when he spoke about his wif
and daughter. "If the Group destroyed my life, I wante
to destroy it. You're one of the prized agents, Cary. E
eryone knows you're Iverson's heir apparent. I knew
would hurt Iverson and Group morale if Michael coul
get to you, and I helped him. Michael's known ever
move you've made since we came to San Francisco."

Cary crossed the width of the terrace in two angry step
and had one hand around Daniel's neck and his gu
pointed under Daniel's chin before Daniel could eve
think to reach for his own gun. He felt the anger an
betrayal scream across every muscle in his body, almos
pleading with him to pull the trigger. Cary had finall
been pushed too far. He had finally crossed the line be
tween professionalism and pure, unadulterated rage.

"If this were another time and place, I'd love to hear all the excuses for your treachery as I tore you apart limb from limb! Unfortunately, I don't have time! Where did Michael take Jessica?"

"Don't kill me, Cary," Dan pleaded and Cary felt Daniel's body tremble.

Cary cocked the trigger on the gun and dug it deeper into Dan's neck. His voice was a deadly whisper as he said, "Where is she, Dan? Do something right for once in your miserable life!"

Cary saw the glint of steel against the moonlight just before Dan swung a long knife at his stomach. By reflex, Cary jumped to his right but the knife sliced the skin on his right shoulder through the fabric of the tuxedo coat and dress shirt. There was rage in Dan's eyes as he swung the knife again toward Cary's face. Cary ducked, then kicked the knife from his hand.

The knife clattered to the floor and Dan reached inside his coat for his gun but Cary drove his fist into Dan's midsection. Dan groaned and fell to his knees. Still feeling the hot slice of pain from the knife wound, Cary bent to Dan's level and grabbed Dan's gun from inside his coat pocket and tucked it in the waistband of his pants.

Cary watched impatiently as Dan whimpered. "I'm going to ask you one last time. Where did Michael take Jessica?"

Dan violently shook his head as he said, "He wants you there. He wants to kill you."

"I love her," Cary said simply.

Dan nodded slowly and met his eyes. "He has a boat in the marina. Slip forty-five." Dan hesitated, then asked in a trembling voice, "You're going to kill me, aren't you?"

Cary looked at the unrecognizable man crumbled at his feet. He knew if Jessica had never entered his life, he would've put a bullet between Dan's eyes without a second thought. The truth was once Cary named Dan as a traitor, other Group agents would probably kill him. Traitors never seemed to survive very long after they left the Group and went to federal prison.

"No, Dan, but someone else probably will."

"Cary!" Cary stood at the sound of his brother's voice. He saw his brother walk into the room, followed by various uniformed police officers and Group officers.

Cary noticed the pain on his brother's face and moved immediately to his side. "What happened to you?"

"I was clobbered from behind. It must have been Michael. Dan was in front of me."

"Michael has Jessica. I know where he's taking her."

Logan turned to the door but Cary grabbed his arm. Logan stared at him, confused. "We have to move now. Time is precious."

Cary stepped closer to Logan and lowered his voice, so no one would overhear. "I have to do this alone."

"Cary, we went through all this—"

"Give me fifteen minutes, Logan."

"Michael will kill you," Logan said, shaking his head.

"Only if he has to," Cary said, with more confidence than he felt at the moment.

Logan shook his head in frustration and asked, "Why are you protecting him? He doesn't deserve it."

"Five years ago, I was Michael."

"I don't like this," Logan muttered.

"You don't have to like it. You just have to trust me."

Logan hesitated, then nodded reluctantly. "Get Jessica. I owe her my life."

"So do I," Cary whispered, then ran out of the room.

Jessica winced as Michael tightened the coarse rope around her wrists. The two stood on a speedboat, moored in the marina. The night clouds hid the bright moonlight, throwing shadows across Michael's face and making him appear even more frightening. Jessica forced herself to stop shaking and start thinking of a plan to get away from Michael and to warn Cary. She refused to allow anyone to use her to hurt Cary. She told herself she was an intelligent, resourceful woman. She could get away from Michael, find a telephone, and call Cary. Of course, imagining herself running away was completely different than actually being free.

Jessica grunted as Michael pushed her onto a cushioned bench on one side of the boat. He began to pace the small floor area, the pistol at his side. He occasionally glanced into the darkness around the boat and cocked his head to listen. Jessica noticed several fishing poles and a bucket lying near her feet.

"You can leave right now, Michael, and everything will be fine," Jessica said in a soothing voice as she moved down the bench. "I won't tell anyone and I'll tell Cary not—"

"Don't mention his name!" Michael exploded, causing Jessica to jump in fear. He dropped on the bench beside her, shoving the gun underneath her chin. Jessica felt sweat roll down her back as she looked into his eyes. "How can you care about that bastard? How can you feel anything for a man like that? Did he tell you what he did?" Michael cocked the gun and Jessica shut her eyes, not wanting his face to be the last thing she saw. "Cary Riley lied! He joined my organization, pretended to care about my country and my cause, then he had my men killed! He pretended to care about my loss, but it was an act! He didn't care that the American government killed my father and brother!" Michael removed the gun from her chin and stared at his hands, all the fight drained from his body.

"He lied to me," Michael muttered, more to himself. He glanced at her and Jessica held his eyes as she continued to push the bucket with her right foot, closer to her tied hands. "I wish there were another way, Jessica, but I must avenge the death of my men. You understand, don't you?"

Jessica grabbed the bucket with her tied hands and swung it at Michael's head. The bucket slammed against the side of his face and Michael instantly dropped off the bench to the ground, clutching his face. Jessica didn't wait to see the complete damage before she jumped to her feet. She jumped off the boat onto the wooden deck and ran down the dock toward the parking lot and the street, where numerous cars passed. She heard Michael jump off the boat and his footsteps pound against the wooden dock as he chased after her.

Jessica ignored his curses and continued running, as fast as she could. She glanced over her shoulder and screamed when she saw how close he was. She remembered how she'd escaped him in the park. But this wasn't the park. Her hands were tied, she wore three-inch heels, and she and Michael were only four feet from the parking lot. Jessica screamed as his hands wrapped around her waist and they tumbled to the ground with a thud. Jessica tasted blood as her chin met the hard, unyielding wood. She scrambled, trying to break free of his grip, but he pinned her to the ground with his weight.

"Get off her," came Cary's gruff voice.

Jessica grew slightly dizzy from the speed with which Michael pulled her to her feet and against his chest, one arm wrapped around her neck and his other arm directing the gun at Cary. Cary stood as frozen as a statue, with his gun aimed at Michael. Jessica drank in the sight of Cary, from his dark eyes to the blood covering his once pristine white shirt.

"Cary, get out of here," Jessica cried, with tears in her eyes. She didn't want to be a witness to the murder of the only man she would ever love. Cary briefly glanced at her and Jessica felt the tears spill over at the pain in his eyes that he tried to hide.

"I'm here, Michael, you got what you want. Let Jessica go," Cary said calmly.

"Drop your gun right now," Michael commanded and Jessica inwardly winced as his arm tightened around her neck. She noticed Cary's obvious hesitation, as did Michael. "I told you he would save his own neck before yours," Michael said into Jessica's ear.

"Let her go, Michael, this is between you and me," Cary replied slowly, not moving an inch.

"I will kill her, Cary! Drop your gun!" Michael screamed impatiently. Jessica tried not to show fear. She tried to be brave, but she didn't want to die. A frightened cry escaped her throat and Cary immediately threw his gun to the ground. Michael grinned and nuzzled Jessica's hair, causing her skin to crawl with disgust. "Could the great agent Cary Riley actually have feelings? I'm impressed. Since you've taken so much away from me, maybe Jessica can be your repayment. A woman like her could help a man rebuild his empire." Cary took a step toward them with fury screaming across his face, but Michael only laughed.

"Jessica is not a part of this." Cary's voice shook. "Anything you want, Michael, it's yours. You want me? You have me. Just don't hurt her."

Jessica felt Michael's entire body tense. "I trusted you, I gave you a home, I called you brother. And then you betrayed me, you killed my men," he spat out angrily.

"I didn't want your men killed, Michael. My cover was blown and your men locked me in the attic. I didn't check in with the Group at the appointed time and they launched a search-and-rescue operation. There was a gunfight—"

"Shut up," Michael commanded hoarsely.

Cary continued in a firm voice, "There was a gunfight. Even though your men were outnumbered and outgunned and in an inferior position, they wouldn't put down their weapons. They were killed, Michael, because they didn't know when to quit, which is the same thing you said about your father and brother once. Do you remember telling me that you never wanted this fight? You told me you wanted to be elected by the people and rule the country legitimately, something your father never did. You can still do it, Michael, but you have to let Jessica go."

Michael suddenly shoved Jessica toward Cary. Cary barely looked at her as he stepped in front of her. Jessica didn't want him to die for her and tried to step beside him, but Cary held her behind him with one arm.

"You're a traitor, Cary Riley, and traitors don't deserve to live!" Michael yelled and Jessica saw the tears in his eyes. She gripped Cary's hand between hers, then noticed another gun sticking from the back of his pants waistband. The hand she held could easily reach the gun and she knew he was fast enough to shoot Michael before Michael had a chance. Her heart quickened as she realized they had a chance. Then she stared at his hard profile and she knew he would never pull the gun. For some reason, Cary felt responsible for Michael. He felt like he owed Michael something.

"I wanted to kill you, Michael, for everything you've done to Jessica, but I can't. Because I know who you really are beneath all of your ranting and raving. I know what a good man you are, no matter how much you try to hide it," Cary said softly. "The police are on their way, Michael. You probably have two minutes before they get here. You can either kill me or escape, but you can't do both."

"We were friends," Michael said, shaking his head.

"Yes, we were. I wasn't supposed to like you, but I did. I understand how it feels to be the only one left, to be the survivor when most nights you wish you had died with everyone else. But, no matter what you do, you can't bring them back, Michael. Killing me or hundreds of innocent people won't change the fact that they're dead."

Michael suddenly cocked the trigger and aimed the gun at Cary's head. "Michael, please don't," Jessica begged.

"Take this chance at freedom, Michael, and get the hell out of here while you still can, before you really hurt someone. Take this chance to return to your country and lead the people like your father should have and like your brother wanted to," Cary said softly. "Don't throw it all away because of me. I'm not worth it, am I?"

Michael turned toward the street as the loud wail of police sirens grew closer. The red and blue bright lights on top of the cars were barely visible in the distance. Michael stared at Cary uncertainly then finally placed the gun in the waistband of his pants.

"Don't ever come to my side of the world, Cary, because then I would have to kill you," Michael said softly, then hopped back onto the boat and started the engine. He took one last look at Cary. Cary raised his closed fist in a salute. Michael hesitated then reluctantly did the same. He directed the boat from the slip and raced toward the open bay.

Logan suddenly emerged from the shadow of a nearby boat. He watched Michael's boat race across the bay and calmly reholstered his gun.

"I thought I told you to wait," Cary said, glaring at his brother.

"I did," Logan said, simply. "And you're welcome." He winked at Jessica then walked toward the entrance of the marina.

Jessica laughed in relief and slipped her still tied hands over Cary's head to pull him close to her.

"I was so scared, Cary. I thought he was going to kill

you," she cried, closing her eyes against the image. When his arms didn't tighten around her, Jessica leaned back to look at him. She shook her head confused at his somber expression. Cary slowly pulled her arms over his head then untied her hands.

"Cary, what's wrong?" she asked, concerned as police cars screeched to a halt at the end of the marina. Several police officers raced down the pier as Jessica watched Cary, waiting for an answer. He never answered as she was whisked into a waiting police car. He remained on the dock, staring at the open bay.

For the second time in two weeks, Jessica found herself sitting in the same hard, wooden chair in Inspector Kerns's sparse, windowless office with a regulation wool blanket wrapped around her shoulders. She sipped the hot coffee from the Styrofoam cup someone had handed her a few minutes ago, and she willed herself to stop shaking. She knew coffee wasn't the answer, Cary's arms were, but he was nowhere to be seen. She hadn't seen him for the entire two hours she had been there.

No one else paid any attention to her either. Inspector Kerns had hurriedly ushered her into his office and shut the door without saying a word. Jessica would have thought she didn't exist if a uniformed officer hadn't brought her a cup of coffee ten minutes ago. He answered all her questions about Cary with an apologetic smile and little else.

Jessica heard the door open behind her and whirled around to face whomever entered, to demand answers about Cary. She smiled relieved and set the cup on the desk before she jumped to her feet and threw her arms around Cary's neck, pressing close to him until his arms drew around her waist. She finally felt safe and protected, even though she sat in the middle of a police station.

Jessica's smile disappeared as she noticed a certain restraint in his touch and her heart sank to her stomach. She knew Cary blamed himself for Michael kidnapping her. She didn't know what to say to him to prove otherwise. She didn't blame him, or Michael, or even Dan. She couldn't blame them, because without the specific circumstances of the last two weeks, she never would have known how much she loved Cary, how much he made her complete, how much he cared about her. She finally pulled away from him, not missing his somber expression.

"Are you okay?" he asked, breaking the silence. "Did he hurt you?"

Jessica forced a smile, trying not to notice the regret in his eyes because she didn't know what that meant to him. "I'm fine. What happened to your arm?" He no longer wore the white shirt. A stark white bandage wrapped around his right arm peeked from underneath the short sleeve of his white T-shirt.

"When Dan told me Michael had you," Cary began in a strange, flat voice that reminded Jessica of the first night she met him, "I felt so helpless and out of control. I felt like I was caught in a riptide and no matter how hard I fought, the result would always be the same. I would drown. I've never been that scared before and I don't ever want to be that scared again."

"I'm fine now, Cary. You have nothing to worry about." Jessica reached for his hands but he stepped away from her. Her heart sank as she realized he couldn't stay with her. When they were kissing each other and dancing at the ball, she wanted to believe their conversation at the pier was meaningless, but it was who he believed he was. The empty look in his eyes and his flat tone told her what he couldn't say in words. He felt he couldn't love her and she would never be able to convince him how wrong he was.

"We would never work, Jess. I was naive to think I could

ever make you happy. I can't. I'm everything Michael said, and much worse. I could never give you the kind of life you deserve, with stability and security and love," he whispered, staring at his hands. "I'm sorry, Jess, about all this, about Michael . . . about everything."

"What are you saying?" Cary sadly smiled and softly caressed her cheek, but Jessica barely felt his touch.

"I'm saying I'm not your other half, and I'm just keeping you from finding him," he whispered.

Jessica knew time continued, but she couldn't comprehend that her life would continue without Cary. He held the other half to her heart, to her soul. He was the only one who could make her feel whole, who could love her like she needed to be loved.

"Cary, I love you," she said quietly, summoning all her courage to meet his eyes and ignore his previous words.

He flinched as if she had punched him. "Your family is here to take you home—"

"Don't walk out that door," Jessica warned, with tears in her eyes. Cary refused to look at her. "You made me love you. You made me trust you. You're going to throw it all back in my face?"

"It's for the best, Jessica."

"For whom? You or me?" she demanded. He looked at her and she could see the self-hatred in his eyes. "I think you want to make things easy on yourself. If you pretend that you're being noble, then you can escape without having to care about someone, without having to give a piece of yourself to someone else. You don't speak to your brother or sister, not because you're protecting them, but because you're protecting yourself. You don't want to love someone, like you loved your parents, and have it taken away."

"You don't know the things I've done—"

"I love you, Cary, and my love isn't conditional. I won't stop loving you if I find out you did something amoral or wrong because of the Group. Every experience with the Group, your childhood, your loving family, made you who you are today. A wonderful, sensitive, caring, good man, whom I love with all my heart."

"You don't know me," Cary said angrily.

"I know all I need to know," Jessica whispered, as tears threatened to impede her ability to speak. "I know your smile makes my heart want to sing. I know your touch makes me want to fly into the sky and never come down. I know—"

"Jess, we would never work. I can't have a relationship while I'm constantly traveling to places and doing things that I could never tell you about."

"How would we know, unless we try?" she demanded desperately. She straightened her shoulders and met his gaze. "Please stay, Cary. I need you."

"You don't need me, Jess," he muttered, shaking his head.

"Maybe I don't need you, but I sure as hell want you." The two stared at each other in silence. Jessica prayed he would walk into her arms and vow never to leave her.

Without looking at her, he said quietly, "Good-bye, Jessica."

Jessica stood frozen to the spot as he walked from the office, closing the door with a dull thud. By the time she snapped from her daze and swung open the door, Cary was nowhere in sight and Jessica stared into Logan's concerned face.

"He left?" Jessica asked, in disbelief.

Logan wouldn't meet her eyes as he nodded. "You have to understand him, Jess. He's scared."

"Of me?"

"Of how alive you make him feel," Logan said softly. Without a word, Jessica walked back into the office and closed the door. She covered her face with her hands and cried.

Twenty-five

Jessica stared out the window of her office, as the phone rang on her desk. She wanted to answer it, she should have answered it, but she didn't move. She had spent the past five days, running for the phone, praying it was Cary. She had been disappointed too many times. For her own sanity, Jessica had to move on with her life, to forget Cary, to forget the life she could have had with him. The phone stopped ringing and Jessica sighed with disappointment.

She refused to allow anyone to see how much his disappearance affected her. She pasted a brave smile on her face for her mother and brother. She arrived at work with the same energetic attitude and left late, as usual. No one would know that inside, her heart broke. No one would know that at night, in the privacy of her room, Jessica had cried so much for Cary that she couldn't cry anymore. She wanted him, she loved him, but she couldn't force him to take a chance on their love no matter how much she wanted to. She'd tried to convince him at the station and he had walked out her life, without a second glance.

Jessica glanced from the window at the sound of a knock on her door. She quickly took the seat behind her desk as Erin walked into the room. Jessica forced a smile,

nly because she knew Erin reported to David, who called
er every night just to curse Cary for leaving her.

"Hi, Erin. Is it lunchtime already?"

Erin didn't respond but sat in a chair across from Jes-
ca. Jessica didn't like the serious expression in her eyes.
ince Cary left, Jessica had been able to evade any at-
mpts by Erin to talk about Cary. Judging from Erin's
rious expression, she wouldn't be able to escape this
me.

"We need to talk," Erin began bluntly.

"I'm really busy, Erin."

"Staring out the window?" Erin said dryly. "I haven't
een fooled by your Susie-Sunshine attitude, Jess."

"I have no idea what you're talking about," Jessica said
nocently.

"I'm talking about you and Cary Riley."

Jessica pretended to search through the papers on her
esk for an important item, when really she was attempt-
g to hold back the tears that she knew would come if
e looked at Erin. "I have a million things to do before
meet with a new client this afternoon, Erin. I would
ve to talk to you—"

"Jess, do you love Cary Riley?" Erin interrupted.

"Yes." Tears blurred her vision and she reached for
e box of tissues she recently started keeping in her desk
rawer.

"Then why are you still here? Why aren't you in Vir-
inia with him?"

"You can't make someone love you back, Erin," Jessica
hispered the awful truth that had been racing through
er head since Cary had left.

"Jess, you're one of the most intelligent women I know.
verything I've learned in this business, I've learned from
atching you. I think you've even taught Peter a few
ings. With all your brains and common sense, you can't

seriously sit there and tell me Cary Riley doesn't lov
you."

"He did, but not enough to overcome his fears."

Erin leaned on the desk with a smirk on her face. "
have a secret to share with you, Jess. Men are human
They don't have all the answers. They don't even hav
half of the answers."

Jessica rolled her eyes, with a bitter laugh. "I know tha
Erin."

"Then help Cary understand that," Erin said desper
ately. "I hate seeing you like this. You're still Jessica La
son, future partner of Jannings & Associates, but you'r
not the same Jessie who's my best friend, who makes m
smile when it's the last thing on earth I feel like doing."

"I'm trying, Erin."

"I know, but you have to try for yourself, not for ev
eryone around you. You have to make yourself happy. I
that involves working one hundred hours a week, the
fine. If that involves sitting on a small farm in the middl
of Idaho and knitting socks for your five kids and farme
husband, then that's fine, too." Erin sighed in frustratio
then asked abruptly, "If you could do anything in th
world at this moment, what would you do?"

"Catch the first flight to Virginia," Jessica answered be
fore she could stop herself.

"Then what's stopping you?" Erin asked, grinning.

"I have work and—"

"Contrary to popular belief, I think this compan
would survive without you. It may actually be good for u
to go a few days without the great Jessica Larson. If any
thing, it would give our crisis-management team a chanc
to test their skills."

Jessica laughed, the first real laugh she had experi
enced since Cary had left. "You think I can really do thi
Erin?"

'If you can handle Peter Jannings, one secret agent
h trust issues should be a piece of cake."

essica abruptly stopped smiling, and asked in a small
ce, "What if he really doesn't love me? What if I read
e signs wrong? What if there are no trust and fear issues,
d Cary just doesn't want me? Then what will I do?"

"Then we'll buy a ton of cheesecake, a few cases of
e, rent every tearjerker movie made, and rage about
n for an entire weekend," Erin said simply, then stood
with a smile. "Somehow, I doubt that will happen."

essica laughed, then frantically searched through the
endar of appointments on her desk. "I guess I could
chedule the Borden presentation—"

"You can call me from the airplane and I'll make all
e calls for you," Erin said, then handed Jessica an en-
ope.

essica grinned when she saw the airplane ticket inside.
ou're pretty sure of yourself."

"I learned from the best," Erin said with a grin. "David
d I bought the ticket last night."

"David? David Larson, my brother? Did he know why
was buying the ticket?"

"I asked David if he wanted you to be happy or not.
e gave me his gold card," Erin said with a twinkle in
r eyes. She glanced at her watch and clapped her hands
citedly. "You have about two hours to pack and get to
e airport."

essica ran around the desk to hug Erin. "Thank you
much."

"David and I decided we owed you for having to listen
us argue for two years."

"You owe me a lot more than a plane ticket," Jessica
urmured then hugged Erin once more. "But, we can
l it even."

* * *

Cary looked up from the pile of papers on his desk surprise as Director Maurice Iverson walked into his fice. He had barely spoken to Iverson or to anyone el since he'd returned from California, five days ago. I had received numerous congratulations on his esca from Michael Lyons, which Cary had creatively written the report, and congratulations over figuring out th Dan was the traitor, but Cary felt like a robot. He reme bered Jessica's scathing words when she'd told him return to his life where he didn't have to care about an one or anything and he realized that's exactly what was doing. And he suddenly realized after the first nig alone in his sterile, cold house that he didn't like his li at all.

There was no one to go to the movies or for a run the park with. There was no one to talk and laugh wi over television shows. There was no Jessica in his li There was nothing except work, and he wanted a more. He wanted to make David like him, make Kar Larson laugh, he wanted to play basketball with h brother in the park, and he wanted to have a long li with Jessica. The feelings hit Cary like a brick and l didn't know what to do about any of them, except fly San Francisco and have Jessica help him.

"Riley." Iverson nodded and closed the door. Cary n ticed his somber expression, which was usual, but the was also a strange glint in his weary blue eyes that ma Cary straighten in his seat. Iverson settled his six fe three inch lean frame into the chair across from Cary desk and tossed a stack of papers in front of him. Ca recognized it as his report from San Francisco. "Do ye really expect me to believe this piece of contrived f tion?"

Cary slowly turned the pages of his report and avoide Iverson's eyes. Iverson had hand-picked Cary from colle to join the ranks and Cary didn't want to disappoint hi but he had to leave the Group. He no longer belonged with these men who moved in the shadows. He belonged with Jessica, his other half. He couldn't return to his old life, his old ways, not while dreaming of her and his potential future.

"I don't understand, sir," Cary replied carefully.

"What happened in San Francisco, Cary? Did you allow Michael Lyons to escape?" Cary set his report on the desk and met Iverson's eyes. He didn't know how to respond, what to tell the man who had been his family for the last five years. Iverson spoke for him. "I'm going to miss you, Cary. I was planning to retire in the next couple of years and even though you're young, I was going to appoint you as my successor."

"You're firing me?" Cary asked, surprised by the turn of events.

Iverson shook his head and smiled, something he rarely did. "I'm not firing you, Cary; I'm just accepting your resignation. I knew after your last assignment you would never be the same. In this job, we all have to erase a certain part of us, a certain humanity, and I don't think you can." Iverson stood and offered his hand to Cary. Cary stood and shook his hand, not certain how exactly to proceed. "I've already sent a letter of recommendation to the special agent in charge of the San Francisco Bureau. He says they have an opening for an assistant director of operations that sounds perfect for you. You could do a lot in that position. A lot of paper work, but very limited field work."

"San Francisco?" Cary wondered how the Director knew that was where he wanted to go.

Iverson glared at him impatiently. "This all has to do with that young woman in San Francisco, right? The woman you demanded be protected at any cost against Michael Lyons three weeks ago? I think her name was Jessica Larson. I've also learned your brother is in San

Francisco. Families are important, Riley. Life is too short not to hang on to them."

"Thank you, sir." Cary tried to hide his smile but couldn't. It was the first time he'd smiled in his office. "Thank you very much."

"Of course you'll have to attend a debriefing, where they'll tell you what you can and can't say. You'll have to turn in your badge, your guns, and all your identification. There will be . . ." Iverson abruptly stopped talking and shook his head as Cary nodded, trying to appear serious and concerned. But, he couldn't care. He could only think about hopping on the next flight to San Francisco and telling Jessica what a fool he was to ever leave her. "You don't care about any of this, do you, Riley?"

"Just tell me where to go and when to be there," Cary responded quickly.

Iverson smiled again, then walked to the door. Cary watched his boss and realized he would miss him and the thrill of the job but he was ready for new thrills; marrying Jessica, having children of their own, and reconciling with his family.

"You were one of my best agents, Cary, but I'm glad you're leaving. I'm glad you have to leave. Take care out there." Iverson turned and walked out of the room, leaving Cary frantically packing his few personal items in the office.

Cary sped down the Virginia expressway, ignoring the speed laws and honking motorists behind him. He knew his race to beat five o'clock traffic was useless but he still had to pack before the eight o'clock flight left for San Francisco. He still would have to return to the Group for a final debriefing, but Cary needed first to see Jessica. He didn't know if Jessica would want him, if she would welcome him or slap his face again. He smiled as he realized that he didn't care. For the first time, Cary Riley looked forward to the unknown. In fact, he relished the thought of demonstrating to Jessica how much he loved her.

Cary finally exited the expressway and sped down the quiet residential street toward his house. His hands tightened on the steering wheel when he noticed the dark rental car parked in front of his split-level house, and a lone figure with dark, long hair sitting on the front steps. Cary pulled into the driveway and remained in the driver's seat for a few seconds when Jessica calmly met his gaze across the front yard. He slowly stood got out of the car and walked to her.

"Hi." Jessica stood, brushing dust from the porch off her jeans.

"Hi," was all Cary could manage. He was in a state of shock. He had been rushing to California to see her and she suddenly stood on his front porch, looking nervous and more beautiful than he remembered. His hands itched to caress her lips and pull her to him and never release her.

"How's your arm?"

Cary briefly glanced at his arm, looking for an apparent mark, then realizing that she was referring to the knife wound. He quickly looked back at her. "Fine."

"You were right. It's so beautiful here with all the leaves falling. In California, fall is like winter and like spring," she joked but neither laughed.

"What are you doing here?" Cary asked, confused, wanting to believe she wanted him as much as he wanted her.

"You've come to California twice and it was my turn to come to you," she answered, stuffing her hands in her jeans pockets and laughing nervously. "Believe me, that explanation sounded a lot better on the plane."

Cary continued to stare at her, not certain what to say.

She began to shift her feet uncomfortably and Cary couldn't stop himself from blurting out, "I love you, Jess." Her eyes grew wide with surprise and relief. Cary felt the familiar stab of intense love as he stared into the face of the woman he hoped to build a long life with. "Once I joined the Group, we were taught not to need anyone, not to depend on anyone, because that would make us vulnerable. But, no matter how hard I try I can't stop needing you. I need to be with you every morning and every night. I need to see your smile, feel your kisses, and hear your laugh."

"I know you're an extremely independent woman and I respect that. I don't want to take anything away from you. I want everything you want for yourself, nothing more and nothing less. And I know this may be selfish and egocentric, but I need you in my life. I'm not a complete person without you and I need to be whole." He saw the tears shining in her eyes and wrapped his arms around her as she placed her lips on his. Her lips promised him what she didn't say. Cary grinned into her mouth, pulling her as close to him as possible, lifting her several inches off the porch. He never knew he could feel so human again. But, loving Jessica made him human.

"You don't know how long I've been waiting to hear you say that," Jessica said when they parted. "I need you too, Cary, more than I'll probably ever admit to you or to myself."

"I'm so damn scared of loving you and being loved by you, but I can't stop myself and I don't want to anymore." He laughed and inhaled the rich, fall air of the home he would miss, but gladly leave behind. "I love you, Jessica Larson, and now that I've found you after a lifetime of searching, I'm never letting you go."

Jessica grinned and wrapped her arms around him, feeling relieved and ecstatic. She wasn't certain how Cary would react to finding her on his porch, but his words were even better than her wildest dreams. She was going to wink, grab his hand, and declare her love since the Fates had thrown him in her path.

"Don't ever leave me again, Cary," she demanded happily.

"I won't, Jess," Cary promised then pulled a plane ticket from his coat pocket and Jessica read the destination with an amazed smile. He had been planning to join her in San Francisco that night. She hugged him again before he said, "I quit the Group or I was fired. I'm not exactly certain, but there's a position open for an assistant director of operations in the San Francisco office that I'm going to take."

"You didn't have to do that, Cary. I would've accepted you whether you were a Group agent, a trash man, or a doctor."

"I had to do it for myself and for our future. I don't want to keep any secrets from you or our children," he whispered, then his expression softened and he kissed her on the lips. "I guess sometimes the Fates know exactly what they're doing."

"Sometimes," Jessica agreed. She smiled through her tears, placing her hand in his. Their hands seemed to fit perfectly, almost as if they were made from the same mold.